"We've had visitors while we were out," she said quietly. "They're gone now but they've left us some presents." She nodded toward the oversized wicker storage bin we kept in the corner. It was normally filled with old clothing, blankets, and other materials we would eventually take to the Safehaven recycling center. I've never pretended to be psychic, but there was a sense of ominous danger almost tangible in the room, and I walked to the basket on shaky legs.

There was a bit of an anticlimax when I opened the lid, because staring up at me was the sweater I'd torn while inspecting the underside of the east pier a few weeks earlier. Hesitantly I reached out and pushed it aside. Beneath it lay four military issue assault lasers, rechargeable, each wrapped in transparent plasticene.

MANAGANSETT PRESS

Don D'Ammassa is the author of:

Horror
Blood Beast
Servant of Chaos*
Caverns of Chaos*
Wings over Manhattan
The Gargoyle
That Way Madness Lies*
Little Evils*
Passing Death*
Date with the Dark*
The Devil Is in the Details*
Living Things*

Science Fiction
Scarab*
Haven*
Narcissus*
Translation Station
The Sinking Island*
Alien & Otherwise*
Wormdance*

Mysteries
Murder in Silverplate*
Dead of Winter*
Death at the Art Gallery*
Death on the Mountain*
Death on Black Island*

Fantasy
The Kaleidoscope*
Elaborate Lies*
Perilous Pursuits*

Nonfiction
The Encyclopedia of Science Fiction
The Encyclopedia of Fantasy and Horror
The Encyclopedia of Adventure Fiction
Masters of Detection Vol I & II*
*Published by Managansett Press

WORMDANCE

Don D'Ammassa

Chapter One first appeared in slightly different form in *Isaac Asimov's Science Fiction Magazine*, 1999

Managansett Press Edition 2015

WORMDANCE

CHAPTER ONE

Sometimes the big events in life announce themselves right up front and you know, this is it, this is going to change my future for better or worse, and I might as well accept it and try to make the best of it. Other times they sneak in when you're not expecting them, disguised as routine or at worst inconsequential occurrences. They might make brilliant images or thunderclaps when they rush upon us, but the memory fades quickly to pastels and background noise, and we are changed but little by their coming and going.

It was on Cille's fifteenth birthday that the wormswell came to our farm. At least, that's the day when we first noticed it. Things move so slowly for wormswell that it's difficult to tie specific events in their lives to such a fleeting moment as a day, even the 26 standard hour day of Aragon. It was my brother Jesper who brought us the news, running recklessly up from the north pasture, windmilling his arms and shouting whenever he could spare the breath. Dad spotted him first, rose up from where he was fitting a new board into the front steps where a rotten one had snapped the day before. His face was expressionless but I could see his hands tightening into fists where they hung by his sides.

"What is it now?" Mom pushed open the screen door and stepped out onto the porch, raising one hand to shade her eyes from the bright double sunlight. It was near high-high noon, and the sky was almost completely cloud free. If either of Aragon's double stars had been as warm as Sol, we'd have risked a bad sunburn just standing outside unprotected.

"We'll know presently," my father answered calmly. "If he doesn't break his fool neck getting here." He glanced in my direction. "Did he say where he was going this morning, Ennis?"

I shrugged and turned back to the stack of cornfruits I had been husking. Jesper and I had had a fight the night before, an ongoing battle because I was tired of having to pick up part of his share of the chores. I'd appealed to Dad and he'd told me the two of us were old enough to work it out ourselves and that neither of us would be happy if he had to intervene, but the fact was that Jesper just wouldn't stick to a job until it was finished. Even if it was something he enjoyed doing, he'd get bored and wander off sooner or later, and if it was something he actually hated - as was the case with most of our duties on the farm - it was more often sooner than later. Don't get me wrong; I loved my younger brother intensely, but love doesn't get the barns clean, or the crab hens back into their nests.

Jesper slowed considerably toward the end, climbing the slope atop which we'd built the house. We tried to keep the wiregrass cut to ankle deep here, what Mom called our "lawn", but two of the maintenance bots had been waiting for spare parts for three months, and the four that were left were barely able to keep up with the tilling and harvesting schedules, so it had grown without interference for some time now. We could see Jesper's head and shoulders bobbing above the silken tops as he advanced. We could probably have heard him if he'd kept shouting from this close, but Jesper was saving all of his breath for the effort needed to push through the chest high grass.

Cille came outside, blinking rapidly in the glare. Her bare arms were improbably slim for a Baxter. We're a big boned, heavily fleshed family, always have been. And working the farm ensures that it's muscle and not fat. At eighteen, I was already as big as Dad, and Jesper, two years behind, was taller than either of us, though we each had a few pounds on him yet. Mom was no slouch either; she worked in the fields when her other responsibilities were out of the way, and she was solid enough to provide a painful whack when the two of us boys deserved it.

But Cille was different. Not fragile by any means, although she looked it compared to the rest of us. Wire hard though, tough enough to have spent twenty straight hours helping us shore up the retaining walls when our small dam let go and the east fields were in danger of flooding. She had another strength as well, one unique in our family. The Baxters abide by themselves, as a family and as individuals. Too much so, I suspect. When things go bad, when we're discouraged or tired or worried, we shrink into our separate selves to work things out. Cille, well, she didn't seem to have moods. She got tired like the rest of us, but she never let it bother the part of herself that was born wondering about the world around her.

"What's going on?" She followed our eyes, lifting a hand to shade her own. Jesper broke out into the open a minute later.

"North field. Down by the new barn." His voice was hoarse from shouting and his breathing was ragged. "Coming up right where we plowed!"

Dad took a step forward. "What's coming up, son? Not bitter grass again, is it?"

Jesper stopped a few meters from us, half crouched over with his hands on his thighs, fighting for breath. "Wormswell," he said at last. "Looks like a big one."

The five of us went off to look.

We'd seen wormswell before, of course. There'd even been a couple of them on our property, though they were both pretty small. Wormswell are Aragon's largest form of animal life, but no one had any real idea how numerous they might be. They lived underground, most of the time, surfacing once every several years to soak up some sunlight and pollinate. Yes, I said pollinate. I'll explain that later.

This one wasn't visible yet, though we could see evidence of its presence from the opposite end of the freshly tilled field. Several saplings were bent back at odd angles where the ground had literally started to rise beneath them. Wormswell moved almost imperceptibly through the earth most of the time, absorbing the soil at one end, removing the nutrients to fuel their incredibly slow metabolisms, excreting whatever was left in their wake. No one knew how deep they went, although it was certainly at least several hundred feet. A few had been unearthed when the spaceport at Aladdin was being built - great featureless sluglike creatures - but their flesh wasn't fit to eat, they posed no apparent danger to anyone, and they'd been accepted and almost forgotten.

Almost, but not quite. Part of their life cycle was a periodic rise to the surface, the only time when their metabolism actually accelerated to the merely ponderous. They broke out into the open and, when the sunlight touched their armored hides, they went through a transformation that had attracted scientists from all over this region of space.

Dad considered the future with a more jaundiced eye. "It's likely going to rip up a third of the field before it's done."

I confess that I was pretty unhappy as well. We'd spent a lot of sweat culling all of the buried rocks out of this field, then plowing what was left in anticipation of seeding. The bluebug infestation had wiped out a third of our pseudowheat crop that year, and we were hoping to recoup some of the losses by increasing the acreage we had under cultivation. The cresting wormswell was near the edge of the field, about forty meters from the new barn we'd had built during the spring. Assuming this individual was about average in size, he'd tear up a line approximately twenty meters in all four directions when he finally broke free. And then he'd sit there for as long as thirty days before slowly sinking back. By then we'd have missed an entire crop cycle, even if we replowed and seeded right away.

"Might be a small one," I suggested hopefully.

"Might be a big one," contradicted Jesper. "Came up awfully fast."

Dad was scratching his head, measuring things with his eyes. "Your brother's right, Ennis. I was up this way day before yesterday. Not even a swell then."

I didn't understand and said so.

"When they surface, they come straight up, faster'n they do otherwise but still damned slow. I think we're going to have to write off this field for the season."

It was even worse than that, but we didn't find out the extent of the disaster until later.

It began to broach four days after that. Dad was driving us harder than ever, apparently resigned to the loss of the north field for the season, trying to find ways to squeeze as much as possible out of what remained to us. After two days widening the arable part of the west field, Jesper and I had pretty much forgotten about the wormswell. Cille hadn't though. She'd been spending half the day working alongside us, hacking at the wiregrass and sawbrush with a wide bladed knife, then helping us carry it to what we'd decided would be the new border of the field. The rest of the time she spent at the house. She was a pretty handy carpenter though sometimes a little too fussy about unimportant details.

But somehow she found time to wander down to the north field and check on our unwelcome guest.

"It broke through today," she announced at dinner that night.

I can't speak for the others, but I was so tired and sore that I hadn't the vaguest idea what she was talking about, and frankly didn't much care just then either.

"The wormswell," she explained unbidden. "It's above the ground, part of it anyway. It hasn't started dancing yet." There was a hint of disappointment.

"Has to get its whole snout out first," Dad answered. "Another day or so, probably." He didn't sound enthused, although the wormdance was a beautiful sight. Jesper and I'd sneaked over more than once to watch the one that'd broken through in our woodlot two years earlier. But I realized suddenly that Cille had never been able to go with us. The first time we'd had one on the property, she'd been away in Aladdin for a term at school; the other time she'd been restricted to the house because of a leg broken in a fall from one of our lofts.

Dad must have remembered the same thing just then because he offered her one of his rare smiles. "You'll get to see it this time, Cille. I promise."

Two days later there was still no dance, and the same two days after that. By then we had a bigger problem, no pun intended.

"We're gonna lose the whole field, aren't we?" Jesper sounded discouraged, as well he should be. The crest of the swell was well over our heads by now and the ground sloped away steeply for twenty meters in every direction. Not only saplings had succumbed; full size trees had fallen along the wooded segment of the wormswell's perimeter.

"More than that." Dad's voice was even more doleful than usual. He glanced toward the barn, the new barn, then back to the wormswell.

"It can't be that big!" I protested hotly.

"The forward collar isn't visible yet." He pointed to the most recently exposed part of the emerging creature. It was a pitted expanse of dark grey, leathery hide. "Three rings need to emerge before it'll start dancing. It'll rise some more after that, not getting any taller but spreading out. That's when it'll take the barn, if it's as big as I think."

Mom didn't say anything but she touched him on the arm. It didn't need saying. We'd weathered three marginal years in a row, borrowed heavily for the new barn to process what was supposed to be the crop from this field. One season's loss would hurt, but we'd get by. If the barn went, well, I wasn't sure then just what might happen. We could even lose the farm.

"There must be something we can do," I blurted.

"Are you kidding? Look at the size of this thing!" Jesper walked closer and spread his arms wide.

"Maybe we could move the barn," I suggested. "Hire a choplifter. Take off the roof. Move all the heavy equipment out of the way, then collapse the walls until it goes back down."

"Every choplifter on the planet's working on the spaceport expansion. Even if one was free, we couldn't afford to hire it." He smiled insincerely. "We might get lucky. Sometimes they don't spread that much. We'll have to keep an eye on things."

The first ring emerged sometime during that night, and three days later the worm began its dance. The barn was intact, for the moment. Apparently our visitor was a lot more cylindrical than average, although the portion of its body that lay exposed to view was better than fifty meters in diameter, and the ground for another thirty meters around its circumference displayed some degree of stress. The near wall of the barn was buckled but the metal hadn't actually split yet, and there were cracks in the foundation. We'd moved out some of the smaller equipment, but that tended to be the less expensive items. We still faced a crippling loss if the wormswell got much bigger than it already was.

We were all there except Mom, adding makeshift braces and tying down the big process equipment, when the dance started.

If you haven't seen a wormdance from close up, you can't know how beautiful it is. Even the holos don't do it justice. The rough hide had been showing more and more cracks every day, and now there was an eruption of filmy tentacles bursting out everywhere. They were pale that first day, translucent blues and pinks and yellows, and they moved with slow, sinewy grace, rising from within the wormswell's body, the longest a full six meters tall, others, more numerous, just brushing our ankles. From the central shaft, fronds of wormflesh opened like unfurling leaves on short stalks, predominantly spatulate but interspersed with other forms, sails of lace, spiky shafts, twisting corkscrews. Everything was in constant movement, movement which would become more rapid as the sunlight poured energy into these organic batteries. That first day it was silent as well, but I knew from the last time that this would not last. As the diaphanous forest of flesh grew taller and richer, its colors deepening, the undulating forms would begin to brush against one another, until eventually there would be an the endless susurration known as wormsong.

We walked our separate paths within the wormdance. Enough of the creature had been exposed by now that the four of us could stand each concealed from the rest. And that's what three of us did, watching with dread and appreciation all mixed together. But Cille felt none of the first, and a great deal of the second. She was caught up in the beauty of it like no one I've ever seen before or since. She ran from one spot to another, pausing to peer closely at a particularly graceful frond, or an interesting splash of color, laughing with delight and calling to us to come see, but then dashing onward to the next wonder before we could respond.

Near the center, there was what amounted to a small ravine cut into the creature's flesh, big enough that I could have pitched a tent inside, set up camp, and remained hidden from anyone passing more than a couple of meters away. It must have encountered a ledge of rock as it made its way through the subsoil. When Dr. Estalla came out to see the wormswell a couple of days later he explained it to me.

"They move and think so slowly, they don't react the way ordinary animals would. Likely this one kept trying to grow through a spur of rock until its body just sort of flowed along the sides, leaving this big scar even after it passed on into softer earth."

I sat there on the edge of that ravine, admiring the show, and struck by how even the agent of a terrible destruction could be a beautiful sight.

Cille touched my shoulder. "Isn't it wonderful?"

For some reason, her joy aggravated me just at that moment. "I don't see how you can say that. We're probably going to lose the farm because of this thing."

"Oh, things will work out. I just know it. Nothing this beautiful could hurt us." But she was wrong.

We finished bracing the barn, but before we could go back, Dad made us inspect the dike. Lake Pudallah sat solemnly behind it, the source of our extensive irrigation system, the power behind the Jackknife and Swift rivers. The rainy season this year had been much more intense than usual and the water lapped against the top layer of the dike system. Runoff from the mountains was still rushing in from the east, but we'd built the dike with a considerable safety margin.

We'd pretty much finished our inspection when a loud crack startled us. Dad glanced back at the wormswell. "That was quick. They don't usually start till the second day."

Our wormswell was pollinating. They're animals, like I said, but they have a very unique method of reproducing. Underground they were pretty much self sufficient, but when the time came to procreate, they surfaced and sucked up the sunlight. In and among the dancing structures were straight pillars that looked like giant asparagus. When enough energy accumulated in one of these, drawn from the energy collectors around it, the wormswell expelled what I guess you'd call a sperm, although they're hermaphrodites. The sperm was fired up into the upper atmosphere where it remained viable for up to thirty local days. If it encountered another, suitable partner before falling to the ground, the united pair would then tunnel into the soil and, presto, the start of a new wormswell.

As orgasms went, this was pretty spectacular.

We settled into a grim routine after that. Everything that was portable enough to be moved was out of the barn, stored temporarily in a prefab shack Jesper and I had set up at the opposite end of the field. The wormswell's exposed surface grew another couple of meters, but the bracing on the barn held and I began to feel more optimistic. Then Dad let us go along when he took Dr. Estalla out to look things over.

Estalla's an exobiologist who supports himself teaching school in Aladdin. He's pretty much the only real expert on Aragon's indigenous life, although he claims he's barely scratched the surface. He'd heard about our visitor somewhere and called up, inviting himself out. Dad doesn't take much to having outsiders on the property, but I guess he figured he'd pick the man's brains a bit.

"Biggest I've ever seen," Estalla told us. "Though there was one over near Tyrada before my time that had a diameter near 100 meters." Ours was 75 meters, but still growing.

"How big do you figure this one's likely to be?" Dad's eyes kept flicking back and forth from the wormdance, which was so fast now it was hard to follow individual shapes, and the barn.

Estalla was silent, walked back and forth, pacing things off. His eyebrows rose at one point. I didn't think this was a good sign. Then he took some kind of electronic device out of his backpack and placed it on a bit of mostly level ground. He watched the illuminated readings for a few seconds, then climbed up into the wormdance, disappearing almost immediately.

"What's he doing?" The tiny pops of the wormswell's ejaculations came every two or three minutes now.

"Just be patient, Ennis. The man knows what he's about." I could feel the tension in Dad's voice, and see it in the way his shoulders never eased up while we stood there. When Estalla reappeared, he wasn't alone.

"Cille! What the hell are you doing up here?"

Oblivious to Dad's clear annoyance, Cille gestured back to the wormdance. "It just keeps getting faster and more beautiful, doesn't it? I saw some new shapes today, kind of like giant ferns except that they coil up into tubes every once in a while. And there's another kind that sprays these silky strands up into the air, and they float down so slowly."

"Isn't your mother harvesting the crab hens today?"

Cille's smile went down a notch. "Yeah, but she isn't going to start until after lunch."

"Then that gives you time to sweep out the moltings beforehand, doesn't it?"

Cille gave him an exaggerated look of reproach, then sketched a salute, said goodbye to Dr. Estalla, and ran back toward the house. Dad forgot her almost instantly.

"Care to guess how big it's going to get?"

Estalla looked solemn, glanced around before answering. I noticed his eyes lingered on the barn. "Can't be precise. Sometimes they don't surface completely."

"Close is good enough." I think Dad had already figured out the answer, or at least the consequences.

"Hundred meters minimum, more likely half again that."

I opened my mouth to say something, but no words came. A hundred meters would put the wormdance inside the barn, half again as much would put the barn inside the wormdance.

"Anyway of keeping it down there? Maybe cover the exposed part so it can't find the sun?"

Estalla shook his head. "That'd just make it spread further, looking for the light."

"How about poison?" I was shocked by this. I'd never heard of anyone killing a wormswell before, not even by accident.

But Estalla was shaking his head again. "Metabolism's too slow. You could give it a fatal dose all right, and a month or so from now it'd start dying and eventually you'd have one gigantic corpse lying in, and under, your field."

"There's got to be something we can do."

"Move the barn," Estalla said quietly. "And be glad it didn't come up closer to your dike."

I glanced toward the lake, three hundred meters away, and realized what would have happened if the wormswell had chosen to surface there. Maybe, all things considered, we hadn't been as unlucky as we might have been. But it still might be sufficient to cost us the farm.

Dad invited Dr. Estalla to stay for dinner, which surprised me. I'd expected Mom to extend the offer, but Dad has never been particularly graceful in social situations. Lack of practice, I guess. He had an ulterior motive, of course. He wanted to pump the man for information, convinced that somehow there was a way to divert the wormswell. I sensed the way his mind was working, but I wasn't hopeful. The creature was just so immense, the idea of affecting its plans in any way seemed to me just so much wishful thinking.

"What would happen if we took the autoscythes in and just cut down all of the wormdance?"

Cille choked on her food. "Dad! You wouldn't!"

"Just theoretically," he said soothingly, but without fooling anyone.

Estalla chewed for a while before answering. "Most likely it would spread faster, bring more of itself to the surface. The shorn parts would grow back quickly in any case. You'd see fresh growth in four or five days. Their regenerative powers are amazing. They can grow faster'n they can move."

"Is there any way to prevent the regrowth?"

"I suppose you could cauterize the area. Build up enough scar tissue and the fresh growth wouldn't be able to break through."

"Wouldn't it just spread out around the scar tissue?" I asked.

Estalla was silent for another bite or two. "Maybe. Maybe not. We just don't know enough about them. They will eventually withdraw if they encounter an obstruction they can't move. It's possible damage to the core of the exposed area would have the same effect, but I wouldn't count on it."

Dad didn't say much more that evening, but I could see in his eyes that he'd made a decision.

Cille and Dad had an argument the following morning. Such a simple thing to say, such a complex and shocking event. I'd never seen her so upset before; no one had.

"You can't do it! You just can't! It doesn't know it's hurting anything. This is its world and it's just acting according to its nature!"

"Cille, if we lose the barn, we'll probably lose the farm. I know it seems cruel, but we have to drive it back underground."

"By burning it? How can you even think about doing something so horrible?"

Dad sighed. "Dr. Estalla said it probably wouldn't even feel pain, just a vague sense that something was wrong. I'm sorry, Cille, I really am. If there were any other way…" His voice trailed off. "I've made my decision."

And even Cille heard the determination in his voice, and subsided. We knew she wasn't happy, but she'd accepted the situation.

We spent the whole day ferrying canisters of synthfuel down to the north field.

We all went to bed early that night, exhausted from the effort, knowing that eventually we'd have to put in long hours catching up on the work that we should have been doing that day. It must've taken Dad three or four tries to wake me up when he came into our room early the following morning. Too early.

I glanced at the window. There wasn't even a hint of the dawn. "What's wrong?"

"Quiet!" Dad's whisper was intense. "You and your brother, get up and dressed. Don't make any noise."

"Wha's going on?" Judging by Jesper's slurred words, he was even less alert than I was.

"We're going up to burn the wormswell. I want to get it done before your sister wakes up. She'll insist on coming up to watch us do it, and I don't want her seeing this. It'll be better that way."

We ate cold biscuits while we walked, using a flasher to light our path. When we reached the wormswell, we could see that some of our bracing had given way, the buckled wall of the barn was beginning to split. There was no longer any question; we were going to lose the whole thing.

We strapped spraypacks onto our backs and attached them to the first three canisters.

"Be careful not to get caught in each other's spray," cautioned Dad as we began walking the perimeter, directing the stream of fuel back and forth, coating everything we could reach with a thin film of flammable mist. The sun was just starting to come up when we finished.

"Get back behind the barn," Dad ordered as he primed the flare. Jesper and I retreated, but we watched as he stood there, hesitating, and I knew that even he was troubled by the destruction of such beauty, no matter how necessary. Then he tossed it and ran toward us, and the night turned to day behind him.

The shockwave knocked us all from our feet and blew the buckled section off the barn. We lay with our hands over our heads, but the immediate fury died away within seconds, and in less than a minute we stood, blinking, and emerged from behind our shelter.

The wormdance was, of course, completely gone, replaced by clouds of smoke and ash. But there was still something moving out there in the forest of death, something that moved deliberately if rather unsteadily, reached the perimeter of the blasted area and then collapsed.

Cille had sneaked out of the house to spend one last night among the dancing structures of the wormswell.

CHAPTER TWO

Dad's gamble worked. The shock of cauterization discouraged the wormswell from rising any further, or perhaps it had discharged enough of its sperm shells for this cycle of its life. For whatever reason, it began to subside the following day. Not that any of us noticed at the time.

Emergency Services flew Cille to the big hospital in Aladdin and saved her life. There were times in the months that followed during which, I am ashamed to say, I wished that they had failed. There are some remarkable things possible with skin grafts, and on some of the bigger colony worlds they can fit you out with a synthetic skin that looks almost normal, although it takes a lot of maintenance and you have to replace it every few years. All of this requires a lot of credit though, credit that we didn't have, and the basic equipment available on Aragon was hardly state of the art.

I'm not trying to say that they treated Cille badly. On the contrary, everyone at the hospital seemed very nice and I think they were genuinely fond of her and sad that they couldn't do more. Dr. Corso convinced the hospital to include her in a research project so that Cille's eyes got replaced for free and I know some of the specialists waived their fees when they learned about our situation.

We all stayed in Aladdin for the first few days. I hadn't been to the capital city in a couple of years and normally I would have been excited at the prospect of seeing the spaceport and the entertainment quarter and all the rest. Instead, I just moped in the room Jesper and I shared at the hostel. Jesper went out all the time, but he discouraged any attempt to accompany him and I don't think he was exploring. Ever since that terrible day, he'd been filled with a bubbling rage that actually scared me at times. I'm not sure where he went or what he did, but he didn't look any happier or more settled in his mind when he came back.

After four days, when it was certain Cille would live, Mom ordered the rest of us to go back to the farm. "It won't do any good for you to stay here right now. Better that you busy yourselves and salvage what you can back home. It won't help Cille if we lose the farm on top of everything else. If we don't get this season's seed planted, we'll never get out of debt."

Dad looked like he wanted to argue, but he remained silent. He hadn't said much at all since the accident, and it seemed to me that he'd shrunk a little, that he wasn't nearly as tall and broad in the shoulders as I remembered. Jesper didn't argue either, just turned and stomped off without a word. I was the one who opened my mouth, insisting that I didn't want to leave.

"What if she wants to see us and we're not here!" My voice cracked with tension and my eyes were stinging.

Mom just came over to me and put one finger on my mouth and talked softly. "What your sister needs now is rest and quiet. She doesn't need to have you sitting around here feeling sorry for her. When she's ready to come home, she's going to need a home to come to, and the best thing you can do for her right now is to help make that possible."

So Dad, Jesper, and I went back to the farm, repaired the barn, seeded and irrigated and harvested, and somehow managed to get through the season with a modest profit. We talked to Mom every day or two over the com. Cille was doing well, she told us. Once she'd been stabilized, they started repairing the damage. The eyes were first, thanks to Dr. Corso. Then her vocal cords had to be completely rebuilt. Mom's voice was a little strained the day she told us about that. "It'll be weeks yet before she learns to use them, but she's conscious a lot of the time now, and alert. We've worked out a little code with eyelid blinks and finger twitches."

After we'd gotten a progress report, she'd ask how we were getting on and we all lied and said things were fine. Even Jesper would join in our conspiracy, and that was almost the only time Dad or I ever heard his voice. He'd turned in on himself and I'm not sure whether he was mad at Dad and I or ashamed of himself or both. But he did more than his share of the work now, and he even completed the jobs he'd always skipped out on, sometimes going on even after Dad and I were satisfied, like he was punishing himself for his earlier laziness.

I ended up doing most of the cooking and Jesper took on the housekeeping. Neither of us did a particularly good job of it. Meals were not congenial, but I'm happy to say they were always edible. Much of the time we ate as we worked. On the rare occasions when we were back at the house, it was not unusual for each of us to take our plates to a different room. We rarely talked about Cille or Mom and never even approached the subject of that night. The wormswell had subsided and the barn was saved though badly damaged, but none of us went up to the north field unless it was absolutely necessary.

Dad flew up to Aladdin a couple of times, but neither Jesper nor I asked to go along. When he came back, his face would be darker than ever and his eyes more shuttered, but he'd tell us Cille was doing fine and that she'd be coming home soon. It was four months before we got to talk to her on the com, voice only, and it didn't seem real to me because it wasn't Cille's voice at all. The new vocal cords gave her a deeper, slightly hoarse tone. I covered my confusion by talking too much, which was just as well since Jesper never said anything after the first couple of minutes, and silently left the room even before we broke the connection.

Another season passed by and we did pretty well. The fields were all in good shape, though the house was a wreck. Jesper's intentions were good, and he cleaned and polished and repaired and even repainted with relentless thoroughness. But it didn't feel like our home any more. It had become a characterless, unknown place, and each of us shared it with two mildly familiar strangers.

It was almost eight months before they decided that Cille could leave the hospital. Her eyes and vocal cords were working fine and she was walking on her own, though she tired easily. Mom told us that she'd need a lot of extra care, particularly at first, and that a therapist would be coming out every few days to check on her progress. A tentative date was set and Jesper and I spent a lot of time cleaning up, particularly Cille's room, making space for some special equipment that would be coming along with her. Dad had set us to work extending the house to accommodate her needs, but we wouldn't be able to finish it in time. We still hadn't seen her since the dressings had been removed, and we thought – or at least I did – that she was embarrassed by her appearance and didn't want us to see her. There was no hint of it during our conversations though. She still talked very slowly because it sometimes hurt otherwise, but she was almost always cheerful, asked questions about us and how we were getting along, made jokes about our housekeeping efforts, and insisted that Jesper and I take care of Dad. "He needs you boys more than he lets on."

In my head I knew that it was Cille I was hearing, but the voice was still wrong and it was hard to accept her identity where it really counted. Not being able to see her didn't help, although I suppose it wouldn't have anyway, since she would never again look as she had the day of her birthday. I later found out that it was Mom's decision to turn off the visual feed. I think she sensed that Jesper and I weren't ready to see what had happened to our sister. I know that I wasn't, and for Jesper it was apparently even worse.

The day finally came. Dad flew up to Aladdin the night before and Jesper and I were up and down all night, waking up to think of some last minute and completely unnecessary adjustment that needed to be made to her room. We'd fixed the rough spot in the front steps because Cille was still a bit unsteady on her feet, and we'd rounded corners on tables and cabinets, added padding in some places, all because Mom said she bruised easily and that we'd need to be very careful that she not hurt herself because some parts of her body no longer felt pain and if she cut herself, she might not even notice until it got infected.

They came out to the farm in a commercial choplifter that carried her special equipment in its cargo bay. They landed behind the house, where it was fairly level, and the crew was out and opening the sliding doors even before the rotors had stopped. Jesper and I stood on the back stoop, and I remember being happy and nervous both at once. Dad stepped out first, gave us a perfunctory wave, then turned back to help a much smaller figure descend. It had to be Cille, but she was wrapped in a scarf and sweater despite the warm weather. We later found out that she nearly always felt chilly, even on the hottest of days. From a distance, I couldn't see anything unusual about her face, but it was too far to make out her features. She stepped down a bit tentatively, nodded to Dad, and then waved to us with what appeared to be genuine enthusiasm. Mom deplaned right behind her and the three started toward us while the cargo handlers began unloading several boxes.

I will never forget the next few moments. There was no trace of Cille in the face of the young woman who came home that day. They eyes were a different color, of course, but they were in some ways the most recognizable part of her. The hair was a wig; her own never grew back. Her face had generally the right shape, but the flesh was twisted and distorted as though it were wax that had melted and run. The color was wrong too; it had a rosy hue that had been added to counterfeit health, but which only exaggerated its artificiality. I felt my breathing stop, maybe my heart as well, but I think my face held its cheerful mask. Cille came to me first, wrapped her arms around my waist and hugged me. I only hesitated a second before hugging her back.

"Not too tight, Ennis," she warned me in that foreign voice of hers. "I'm still a little tender in spots."

I patted her shoulder tentatively, noticed the twisted flesh on the back of her neck, and closed my eyes. "Welcome home," I said unsteadily. "We've missed you."

Then she hugged Jesper and I saw the look in his eyes as he raised his hands, not quite willing to touch her, though he didn't pull away. I saw panic there, panic and guilt and horror, and I wondered if the same emotions were visible in my eyes as well. Then we were all going inside, and Cille complimented us on how nice the place looked, and Mom kept her silence but I could almost see her making up a list of things that needed to be done to turn the house back into a home.

The choplifter was gone a few minutes later and Jesper and I lugged the freight inside. Most of it went into Cille's room, where Mom supervised its installation. The rest consisted of medicines, dietary supplements, and some items that needed to be added to our large bathroom. Dad pointed out where Cille's new room would connect to the existing house and Mom nodded her approval. Cille was tired and lay down for a nap as soon as we were through, and Mom put us all to work right afterwards. "Jesper, bring me a dozen fresh eggs. Ennis, get one of the cured hams from the larder." Dad got sent to pick some greens for a salad, while Mom surveyed the cooking utensils and selected the ones she wanted. I noticed that she washed each of them before use, although she never said one reproachful word. I'm not sure if she really thought they were dirty, or if it was just her way of re-establishing ownership of the kitchen. Or maybe it was just nervous tension.

My hands were shaking so bad that I had trouble untying the ham from where it hung, and nearly dropped it on my way back. All I could think of was that if the doctors had spent so much extra effort on Cille's face because it always showed, then how bad must the scarring be on the rest of her body? Imagination roiled my stomach and I had to fight to keep from retching. I passed Jesper coming in from the crab hens, and his face was set, though a bit pale. Mom gave him a funny look when he delivered the eggs, but she didn't say anything. She probably recognized that something was wrong, but she was using up all her mothering on Cille just then.

The meal was uncomfortable, at least for everyone except Cille. Rested, she seemed full of energy, chattered away about one thing or another whenever she wasn't actually eating. She spoke more slowly than before, and I was still having trouble with her voice. It made her sound older, but then, I guess she really was older, and in more ways than one. I wondered at first if it was an act she was putting on to convince us she was okay, but then I decided otherwise. Cille was genuinely excited and pleased to be home, out of the hospital, back where she felt she belonged. I kept sneaking glances across the table when I thought she wouldn't catch me, fascinated by the gnarled cheek, the slightly asymmetrical nose, the distorted lips and mismatched ears, and I kept asking myself how she could possibly find anything to be happy about when she faced the rest of her life looking like that. I started to feel angry at her because she had no right to be happy in the midst of so great a tragedy, and then I felt ashamed of myself, and my emotions got so confused I didn't know what I was feeling.

"Something wrong with the food, Ennis?" Mom was looking pointedly at my plate.

"No, of course not. I'm just not very hungry. Slept late and had a big breakfast." Hadn't slept much at all, actually, and hadn't eaten since the night before.

We had caffee afterwards, steaming mugs of it, and I managed the hot, bitter fluid better than solid food. Cille drank cool rosewater tea instead. "Really hot food still hurts a little," she explained easily.

"Is there much pain? I mean, anywhere else?" The words spilled out of me before I realized I was going to speak, and I flushed, wanting to drag them back.

Cille didn't seem at all uncomfortable though. "I ache a little all the time, although the doctors say most of that will go away eventually. If I stay in the same position for too long, sometimes my muscles don't work right for a while. And if I get a bruise, it either hurts for days or it doesn't hurt at all, depending on where it is."

Then Dad changed the subject and the meal ended. Cille offered to help clean up, but Mom shook her head. "Not yet. Ennis will help me. We'll put you back to work soon enough, but not so soon that you make yourself sick. I've spent enough time nursing you."

When I turned in that night, Jesper was sitting on his bed, still dressed. For the first time in months, he initiated a conversation. "Do you think she forgives us?"

It was a question that had been rattling around in my own head for a long while, but it seemed harsh and alien actually hearing it out loud. I sat down on my bed and started pulling off my boots. "Seems like. Cille never had it in her to feel badly towards a person. And it was an accident, anyway. We couldn't've known she was there."

"Do you believe in God, Ennis?"

Now that was a complicated question. Mom and Dad had both been raised as Neo-Christians, but neither had attended church after they left their parents' homes. They didn't have much opportunity once they married and came to Aragon. There were churches at the big settlements, Neo-Christian, Islamic, and Paniversalists, but it wasn't practical for them to travel that far to attend, and none of us kids had ever been to a service except a wedding here and there. The subject didn't come up very often, but Mom had told me once that she believed there was some kind of guiding intelligence in the universe, but that she wouldn't presume to give it a name or describe its nature, and that I'd just have to decide for myself when the time was right. Dad was a little more orthodox, or maybe he just pretended to be for our sake.

"I suppose," I answered finally. "Some kind of god anyway."

"If there's a god," he continued in a flat monotone, "then how could he do this to her?" I didn't answer, and the question may have been rhetorical in any case. "I mean, if anyone should have been punished for what we done, it should've been us. You and I and Dad. Or at least Dad, since it was his idea." His voice had started to rise.

"You just put that idea out of your head," I said with some heat. "Dad only did what he thought was best for us. And we did as we were told because we believed the same thing." I paused and wet my lips with my tongue as I searched for the right thing to say. "And if what you and I and Dad are feeling right now isn't punishment, then I don't know what is."

A few seconds of silence passed. "It's not enough."

I pulled off my trousers and swung my feet up onto the bed, suddenly very weary. "What's not enough?"

But he didn't answer. Instead, he rolled over onto the bed, still fully clothed, and didn't speak again. I half sat up, waited for a few minutes, couldn't think of anything else to say and finally settled back, willing myself to fall asleep. Sleep was a long time coming.

In the morning, Jesper's bed was empty. About half of his clothing was gone along with some food and other odds and ends. It would be years before any of us saw Jesper again.

We searched for him, of course, and you'd have thought someone would have found him pretty quickly. There wasn't much more than a quarter million people on Aragon back then, one settlement big enough to be called a city, maybe a dozen towns, twice that many villages, a few score remote farms like ours. The Colonial Police were polite but hinted pretty openly that they had more important things to do than search for runaway teenagers almost old enough to strike out on their own. Jesper had just turned sixteen, and since Aragon's year is pretty long, that made him legally an adult by the standards of most worlds.

"He'll come back when he's ready," Mom told us, and it seemed to me that she forgot about him after that, although from the perspective of time I'm sure that wasn't the case. Cille still needed a lot of care. She'd been at one of her high points when she'd come home; there were other times when she was physically weak, trembled all the time, had difficulty eating, and sometimes suffered terrible chills. Most of her natural resistance to infections had been weakened, so she was constantly taking medication. Through it all, she was upbeat and cheerful.

"Doesn't she ever get sad?" I asked Mom in one of those rare moments when I felt like talking about Cille's condition. It was a delicate tightrope, because the one subject that never came up was the cause of her accident. I don't think Mom blamed us for it, but she didn't hold us blameless either, and if that's a confusing way to put it, that's because it was a confusing situation.

"In little ways, yes." We were sitting on the front porch together, one of our rare moments of quiet companionship. "She hides them, even from me, but every so often I catch her looking at her reflection in a bright surface." We'd removed all the mirrors from her room before she'd come home, but she'd demanded their return. "And she's impatient with her body a lot of the time. There are things she'd like to do that are physically impossible right now, and some that probably always will be. And she'd always planned to have kids of her own some day." Her voice trailed off.

"Can't she?"

"She's still physically capable. An implant is possible. But it's not the same, raising a child on your own." She didn't have to tell me how unlikely it was that Cille would ever marry. I'd grown used to her appearance now, but I still flinched away occasionally, and sometimes her warped features came to me in nightmares.

"Where do you suppose Jesper's gone off to?"

"Out in the wilds, most likely. They've seeded enough human compatible vegetation to let him live off the land even away from settlements. He'll be back when he's ready."

"He might have gone offworld." I remembered the time we'd gone in with Dad to tour the spaceport, and how fascinated Jesper had been, watching the landing craft arrive and depart.

But Mom shook her head. "Not likely. He doesn't have the skills to join a crew, and it would take years for him to earn enough to buy passage."

"He could've stowed away."

She laughed, although there wasn't much humor in it. "I dreamed of stowing away when I was a young girl. It happens a lot in the trivideos, but not very often in real life. They have security systems, you know. Weight sensors and life detectors and such. I can't say it's impossible, but chances are still pretty good your brother is right here on Aragon somewhere."

I turned nineteen, and then twenty. Cille was doing some of the housework again and, despite protests from the rest of us, occasionally came out to work a bit in the fields. We were all worried about this and tried to put our collective foot down, but Cille pointed out that she was now legally an adult and responsible for her own life. So we negotiated a surrender in which she agreed that she would never go off on her own without letting someone know where she was, that she'd always carry an emergency com unit, and that if she felt at all distressed, she'd break off work no matter how close she was to finishing whatever chore she'd taken on.

She also started to read about then. Well, actually, she'd always been more of a reader than the rest of us, mostly adventure stories and humorous pieces. But now she started spending part of her share of the profits (and we were finally making some pretty hefty profits) to pay for access to the Aladdin Central Library. Since she was constrained from working physically for more than a few hours each day, she had plenty of time for reading. And it wasn't just fiction either. She was studying history, political science, psychology, and other fields, and not layman's surveys or popularizations. At supper one evening she announced proudly that she was enrolled in a degree program at Aladdin's Virtual University. We all acted real pleased but I don't think any of us actually understood why she was bothering. Aragon wouldn't be much more than a rural backwater for the foreseeable future, and it was the technical schools that were training the virtual coders, maintenance techs, and other professionals who would drive the planet's economy for the next couple of generations.

Like I said, the farm was finally turning a profit. We had to hire two contract workers to make up for the loss of Jesper, particularly after we opened up the west field for planting. That brought us up to six major crops and made us the third largest farm south of Aladdin, although there were a lot of bigger places to the north where the land was smoother and water more plentiful. Both field hands were about my own age. Jeb Booker was tall and thin and an able worker, but he had trouble with complex instructions and tended to become unfocused if left on his own. Zai Kreller was from one of the fringe worlds, raised in a strict religious community until she managed to escape through the good services of an underground resistance movement. She didn't talk about it much and I didn't take to her at first, but she never even blinked when she first met Cille and always treated her as though there were nothing remarkable in her appearance, and I warmed to her pretty quickly after that. Jeb was pretty good with Cille as well, but I noticed that he always kept his eyes slightly averted when he talked to her, and he had a tendency to stutter in her presence, although he never did otherwise.

Jeb was a good looking guy and I thought Zai might be interested in him for a while, but nothing ever came of it. She had kind of a craggy nose and her mouth was too small for her face, but I thought she was good looking in an exotic sort of way. But then again, she was almost the only young woman I knew other than Cille. In those days, we didn't get into Safehaven, the closest town, for more than a handful of visits in a year.

With the two of them to help, Dad and I found time to go over the accounts together and he introduced me to the business side of farming. Happily, I had no trouble understanding the system of debits and credits, or the terms of the contracts we held with the wholesalers who bought the bulk of our produce. I even made some suggestions about simplifying the way we accounted for things that Dad approved of and adopted. "You've got a head for this, Ennis. I've always hated this part of farming and it would be good for both of us if you started taking on some of the management work."

That year, Dad sent me to Aladdin on my own to take care of the annual supply contracts, though he briefed me pretty thoroughly beforehand. I'd gone with him the previous year and sat through the negotiations, but this was still a pretty big responsibility for me and I was proud and nervous all at the same time. "You're going to have to do it sooner or later, Ennis, and right now we've got the upper hand, so you ought to be able to get us some good terms."

I walked to Gansett Village and went by hoverboat to Junction and from there to Aladdin, by flitter, arriving early in the evening. There was a lot of new construction going on. Aragon was well situated to become a major trading hub as this sector was opened up. A lot of commercial exploration vessels were stopping for supplies and recreational visits, and there were even rumors that the Navy was going to establish a base in the system. The spaceport itself was being expanded, and a new power plant was in the works.

I spent the evening exploring, cautiously. In all honesty, I was a bit overwhelmed by the number of people around me. Safehaven was a fair sized town, but there were never enough people around at any one time to make up what you might call a crowd, and the other communities nearby were even smaller. I'd occasionally visited Gansett Village and the Malcolm Cooperative, although not as often since the accident, and only once with Cille, who didn't seem upset when heads turned in her direction, although I felt unaccountably embarrassed and was greatly relieved when we finally headed back home. Gansett had about five hundred residents altogether, and the Cooperative about half as many, while Safehaven outnumbered the two combined, though not by much. So put more than twenty or thirty people together in one place and I called it a crowd. In Aladdin, it was hard to find any place where I couldn't see that many people without even turning my head.

I bought some roasted cornfruit and some crab wings from a sidewalk vendor and ate them sitting on one of the benches facing the spaceport. Jesper had been fascinated with the idea of traveling to other worlds, visiting exotic places, maybe even meeting one of the alien races we knew were out there. I wondered again if he'd managed to get off Aragon somehow. Dad checked now and then and there was still no record of his being legally employed anywhere on the planet, but about a third of the jobs held here were unofficial and unreported. He might have earned and saved enough to buy passage by now; it had been more than a year. I was mad that he'd gone off and left us, but I kind of understood it in an inarticulate sort of way, and I hoped he was well. Personally, though, I had no interest in seeing the universe. I was born a farmer, I figured, and a farmer needs to keep his eyes on the ground, not the skies.

The next day I met with the brokers we usually dealt with, Hobson and Izrahan and Shiino. Akira Shiino never gave any sign of surprise that I was representing the family, dealt with me fairly from the outset, and I ended up with the small increase in pricing that I'd expected and an early delivery bonus clause that I hadn't. Hobson couldn't conceal his pleasure at dealing with an obviously untried youth and tried to doubletalk me into accepting a convoluted penalty clause, pressed the issue until I stood up and thanked him for his time and started for the door. Then he got all red in the face and insisted that I sit down again while he considered an alternative, and his second offer was fair if not generous, and we shook hands over it. He laughed a bit nervously as I was leaving, called me a "good lad", and sent his regards to my father. Izrahan appeared to be offended that Dad hadn't come himself, questioned my authority to sign a final agreement, and his initial offer was so insulting that I not only didn't counter, I refused to listen to any modifications. Dad had never liked the man anyway, and the agreement with Shiino was sufficiently open ended that there would be no problem marketing all our produce. It was still best to have at least three outlets, but this would give us a year to find a replacement for Izrahan.

I returned to the hostel feeling pretty pleased with the day's efforts, and rewarded myself with a good meal in the main dining room. I tried real beef for the first time, and decided that the synthetic version was just fine, particularly given its much lower cost and consistent texture. About the time I was leaving, there was a sudden rise in the noise level in the lobby and I wandered out, curious, casually eavesdropping on a couple of conversations.

Apparently there'd been a new arrival at the spaceport, a skiff from a corporate lancer searching for potential mining sites. They'd found one of the big commercial explorer ships lying dead in space, hull ruptured, crew dead or missing, selected equipment removed from the ship. It had obviously been attacked by another vessel. Piracy in space was rare but not unknown, but pirates usually preferred cargo or passenger vessels. Some of the equipment aboard a research ship was quite valuable, but would be hard to dispose of profitably.

The speculation I heard that evening ran the gamut from alien warships to corporate infighting. A generation or so back, a commercial exploration crew had found what appeared to be a paradise planet, habitable, mineral rich, geologically and climatically stable. They were still gathering data when another ship warped in to the same system, representing a rival corporation. The newcomers acknowledged the prior claim but orbited anyway, asking if they could cycle some of the crew down to the temporary camp to visit and compare notes and stretch their legs. Everything appeared amicable and both crews seemed happy to see new faces. On the tenth local day, however, a bomb exploded in the first ship, killing everyone aboard, planted by one or more of the visitors. The landing party was slaughtered by the newcomers the same day, and they might have gotten away with it if the first ship hadn't already commed to one of its fellows with an invitation to come see the prize. They arrived in time to discover the killers towing the derelict into an orbit that would have taken it into the system's primary.

It was mildly exciting news and I listened with some interest, but concluded later that the incident was not relevant to my life. Rarely have I been so mistaken.

CHAPTER THREE

It was almost two years before Cille and I actually talked about her accident. That was mostly my fault. Opportunities had come up from time to time, and I'd always shied away from them, found something else to do or changed the subject. I told myself on each occasion that it was too much to ask her to speak of such painful things, but the truth was that I was both embarrassed and guilt ridden and it was for my sake rather than hers that I never confronted the issue.

Cille was a few days shy of eighteen when she finally lost her patience with me.

Over the previous year, she'd regained most of her strength. There were still things she had to do for herself medically that wouldn't ordinarily have been required, and she continued to be particularly vulnerable to infection, but for the most part she was functioning normally. Doctor Tanaga gave her some new concoction every few months and made no secret of the fact that at times the medications were experimental. Her stamina wasn't what it had once been, but she worked around the farm at least a few hours every day, and spent so much time on her studies that she had already earned a degree in Commercial Management and was working on another in some arcane discipline called Socio-Industrial Evolution.

Mom said something at dinner one night about Cille's approaching birthday. "You'll have full citizenship privileges now, you know, which means you get to cast a vote at the regional council instead of just for local issues." It was customary to celebrate when someone came of age to become a full, independent citizen, but this had all reminded me of her birthday three years past, and I felt a queasy sensation and excused myself from the table.

Cille came looking for me a while later and found me sitting on the back stoop. "It's chilly out here tonight."

I nodded without looking at her. "The season's been cooler than usual. Good for the cornfruit, bad for the pseudowheat."

"Any decision on the new expansion?"

I nodded. "Dad and I decided this afternoon. We're going to clear the land all the way to the Jackknife River and incorporate it into the east field. We've claimed everything down to the Rollers on the southwest. Dad says we won't have time to plant it all this year, maybe only a third, but that'll establish our claim and the river gives us a good natural border. The soil tests have been pretty good."

"Does that mean we hire another hand?"

"Nope. We just put down a deposit on an autotiller. Second hand, but in good condition. That'll free up Jeb and Zai enough for this year. After that, we'll have to see. It's kind of a balancing act. You need profit to expand, and you need to expand in order to increase your profit."

"How big do you see us getting?"

That was a good question, and I wasn't sure of the answer. Most of the farms in this area were down south of us, clustered around Safehaven, a town with ambitions to become a city, but those were much smaller than ours, having clustered together early in too confined a space, making it impossible for some of them to expand unless they engulfed their neighbors. The Malcolm Cooperative, a good sized communal farm sat across the Jackknife to our east, but it was a rigidly planned organization that was designed not to grow larger. When Mom and Dad arrived, back before I was born, they were part of an organized settlement group from Lucaster, a mostly agrarian world in itself. Most of the people who came in that group settled around Safehaven, the Harwells and the Ngandas and the Chandlers and such. Each of them had a profitable farm, but they had all kind of grown up against one another. Only the late comers on the circumference had any real opportunity to expand, and even that was limited by natural barriers like the Rising Hills and the Rollers, and the contiguity laws. .

Mom and Dad chose to distance themselves from the rest of the settlers, found a spot just south of where part of the Jackknife splits off into the Swift at the top of Lake Pudallah. Our irrigation dam was on one channel of the Swift, and the north field's last expansion gave us the fast flowing water as our northeastern border. This year we were claiming all the land due east of us right up to the Jackknife. We couldn't go south very far before running into the Chandler and Tonobi properties, but there was still the west, a broad expanse of fertile land on both sides of the Swift. Unfortunately for us, although every adult could legally claim undeveloped land, there was a limit to the acreage per person, and we were starting to press up against our collective allocation. There was enough leeway for one more big acquisition and Dad had been talking about establishing ourselves on the west bank of the Swift, but there were logistical problems and other issues that had to be addressed. I had different ideas. Dad thought I was getting ahead of myself, but I chafed at our inability to expand west and south along the Swift. It would give us a strong position on both watercourses as well as the junction at Lake Pudallah. The law was designed to make it difficult to accumulate large land holdings, but there were ways around it. And once Aragon was an independent world, the laws would almost certainly be altered.

"Pretty big, Cille. If we're willing to do the work to take it, there's no limit to what could be ours one day."

We sat silently for a while, but I knew there was something on her mind and that she was working around to saying it. I was less certain that I wanted to hear it, but if I'd made an excuse to leave, Cille would have known and I wasn't that craven.

"Why don't we ever talk about it, Ennis?"

"Talk about what?" But I knew immediately what she had in mind, and my stomach kind of clenched.

"The accident."

Well, it was said at last, and there was no way I could think of to change the subject now. She'd made it clear that this was why she'd come out to talk to me. What went before was just to break the ice. I felt a rush of anger, which didn't make me feel any less guilty.

"There's not much to say. It happened. We made a mistake and you nearly died. I'm sorry for my part in it and I'd take it back in a heartbeat if I could, but I can't."

"That's why Jesper ran away, wasn't it? He felt responsible."

I sighed. "Jesper and I never talked about it either. I don't know what was going through his mind that day. Running off doesn't seem like the right thing to do. A man should face his mistakes."

She shifted a bit and her voice was suddenly different, a tone that I realized was anger. Cille didn't get angry. She got exasperated, grouchy, and sometimes mildly sullen but never angry. It was so startling that I turned and looked at her directly.

"Is that all I am to you, Ennis? A mistake that you have to face?"

"I didn't mean. . ." but she cut me off, her voice rising.

"Not that you face me very much anyway. I think this is the first time you've looked me in the eyes in months. Most of the time you're studying something hovering just over my shoulder, or caught in my hair, or if you have to look at my face you let your eyes get kind of unfocused and glazed, like you're looking right through me at something else."

I felt my own temper beginning to rise. "That's not fair. I just don't want you to think I'm staring at you."

"And why should I care about that?" She raised her hand and touched her twisted face. "Do you think I'm ashamed of this? It happened, like you said, and it was a terrible thing. But I don't need to be ashamed because it wasn't my fault." She leaned forward suddenly and grabbed me by the shoulder, and her fingers pressed painfully into my flesh. "And it wasn't your fault either, Ennis. Not yours, not Jesper's, and not Dad's. You were all trying to do the right thing, and it went wrong. Life isn't perfect. We all try to paint a beautiful life for ourselves, but the problem is we're all using the same canvas and sometimes the brushstrokes interfere with one another or someone's hand slips. Feeling guilty when something goes wrong won't make it any better. Neither will feeling embarrassed. This is our life now, Ennis. We have to go on from this point. We'll both make more mistakes, sometimes big ones that we'll regret for years after, but we have to do the best we can at the time and move on."

I wanted to argue with her, explain that we should have told her what we were doing, or checked on her before we left that morning, but when I tried to talk, my voice broke and I realized that I was crying and I hadn't cried since the night we burned the wormswell. Cille put her arms around me and I held onto her as well and we stayed that way for a long time, until it was dark and too cold to stay outside any longer.

And from then on, I never had any trouble looking into her face and seeing the beauty that was still there, and I felt a load of guilt lift from me and vanish. Not all of it, mind you, but enough that life seemed a little more bearable.

That was the year things started to change on Aragon. Well, that's not fair. Things changed every year, but it was about this time that the changes started affecting us at the farm. The Concourse or Worlds is a pretty loosely constituted arrangement, but they have strict rules about new colonies. Most of them are opened up by one of the big trading corporations, and they administer the law in accordance with guidelines from the Concourse's executive council, which is made up of representatives from all the member worlds. There's a complex formula that determines when a colony is considered a viable political unit, a combination of population level, infrastructure, commercial viability, and other factors. Corporations have been known to manipulate some of the components in order to prolong their domination of a colony, but generally that's not the case, because the Concourse provides attractive financial incentives for the corporations to turn over control as quickly as possible. Before that could be accomplished, the local population was charged with forming a government and a body of law. There were certain minimum safeguards required of all Concourse worlds, and a handful of colonies – mostly those settled by extremist groups – had rejected elements among those safeguards. No one interfered with them, but they were not allowed to become members of the Concourse, and there were restrictions on emigration, trade, technology transfer, and other matters. Jai Kreller came from one of these, had claimed refugee status after her escape.

Aragon wasn't quite ready for independence, but it was close enough that there was already some maneuvering going on. Aladdin was our biggest city, but Tyrada and Casper were growing rapidly as well. Even Safehaven was a real town now, its population having passed one thousand. Immigration had tapered off and the southern continent was still closed to all but research parties, but natural growth was steadily increasing the population, the mines out west had brought a lot of capital investment, and there was already a manufacturing district in Aladdin. Abe Longfeather, the company administrator, appeared to be both able and fair minded, and he was actively encouraging the formation of an independent city government in the capital.

Dad had words with Sobriety Carter on the subject. Like I said before, Dad wasn't too happy having outsiders in our home. I think this was one of the few bits of tension between him and Mom, although she never let on to us directly, just hinted from time to time that she'd kind of like to have more people out to visit. Anyway, one afternoon Sobriety Carter called and asked if he could stop by and wouldn't take no for an answer. An hour later he and Cindy Aguilar came up the Jackknife in a small powerboat and Dad met them at the east dock and brought them back to the house.

I'd been planning to work with Jeb in the new plot along the river, but Dad told me to stay at the house. "If this is what I believe it is, you need to be here as well. If you think dealing with the wholesalers was a chore, wait till you get introduced to politics."

So Cille served us caffee and cake while Dad, Mom, and I listened to our visitors. Their argument was a simple one. They wanted Safehaven to be government center for a new district which would include the Malcolm Cooperative, Gansett Village, and Managua, a new settlement up to the northwest beyond the split between the Swift and the Jackknife. Our farm would have to be included for the plan to make any sense; we were now the largest landholders in the area and the four named settlements all abutted our property, or faced us across rivers.

"What does Ned Grant up in Gansett say about all this?"

Carter scratched his head. "Well, we haven't broached the subject with him yet."

Cindy Aguilar spoke up for the first time. "We all know how thick headed Ned can be, and the people up there generally follow his lead. The council figured that if we could get everyone else to sign on to the plan, he'd find it harder to hold out."

Dad ran his fingers through his beard, not saying anything. It was Mom who asked the question I'd been wondering about. "This council you keep talking about. Just who exactly is on it?"

"Most of the big landholders in Safehaven," said Carter. "All but old Harwell. And there's Needham, the banker, and Shikuro, and a few other merchants."

"Anyone from the Cooperative?" asked Dad.

"Well, they're anarchists," Carter complained inaccurately. "Damn it, Jon, you know how those people are. They want nothing to do with government, or the rest of us."

Mom spoke up, and I could tell she was annoyed. "That's nonsense, Sobriety, and you know it. When we had the bluebug infestation, they helped all the farmers clear their fields. Even yours.

They mind their own business and don't like interference from the outside, but they're sociable enough and they help when it's needed."

"All right, I didn't mean to be critical. But we asked them to send a representative when we were getting ourselves set up, and they told us they weren't interested."

"So you haven't talked to the Cooperative and you haven't spoken to Ned Grant." Dad's voice was nice and level and he spoke each word so precisely that I knew he was fuming underneath. "So who came down from Managua to be on your council?"

Carter chuckled. "Those fellows don't even have a permanent power station yet. They've got too much on their plate to get involved in regional politics for a while. Hell, Jon, if you hadn't loaned them the equipment to run a channel from the Swift, they wouldn't even have running water."

"So let me see if I understand this. Everyone on the council is from Safehaven, and all of them are farm or business owners. But you want to set policy for three other communities, whose combined population outnumbers you by a fair amount? What makes you think they'll agree to your little coup?"

Cindy's eyes flickered with nervousness; she'd picked up on Dad's anger. Carter licked his lips and hesitated, but it was Cille who answered for him.

"Managua won't be viable as a separate community for another year or two, and until then they're depending on getting their produce to market by piggybacking on the hover barges we've contracted for as well as the one we owned outright, to say nothing of trading labor for use of our tilling equipment. Gansett is more independent and they could probably raise the credit to run their own barge down to market, but that would mean delaying construction of their new processing plant for at least a year. The Cooperative isn't beholden to us at all, but they're pretty well withdrawn from the outside world in matters like this, and the incorporation would engulf them as a matter of course."

Dad nodded. "So the reason you're here, Sobriety Carter, is to convince us we should help coerce our neighbors into acquiescing to your plan. Safehaven doesn't have any leverage with them, but we do. Should I ask who heads this council, or do I already know?"

Cindy Aguilar answered, but her tone was defensive. "Sobriety was elected by the members, Jon. Outside of yourself, he's the biggest property owner in the region."

My father was suddenly standing. "Thank you for coming by to present your viewpoint. I'll take it under advisement."

Any of us Baxters could have told Carter that it was time to pick up his hat and go, but he was either insensitive to the tension in Dad's voice or indifferent to it. "We were hoping to have your agreement on this today, Jon. Ned Grant has been talking to the Managua people about jointly financing a harbor on the Jackknife north of the split. If Gansett and Managua grow toward each other, they could merge and form a good sized town."

"Bigger than Safehaven, even," said Cille slyly. "And they'd have a harbor upriver of the split. Good transport down the Jackknife or the Swift. I hear there's talk of opening up a new settlement down the Swift a ways."

Carter's head bobbed. "Your daughter's got the right of it, Jon. We've got to get ourselves established first if we want to be regional capital. Damn it, man, you have to throw in with us or this whole thing could hang in the air for a couple of years and who knows what might happen then?"

"I don't take kindly to people coming into my home and telling me what I have to do, Sobriety Carter." Dad wasn't hiding his anger now, and Carter stood up, almost defensively. "Neither do I care for people who want me to use the problems of my neighbors to accumulate power for myself or others. There's plenty of time yet before we have to worry about councils and governments and who's going to be calling the shots for everyone else. Now I do think it's time for you to thank my wife and daughter for their fine caffee and baked goods and apologize for taking up our valuable time. When I have some thoughts on these matters, I will certainly make certain you're aware of them, but right now all I can think of is that I came to Aragon to get away from the kind of political infighting that you're talking about here, and I don't much like having it thrown in my face this way."

Carter left in a huff, Aguilar in embarrassed confusion. None of us walked them back to the river. Dad calmed down after a bit, and then Cille broke a long silence. "You're right, Dad, but you're wrong as well. The change is coming and it's coming fast."

"I know it, Cille. That doesn't make it sit any better." He glanced up at me. "Ennis, you finished surveying the Rollers yet?"

The Rollers was the name we gave to the land south and west of our holding, which extended all the way to the Swift, and south almost as far as Carter's farm and those of his neighbors. I'd scouted the area thoroughly in order to present it as an alternative to Dad's proposal that we cross the Swift. "Pretty much. Most of the soil's good, a few sour spots. Heavily forested, not much level ground, but the hills are gentle enough. It'll be more expensive to farm but it should be profitable eventually. Carter's been pushing up in that general direction a bit, but it looks like he's just anticipating a service road rather than looking for fresh cropland."

"If we hired another hand or two, could we clear a significant portion of it over the next year?"

I didn't need to calculate, and I'm sure Dad already knew the answer. "No. Random cutting doesn't establish ownership. We'd need to clear in such a way as to make the land tillable, which means trunk removal." And native Aragonian trees had thick roots that ran horizontally and intertwined with one another, as well as tap roots that ran deep. "We could probably add two or three plots, less if the winter's bad or the spring's wetter than average. Why the rush?"

"To keep them from putting through an access road." It was Mom, who was obviously well ahead of me. "They'll want a way to reach the Swift above the new settlement. If the newcomers are dependent on Safehaven for supply and transport to market, they'll be forced to bow to them politically as well."

"If there was any way we could take that land pre-emptively, an overland route would be less profitable. It would have to be longer and wind through the Rising Hills to the south. River transport is still more economical." Commercial flitters could fly over the hills, actually, but the fuel expenditure would make it prohibitively costly.

I didn't get it and I said so. "Even if Carter and his friends build a pier on the Swift, no one has to use it. They can just bypass it and continue up to the Jackknife. We're the only ones who could stop them, because of our dam." And even as I said it, I knew the answer. "Unless they built their own dam."

Dad smiled, pleased that I'd figured it out for myself. "There's a half dozen spots where the Swift narrows enough. I don't think they'd even actually construct one. All that would be necessary would be to do some preliminary work and drop some hints. Use our transport or we'll restrict your water. From the Rollers south to the new settlement, the Swift runs through deep ravines. There's no place to build anywhere along the way."

I shook my head, which was starting to hurt. "But doesn't that mean we're going to have to go into the transport business full time?" We'd been providing space for a token fee to the Managuans ever since they established themselves, and occasionally to the Cooperative, Gansett, and even a couple of farmers from Safehaven. But it had always been a windfall or a favor, was never intended to be a formal part of the family business.

"So I propose," said Dad. "I call for a vote."

Mom and Cille raised their hands immediately, and so did I after a brief hesitation. And that's how Baxter Transport got started.

"But we still can't get that land cleared," I said unhappily. "We'd need a minimum of a dozen hands to clear enough land to block off road construction, and we'd have to do at least some planting or Carter and his cronies will be screaming illegal land grab. That's another two or three. We might be able to borrow enough to pay for all of that, but it would stretch us thin." I did some quick mental calculations. "We might just have enough left on our claim entitlement to block them, but we might also be a little short. There's a lot of acreage there."

"If necessary, we could be selective about what land we take," Cille commented. "Our credit level is the more serious problem. Can we afford to divert resources right now?"

"Can't touch Jesper's share either," cautioned Mom. "It still belongs to him and we don't have the right to use it without his permission." It was the first time Jesper's name had been spoken by either of my parents in my presence for over a year.

"Maybe we could just clear enough to make a road impractical," I suggested. "Block access to the Swift."

Dad shook his head. "Has to be contiguous to our property to establish ownership. Otherwise it's a separate holding and you have to prove you've got enough credit to run independently or the company court won't uphold the claim."

"How about the cooperative?" Cille was standing in a corner, leaning back against the wall.

Dad looked puzzled. "The Malcolm people don't want to expand, Cille, and they certainly wouldn't want to split into two communities. The whole basis of their setup is that they're a single extended family."

"I don't mean the Malcolms. Didn't you tell me the Managuans were overly automated?"

"Yes and no. Their automation is out of balance. They have good harvesting equipment, better than ours in fact. Half a dozen hands can bring in all their crops. But their land is rockier than they thought and they didn't bring in autotillers, which is why we're leasing them one of ours."

"So for a good part of each season, a large portion of their population is going to be sitting around watching the bots bring in the crops, right?"

Dad's eyebrows went up, and probably mine as well. "They'd only be available for about a third of the year, and always in bits and pieces, but there's maybe eighty, ninety adults with nothing to do for a good bit of the time. So what's their incentive?"

"We drop the fees for the autotiller. Give them a reduced rate on transportation for ten years, or a percentage of the yield from the new land, or some combination of the two. They would have to wait for the payoff, and take the risk that the whole thing might fall apart and they'd get nothing, but coming out here to Aragon was a gamble in the first place, and all they're risking is a little sweat and blood."

We were all quiet for a while. I was mentally looking at a map of the area. What we were proposing would substantially increase the size of our property. We'd be as big as the entire Safehaven community excluding its surrounding farms, and we'd be strategically positioned to dominate the Swift River. We were also talking about changing the very nature of our business from straightforward farming to a wider variety of enterprises. But we were headed that way sooner or later; Carter's visit had just precipitated things. It was another hour before we stopped talking about it, but when we went to bed that night, we'd taken another vote, and Dad and Cille were delegated to approach the Managuans and present our case.

It didn't go entirely smoothly, as I found out later. Strictly speaking, the Managuans didn't have any official leaders, although in practice there were a half dozen voices who spoke louder than the rest, or at least were more listened to. They're not a Utopian community like the Malcolms, and had been organized hastily and clumsily when the drought on Tanith wiped out the local economy. At least one of the settlers pointed out that we Baxters were going to be the big winners if all went as planned. Dad conceded that this was the case and countered that everyone stood to gain, and that they were free to reject his offer and make a counter proposal if they wished. And then Cille had spoken up.

"There's no reason why you couldn't do this yourselves, without the Baxters." She waited for the murmuring to die down. "You've got the manpower and we haven't. Your land abuts the Swift, and the territory in question includes the opposite shore, so the law is satisfied and you can clear it and claim it as a community or as individuals. We'll continue to lease you the autotiller and sign a long term agreement on transport if you want, although it would make more sense for you to develop your own, since you'd control both sides of the Swift."

Someone shouted from the assembly. "But you Baxters have the dam at the Jackknife. You could charge us to bring our produce upriver."

Dad shook his head. "Company policy prohibits restraints of passage on any navigable waterway. And even if it didn't, you could build yourselves a new pier north of our dam."

There was a good deal of murmuring, and some arguing. Akiura Song, one of the more influential Managuans, suggested quietly that Dad and Cille leave and let them talk things over. "Give us a few days, Jon. Most of the people here like and trust your family, but you've caught us by surprise with this, and it has significant implications. We've only been here on Aragon for a little over a year, and you're suggesting a pretty radical change from our original plan."

"I understand completely. We'll wait as long as we can. I don't want to be an alarmist, Aki, but you have to realize that the people in Safehaven can add up the figures just as well as we can. The land below them on the Jackknife is much too rocky for development, and beyond that is the salt lake and the desert. The Swift leads to the new settlement, and there's arable land below that as well. If Safehaven doesn't tap into the Swift, they're doomed to stay pretty much at their present size. Even Gansett Village could outgrow them in time. They could run a road through at any time, and they probably would have already if there wasn't such a long waiting list for heavy construction equipment. If we're going to do anything, it will have to be this year."

It was three days before we heard from them. Apparently the debate ran pretty hot and heavy for a while, and the decision might not have been made at all if Sobriety Carter hadn't inadvertently lent us a hand. He paid a visit to the Managuans on the third day and offered to hire fifty adults to work on construction of an access road from Safehaven to the Swift. They voted that evening to accept our proposal, with the terms exactly as presented.

Happily, it was our best year to date commercially. The pseudowheat came in so fast that we actually got four crops in a single year in one field, and the usual three in all the others. We put in a half field of the newly bioengineered rubbage and it did well, although we ran into some resistance at market because of its unpleasant appearance. Tasted fine though, and Mom experimented with it so much that I got rather tired of it. She published a collection of her recipes through the planetary net and it was accessed so many times that she accumulated enough credit to replace a lot of our aging kitchen equipment. Then bluebugs attacked the crops around Tyrada but spared us and prices for cornfruit in particular jumped toward the sky. I was sinfully pleased when I heard that Sobriety Carter had switched from cornfruit to soy, hoping to boost his sales to the stockbreeders up north of Aladdin. I could have told him his transportation costs were going to be so high that he'd be priced out of the market, but I didn't.

Surveyors came out and laid markings for a road from Safehaven to the Swift. I know because some of the Managuans clearing for us called me out to see their pickets and tags. We were on pretty good terms with our new workers by then, because Cille and I talked Dad into increasing their share after they sent us so many helping hands that we had trouble keeping them all busy. Well over a hundred at one time, although we ended up sending a couple of dozen home because we just couldn't use them. We left the surveyors' artifacts in place and cleared all around them, little islands of forlorn hope in an ocean of cleared fields.

I had expected to get no more than three sections seeded by the end of that year, but we actually managed seven, with nine more sufficiently cleared that we could have cultivated them as well. There was some concern that we were going to outrun our market and drive the prices down, and while I wouldn't have minded putting Carter and some of his friends out of business, the downturn would have affected the Cooperative and the Managuans and even Gansett Village as well. Fortunately, the company accelerated the development of Goodhost, the new settlement south on the Swift, and we negotiated a very profitable contract to supply them for the first two years.

Cille and I visited Safehaven a few days after the contract was announced, and as luck would have it we ran into Sobriety Carter and his wife while we were sightseeing. I nodded and half turned away and I thought that would be it, but he came over to speak to us, his lips thin in a reddening face, his wife trailing behind looking worried.

"I understand you Baxters are claiming the Rollers." His voice was hoarse with tension.

"We're developing most of it, yes, but we've formed a limited cooperative arrangement with the Managuans. They'll get most of the profits for the first five years, and a share for twenty after that."

"While you get the land title."

I carefully didn't smile, but I nodded.

"I suppose you didn't know that we were planning to run a surface road through that area."

"Oh, we knew. Saw your markers. Smart idea you abandoning that. It wouldn't have paid you back for a long time. Goodhost is too far south, Managua too far north."

I was gloating inside, but I think I managed to keep it out of my voice. Didn't make any difference in the long run, because Carter just got furious anyway.

"Don't play innocent with me, boy. Your father claims he's not interested in politics, and fool that I am I fell for it. As soon as my back's turned, he's making deals with someone else to cut me out of the picture. Well, I remember my friends and I remember my enemies, and I particularly remember treachery. I'm amazed that any of you Baxters has the nerve to show your face here in Safehaven."

And then he made his mistake. He turned toward Cille, who had remained silent throughout, and said what he shouldn't have. "And I'm even more amazed that your sister has the nerve to show what passes for her face anywhere at all."

I don't remember hitting him. Cille told me afterward that I landed three blows so fast that he was unconscious before he hit the floor. Broke one of my fingers and bruised a whole lot of knuckles, and I never realized before how good it could feel to be hurt.

CHAPTER FOUR

Although we'd taken some of the steam out of the drive by Safehaven, or at least by Carter and his cronies, to dominate the area, we hadn't derailed it, and we'd made ourselves some powerful enemies in the process. Like it or not, we had to accept the fact that Carter and those allied with him had at least taken the initiative to create the rudiments of a local government, and it would have been foolish for us just to ignore the changes that were underway. The official company estimate was that Aragon would be ready for autonomy within no less than two and no more than four years. Some of the other locals who wanted Safehaven to become predominant came out to talk, and most of them were nice people and all of them nicer than Carter, so we reached an accommodation. Dad talked to Ned Grant, Cille and I visited the Managuans, and Mom paid a visit to the Cooperative. Grant huffed and puffed and finally agreed to join the council as an ad hoc member, the Managuans were happy to send an entire delegation, and Mom even talked the Malcolms into sending an "observer". It was agreed in principle that Safehaven was to host the discussions because they had the only comfortable building large enough for the expanded group, and everyone except Carter was careful to avoid hinting that the arrangement was anything other than temporary, and even he had the sense not to let anything inflammatory slip where Ned Grant could hear him.

Dad and I attended the first couple of meetings together. I didn't want to go particularly, but he insisted. "This is your future more than mine, Ennis. You need to have a hand in shaping it."

I heard some subdued rumbling about the size of the Baxter holdings, but it was mostly sour grapes. We were still within the legal limits. Company policy set a cap on how much land each individual could claim. Since Jesper and I were technically the claimants for our original farm, Mom and Dad and Cille used their entitlement to establish our ownership of the Rollers, but that had pretty much used up our collective quota. In fact, there was one remaining plot of land in the Rollers we hadn't cleared, a triangular piece with a small bit of shoreline. We had some concern that Carter might still run a circuitous road around our property and link to it.

"Can't we get some of the Managuans to claim it? There must be dozens of them who haven't taken their full allotment." We could buy land that had been properly claimed and add it to our own, but whoever originally claimed the plot would not have the right to replace it. The company frowned on land speculation.

"Won't work," Cille told me. "It's not contiguous, for one thing. And they'd have to demonstrate the ability to cultivate the land. As a cooperative, they qualify, but as individual homesteaders, none of them have the resources."

The solution came from an unexpected quarter.

We were all sitting around having supper, the family, Jeb Booker, Zai Kreller, and two temporary hands we'd hired for the season. Just as we started to clear away, Zai asked Dad if she could speak to the family some time on a business matter. I felt a little pang of dismay, because I figured she was going to give notice. She'd been saving her wages ever since she'd arrived, and we were paying her pretty well. It made sense for her to homestead on her own, but she was going to leave a big gap if she moved on.

So after the supper things were disposed of, the five of us sat around the table and waited for her to speak her piece.

"I want you to know that I very much appreciate all that you've done for me. The last two years have been the only time I've ever felt as though I had a family." Zai's homeworld, Allahabad, had been settled by The Golden Scimitar, an Islamic fundamentalist group that reacted strongly against the reformist movement within mainstream Islam. Women were essentially chattel, disenfranchised, and had limited civil rights. They expressed no interest in joining the Concourse, and would not have been accepted if they had applied.

"We've been very happy to have you with us," Mom answered. "And you and Jeb have both been more than just employees."

Zai nodded and looked down at her hands, which were clasped tightly in her lap. She'd always been awkward about emotions. I'd rarely seen her express anger, and the only time she smiled was when she was particularly satisfied with some task she'd been working on.

"As you know, I've been saving most of what you've paid me. I have enough now that I can qualify for homesteading and I've lived on Aragon long enough to place a claim."

I nodded to myself, pleased in an unhappy sort of way that I'd guessed correctly. But Zai had another surprise for us.

"We'll be sorry to see you leave but I'm sure we all understand." I thought I caught a hint of sadness in Dad's voice. "Did you have a location picked out?"

She nodded, and to my utter amazement, seemed genuinely amused for a couple of seconds. The expression was so alien on her face that I had trouble reconciling it with my image of her. "There's a small section of the Rollers just beyond your property line that runs from the Swift back to Barbecue Hill."

It was the section we'd wanted to include in our own, but which had exceeded our quota. Dad was caught completely by surprise, so I spoke up. "The choice is yours, Zai, but that's not prime land. The soil samples weren't promising, the terrain is rugged, and the property itself is an odd shape." It was a fair evaluation. The land was of strategic value between Safehaven and ourselves, but as farmland, it was far inferior to what she could have claimed elsewhere, in Goodhost for example.

"I've visited the property. It will support some marginal crops but, as you say, it would likely never be self sufficient."

"Then why?" Dad and I asked the question simultaneously, but it was Cille whose eyes lit up with understanding even before Zai explained.

"You need that piece of land to control local access to the Swift. I can claim it for you, and we can put in some token planting to meet the letter of the law."

"But then you'd never be able to claim property for yourself," I said quietly. "We can't ask you to give up your own future that way."

She shook her head and our eyes met, though briefly. Her childhood training had been to look down or away in the presence of a male. Any male. "I don't know that I'll ever want land of my own. That's never been one of my priorities. But if the situation should change, I would hope that your family would purchase the homestead from me. I know it has little intrinsic value, but that combined with the credit I'll have saved should be more than enough to allow me to provide for myself."

Mom protested a little longer, but not strongly. We all recognized that this was something Zai really wanted to do, and it was an elegant solution to what might be an irritating future problem. We told Zai we'd sleep on it, and after she left we talked some more. In the morning, we accepted her offer, but conditional upon her selling the land to us promptly for a price that was nearly double its actual value. She hesitated and I thought she was going to argue that we were paying far too much, but then she nodded and we shook hands and for all practical purposes, the Baxter family owned the Rollers from end to end.

We had wormswell that year. It was a small one, but it still managed to rip up almost half of one of our lesser fields, and it cost us a considerable amount of credit. There was never any talk of doing anything to drive it off, of course, and for the first few days after Zeb reported its existence, we all walked around the house on tiptoes, none of us wanting to say the wrong thing. Cille defused the tension by announcing that she was going to walk down and take a look and inviting us all to go along. I was probably overcompensating when I started to volunteer, but Mom gave me a look that told me to be silent, and eventually she and Dad went down together.

They were gone a long time and when they came back Cille was the same as ever, but Dad seemed a lot happier than he'd been for years. Cille went down regularly after that, every few days until after the wormdance was over and the swell subsided, and sometimes I went along. It wasn't as elaborate as the one that'd nearly taken the barn, but it was still fascinating and beautiful to watch, and when it finally sank back into the ground, I didn't even much resent the loss of credit.

Mom and Cille went off to Aladdin a few weeks later to meet with the doctors. We had a pretty substantial credit balance by then, and we overruled Cille and insisted that she investigate cosmetic surgery to restore her skin. They were gone for four days, and when they returned, Mom looked grim, although Cille was as sunny as ever.

"Syntheskin isn't nearly as expensive as it used to be," she told us. "It would only cost about ten years revenue from the farm. The good news is, Doctor Tercata believes that it will be half as expensive in five years."

"What about skin grafts?" Dad had stopped avoiding the subject since he and Cille visited the wormswell together, but I could still hear the strain in his voice.

"We can afford them," Mom answered. "But Cille objects."

"How can you object?" I asked. "At least your face and hands."

Cille rounded on me, and I could tell she was angry. "Yes, they're MY face and hands. And I'm the one who'll make the decisions about what happens to them. No one else." She took a deep breath. "Look, these weren't ordinary burns. The wormswell burned along with me and enzymes from its body were mixed in the wounds. The flesh just won't knit properly, even with grafts. I could go to Aladdin and spend a few months in the hospital and have half a dozen operations, and some of the scarring could be smoothed over, and some of the discoloration would go away, although it might come back. But I still wouldn't look anything like normal, I'd lose another big chunk of my life to the hospitals, there'd be some minor but persistent pain for months afterward, and for all of this we'd have to spend a considerable portion of our savings as well."

"The credit isn't an issue," insisted Dad.

"No, it isn't. Please understand, if the treatment could restore me the way you want it to, I wouldn't argue. In a few years, we might be able to afford syntheskin. I promise not to be stubborn or unreasonable if you all want to spend the family fortune, as long as I think we'll be getting what we're paying for. But skin grafts are a bad choice, and since it's my decision, that's how it's going to be."

And so it was.

The Navy was dragging its feet about establishing a base near Aragon, but they did station a pair of small warships in orbit. I saw men and women in uniform around Aladdin when I negotiated with the wholesalers that year, even talked to one woman briefly when we were seated at adjacent tables in a small cafe. I asked her if she thought she'd be in system for long. She was an attractive woman about my age, and frankly I hadn't spent much of my life around women who weren't my relatives, and I was beginning to get anxious about it.

"That's up to the politicos," she told me. "As far as I know, we're on temporary assignment and due to be rotated out pretty soon. We got diverted from Terranos to finish our tour here."

"Is that normal?"

"Not really. But there's been some trouble in this sector. A few ships gone missing. A transmission that was either very distorted or not from a human source. I have a brother whose ship got moved from Varos to Siluria on short notice, and there have been a couple of other reassignments that follow that pattern. I'd say the Concourse is being cautious and beefing up its frontier forces a bit."

I bought her a drink, and she bought me one, and Lieutenant Lura D'Ambrea rescued me from my virginity later that day. She promised to let me know when she was next scheduled to come planetside but I never heard from her again.

That was the summer Dad decided I should go to live in Safehaven for a while. I didn't agree, and I was pretty heated at times defending my position. Dad rolled over every one of my objections.

"The contracts are set for the year. You told me yourself that Zai and Jeb are both good supervisors, and if we need more help, there are plenty of Managuans who'll jump at the chance to earn some extra credit. The bluebugs have passed us by this year, and your mother and I can muddle through the bookkeeping while you're gone. If anything comes up, you're only a couple of hours away by foot and less by flitter."

I seized on the last as a reason not to transplant myself. "The council is only meeting once or twice a week. I can take the flitter down and back; I don't mind the travel time."

"Which means we'd spend two days a week without the flitter, to say nothing of the expense." There was no road connecting us to Safehaven, so I would have to have flown at treetop level, which was prohibitively expensive. He shook his head. "That's all beside the point anyway. Your mother and I want you to spend some time away from the family, meeting other people, maybe even a girl. You can't spend your whole life working the farm, Ennis. It's not natural."

"I've got plenty of time to worry about that." I was only twenty two, after all, and it wasn't as though I were completely inexperienced, although I hadn't told anyone about Lura D'Ambrea.

I was still resisting, even though I was pretty sure I was going to lose, and then Cille drove me from the field of battle in complete disarray. She knocked on my door later that evening and I invited her in, and she came over and sat facing me. Her voice was as serious as I'd ever heard it, and she let me have it right away.

"Ennis, you're going to stay in Safehaven for a few months, and I don't want to hear any more arguments."

I settled back in my chair and smiled like I thought I had any chance in the world of getting my way, but I already knew the battle was lost. There's a tone that gets into Cille's voice sometimes that's hard to resist. There's a kind of absolute certainty that goes beyond reason and rationality. "I just don't see what good it's going to do."

She hesitated, but for my benefit only, letting me think things through myself. There was no doubt in my mind that she'd already examined the situation from every possible angle. "Some day you're going to be running this whole farm, Ennis. Mom and Dad have worked hard all their lives, and it's time we started letting them enjoy themselves while we shoulder some of the load."

I nodded. "And if I'm not here, they'll have to work harder than ever. The new irrigation system is running behind schedule, one of our barges is infested with river roaches, and we're going to need to cut a supply road through to the Rollers if we want to get the last of it under cultivation."

"Were you planning to run the trenching machine yourself to finish the irrigation project? Or scrape the barge hull with your own hands? "

"No, of course not."

"Then go to Safehaven. I've already spoken to the Lounts and they promised a quote on the barge. Jeb is going to promote Flo Balcombe and put her in charge of the autotilling so he can personally oversee the construction crew and get the irrigation project back on schedule. We're on a waiting list to lease the autopavers, so there's nothing you could do about that anyway. "

"We could start clearing the land."

"Good point. I'll talk to Dad about hiring some Managuans to start on that. I don't mean to hurt your feelings Ennis, but the fact of the matter is that it's not essential that you be here every day, or even most of them. We have good people working for us, and good systems, and the farm pretty much runs itself. If an emergency does come up, we'll have you home or talk about it over the com."

"So I'm going into exile?"

"No, call it a working vacation. We need to have a strong voice, Ennis. Sobriety Carter and his faction are ambitious, wealthy, and they don't like us very much. Ned Grant is a good leader and a hard worker, but he's not sophisticated enough to outmaneuver the lords of Safehaven. He'll blow his stack and storm out and never realize that's what they wanted him to do."

"Well then how can I stop them? I don't have any political experience. They all look down on me as just a big kid and talk past me like I'm not there."

Cille shook her head. "That's a lot of nonsense, Ennis. Dad says you negotiated the most favorable terms with the wholesalers that we've ever seen, even though there's more competition than ever."

"Yeah, well I had the leverage of size. We're the biggest diversified producer south of Aladdin. It's easier and more profitable for them to deal with us than with ten smaller farmers producing the same volume. And since we talked the Managuans into letting us represent them as well, we'll be in even a stronger position next year."

She was nodding now. "So what makes you think you don't have the same advantage politically? Who's the largest depositor at the bank in Safehaven?"

"How would I know?"

"The Baxter family trust, Ennis. Who's the biggest customer for seed? Who has the biggest call for servo maintenance? How much of the stock those merchants sell in their stores comes in on our barges?"

Reluctantly, I began to see her point. "But they'd listen to Dad much more readily than to me."

"Then make them listen to you, Ennis. And listen to them as well. Maybe they're right, despite their posturing and politicking, and maybe Safehaven ought to be the district capitol. If you decide that way, then help them sell the idea to Ned Grant and the others. In the long run, what helps this district, and the people living in it, is going to help us as well. I'm telling you, go to Safehaven and sit with all those older people and show them how a real grownup acts."

Like I said, I knew from the outset I was going to lose the argument, and at the end I didn't even feel so bad about it.

Cille stopped at the door on her way out, looked back over her shoulder and grinned at me. "And find yourself a girl while you're at it."

Once I got there, it wasn't so bad. Parts of it anyway. There was a small hostelry, only six units, but I preferred to cook my own meals and have a little more room, so I rented Mara Nganda's three room cottage for the season. Mara had broken the family trust and sold off her claim to the Chandler's, as much to annoy her parents as to get the credit. She used part of that to buy the cottage, and now she was going to Aladdin for a year to finish her degree in xenology, after which she planned to emigrate.

The council met every four days, twice weekly, regular as clockwork. Ned Grant came down by skiff most of the time, usually with Aki Song, rather than take the settlement's flitter. They occasionally brought others with them, but rarely the same people, and I couldn't keep track of all the names and faces. The observer from the Cooperative was Karl Mancel, a very large man who never volunteered anything, and answered every question briefly and guardedly. Mom had tipped me off that the Cooperative people distrusted government on general principle. The company had sent a legal adviser, Fayid Souk, whom I initially disliked because I thought he was patronizing us. Then one night I ran into him in one of the town's two taverns, we started talking, and after a few drinks he confessed that his attitude was deliberate.

"These district councils tend to devolve into endless squabbling unless they have an outside force to resent. The company has learned over the years that sending someone with an abrasive personality helps to speed up resolution of the personal rivalries and petty differences of opinion."

Needham, the banker, was one of the original members, though he boycotted for a few weeks when Ned Grant casually mentioned that Gansett Village was chartering its own bank and would be pulling its account by the end of the year. Then there was Shikuro, the grain merchant, Cindy Aguilar, and three of the local farmers, Sobriety Carter, Abe Chandler, and Tami Pakarang. Abe echoed everything Sobriety said, but Tami seemed to have a mind of her own, and was the most open to suggestion. Needham was bound and determined that everyone accept Safehaven as district capital, and he brought it up so often I think he even annoyed Carter. I couldn't figure out where Shikuro stood; he asked a lot of questions but kept his opinions to himself.

We spent most of our time adapting the Concourse's basic code of laws to our own circumstances. There were some portions of it which were inviolable if we wanted to become a member, and no one challenged any of these. We had more flexibility with trade, post-company land development, environmental restrictions and set asides, and the details of our civil and criminal laws. Not that anything we determined was final, of course. Fayid advised us that it appeared there would be either eleven or twelve districts. Aladdin and Tyrada were the two most populous; we ranked ninth, eighth if the projected population of Goodhost was factored in. Next spring, we would be sending delegates to Aladdin, which was the de facto planetary capitol, to reconcile the differences among ourselves.

I had wondered what I could possibly do to fill up the three day gaps between meetings, but I needn't have worried. I was courted and cajoled and shouted at and pleaded with almost every time I stuck my head outside the door, and sometimes even when I stayed in. Carter wouldn't deal with me, but he sent Cindy Aguilar, who made the best case she could, and Abe Chandler, whom I found overbearing and poorly prepared. Needham frequently invited me to stop by the bank and talk, but I rarely got around to it. I had supper with Ned Grant and Aki Song a couple of times, and even to my inexperienced eye it was obvious that there was some chemistry developing between the two of them. I felt a pang of jealousy. Aki was only a bit older than me, and she was very attractive.

A lot of non-members wanted to plead their case as well, each lobbying for some particular issue. The Tonobis wanted tight environmental controls, Nganda was interested in regionalized power grids, several of the local merchants were concerned about tax schemes. Karl Mancel objected to almost anything that might limit the autonomy of the Cooperative, and Ned Grant wanted the Jackknife and Swift Rivers declared public resources.

Not that it was all work. I got to know my immediate neighbors pretty well. Suki North ran the local med station, a very petite young woman who was having a not particularly secret affair with Abe Chandler's youngest daughter. Sean Mercuriopolous owned one of Safehaven's taverns and tended the autobar himself. He was a big bear of a man with a high thin voice that seemed startlingly inappropriate for him. I got along well with both, and Suki in particular filled me in with all the local gossip. I wasn't too surprised to hear that Sobriety Carter and Cindy Aguilar were having an affair; they'd been awfully chummy at council meetings. On the other hand, the stories about Martin Harwell were frequently disturbing.

Some unkind souls were heard to remark that the biggest contribution Martin Harwell could make to the town of Safehaven would be to throw himself into the jaws of a harvester. Those of a more charitable frame of mind recalled stories of Martin's childhood, an abusive father, a mother so drained of spirit the neighbors were speaking of her in the past tense years before she actually passed away. To say nothing of the difficulty of growing up as the only Decant in a community of normals. Decanting was outlawed on most Concourse worlds, although that prohibition was not one of the requirements for membership, but the form of genegineering that had been done on Martin was now proscribed.

Edina Crowley, Safehaven's comline specialist, joined Suki and I for lunch one day and Harwell's name came up. "Nothing good could come from that household. Ignorance breeds ignorance, and few men were richer in dullness of mind than old Ben Harwell. Gave his seed to a corporation to play with and then complained because they didn't give him back the superchild he'd expected. Bloody idiot."

The genegineers on Omar had altered Martin's DNA during the fetal stage and bred an approximation of what they were after, two and a half meters tall, heavily muscled, more resistant to Omar's few but virulent human compatible diseases. Old Ben figured he'd be sire to a super farmer, but then wastewort devastated that world's croplands and Ben was only one of tens of thousands who lost nearly everything. He salvaged what he could, liquidated everything, and emigrated to Aragon to start over. Martin grew like a weed, with faster than normal reflexes, a high tolerance to pain, and heightened hearing and vision that were probably only marginally helpful in farming. In some ways, Martin was superhuman all right, but something was lost in the process, because he never seemed to display any emotion except spite. He did everything coldly and calmly, but he could be real nasty when he wanted.

Eight years back, Ben had died under rather questionable circumstances. One morning Martin went out to the barn to harvest the eggs from the crabhens and found his father impaled on the tines of the autotiller. The coroner who flew down from Aladdin concluded that the deceased had fallen from the loft while moving bales of pseudowheat, but no one ever offered any explanation for Ben's decision to perform an onerous duty usually delegated to his son.

Martin just shrugged his massive shoulders when asked. "Pa wasn't never one to explain hisself to me."

Martin's interaction with the rest of the town had been minimal for the first two years following his father's death. The Harwell farm was tucked up past a handful of small holdings that lay between the Carter and Tonobi farms; he didn't cultivate enough of his land to provide much of an income but it was sufficient to support a single person with limited aspirations. If bare existence can be termed prosperity, then Martin Harwell prospered.

His neighbors, without exception, loathed him.

"Summer days, the stink from his place drifts down over my property," complained Cindy Aguilar. "We have to shut the windows and run the air spargers just to breathe the air. He never cleans up when the crabhens molt, just plows it out into the yard."

Dan Kater appealed regularly to his neighbors. "He's always dumping his trash out on the property line. We've got to do something about it." He filed a formal complaint with the company, and an administrator named Dowdell made a special trip to investigate, but other than urging Martin to show more consideration for his neighbors, no official action was taken. Martin responded to this provocation by arranging a variety of rusting, decaying equipment and old packing cases into a chaotic fence separating his land from Kater's property.

Tami Pakarang tried to bring suit under corporate law when Martin shot her suckercat out of the tree where it was drawing sap, but it was on his property at the time. Abner Valentine went for him with a hand laser after Martin caught Abner Junior stealing fruit and whipped his ass, but it was Abner who had to pay the company fine and submit to counseling. By the time of his twenty-fifth birthday, Martin was cordially hated by everyone who knew him, and even some who'd never made his acquaintance.

"I'd just as soon he took his business elsewhere." Kani Shikuro repeated that sentence every time Martin Harwell's name came up in conversation. His was the larger of the two seed and supply stores in Safehaven, and that's where Martin did his infrequent and parsimonious shopping for local produce he couldn't, or wouldn't grow for himself, and the occasional offworld delicacy. "When he comes in, everyone else finishes up quick and checks out. I've even seen some spot him squinting at the price of something or another, and walk out and down the street to Del's Depot."

Even Tish Campbell, who converted to Paniversalism after her husband was killed by a wiresnake and spent all her time working for charitable causes found it impossible to come up with anything good to say about Martin. "He needs to rise above his limitations," was the best she could manage.

I heard all that and more about Martin Harwell, not much of it good, before I ever chanced to set eyes on him. But Melody Miller was a different matter entirely. I got to know her pretty well.

CHAPTER FIVE

There were a lot of personality conflicts in Safehaven, business rivalries, personal animosities, family quarrels, exaggerated misunderstandings, political differences, even some mild religious intolerance. But everyone liked Melody Miller.

As colonial towns went, Safehaven was pretty well established. The first generation was growing older and the next was starting to drift away in some cases, but otherwise it was pretty much the same group of faces running things as had been right from when it was founded. It was a conservative community, suspicious of outsiders, jealous of its status, even mildly hostile toward new neighbors like the Cooperative, Gansett Village, and Goodhost. Safehaven minded its own business and didn't welcome changes, and Melody was a newcomer, moved down from Aladdin just over a year before I rented the cottage. Safehaven was one of the very first settlements on Aragon, back when it meant something to come out as pioneers. The town wasn't sited in a particularly optimal location, what with the swampland below them where the Jackknife dived underground, but there was unusually good cropland in the area and the company decided it needed to expand its settlements southward. Anyway, the people landing now, well, a lot of them are city folk that overflowed from the more settled worlds, and another lot of them are refugees rather than volunteers. They don't like being here, and if they have to stay, then they're going to do their best to recreate the environment they left. I'd noticed this on my one visit to Goodhope. The company was investing a lot of credit there to make it work, but half the people I talked to didn't know the first thing about turning wilderness into farmland, and most of them had no idea how much work was involved.

But Melody Miller was different. Melody was an eminently likable person. Invariably cheerful, gifted with an infectious smile, she had a wondrous ability to make a place for herself in the most diverse situations. She talked fieldball with the guys at the taverns, compared recipes with Edna Crowley's sewing circle, argued the relative merits of literary figures like Ernest Hemingway and Paul Alan Sheffield, and made herself a modest but adequate living doing freelance researching and writing by patching into the state of the art data center in Aladdin.

At least one local woman and more than one unattached young man - and some not so young and some not unattached - made advances in her direction, and although each and every one of them was rebuffed, Melody always managed to remove the sting. None of her admirers were resentful, and even her rivals could find nothing bad to say about her.

"She's just...Melody." Jill Garner shook her head, unable to explain exactly how she felt. "What's there to be upset about?"

Melody was undeniably attractive, though in an atypical fashion, tall, not particularly tall but solid. She went for a run every morning at sunup, and her bright red body suit turned heads all the way down Little Main Street, up past the Doppler Link, and around the scattering of native trees that extended the north end of the town center right out to the Jackknife. She ran the circuit every morning, weather permitting, and sometimes again at the end of the day. Melody also spent a lot of her free time rock climbing in the Serrated Hills southwest of town, swimming in Wallaby Pond, or playing power tennis against one of the recreation bots at the rec center.

That's where I met her the first time. There weren't any human opponents in town who could make the game interesting enough for her, but she pretended otherwise. It was a pretty humiliating experience, even if I was a novice at the sport. She moved with a fluid grace that was beautiful to watch, her reach was long, her arm powerful, and she could cover the width of the court so fast that it hurt my eyes to follow her. Otherwise, she didn't hurt my eyes at all. Melody's face was not, in conventional terms, pretty, but that magnificent smile and her radiant good health transformed it into a kind of beacon.

Melody was still turning away advances by the time I showed up, but they were proffered more as gestures of friendship and tradition than out of any serious intent. I had my turn and she put me off with minimal pain, although my ego was mildly bruised. Much to my surprise, I'd attracted quite a few admirers of my own. Jill Garner and I had spent a couple of nights together, but she had offworld ambitions and we both insisted there wouldn't be anything serious between us. I was more interested in Kelli Nganda, and we'd shared a couple of meals and a long, quiet walk along the river, and I thought our friendship might turn into something more intimate with time. Kelli had skin so dark it looked purple in the right light. Her mother had died and her father wasn't a big fan of the Baxters, but his attitude toward me changed not so subtly thereafter and I guess he had calculated the advantages if one his daughter married into the largest landowning family in the area. Or maybe I'm being unfair and he just accepted that I treated Kelli well and made her happy. With Mara uninterested in remaining in Safehaven, there was only Kelli and her younger brother, Lemayel, to take over, and Lemayel had Fagin's Syndrome and was rarely seen in public.

I pined after Melody a bit, but not for too long, and she was too nice a person for me to feel particularly hurt or angry. She had a gift for disarming hostility and was certainly one of the most likable people I'd ever met. Smart as a whip, too, and definitely a woman who knew her mind and what she wanted to do with her life.

Which is why I was as shocked as the rest of the community when she started seeing Martin Harwell.

Martin had retreated from active interaction with his neighbors in recent months, though all I had to do was mention his name to provoke a torrent of invective and unpleasant anecdotes. Dan Kater was still trying to get someone to back his petition to the company to force Harwell to clean up the trash dump. Most of the adults in the community, their children, and even their pets had all learned to avoid the Harwell property as well as his physical presence. A contagion of selective blindness had enveloped Safehaven. Martin could walk through the town in broad daylight, and no one would recall having seen him, though he was hard to miss, or even having moved out of his way. Kani Shikuro frowned when he found Harwell's infrequent credit slips in the day's receipts, wondering how he'd come by them. "Damned if I can remember him stopping by." But you could see the hostility lurking in his eyes even if it wasn't in his voice. In my inexperienced but reasonably objective opinion, it appeared that Safehaven had reached an accommodation with Harwell, an unofficial truce if not an actual peace.

That all changed when he showed up at the First Landing celebration with his arm around Melody Miller.

The picnic was held outdoors, in the gardens behind the community databank. Several hundred people attended, with arrivals and departures changing the mix constantly during the course of the day. Brightly pennanted pavilions had been set up in various places, hawking fresh cornfruit and fried crab hen and dark, rich mugs of barley beer. I was there with Kelli Nganda and she was being more affectionate than usual, so I was thinking about asking her back to the cottage for a while. I was so preoccupied with my plan in fact that it took me a while to realize there was a quiet but palpable disturbance washing up around us.

The progress of Melody and Martin through the crowd resembled that of a magnet through iron filings. One pole drew people close, the other repelled with equal force. More than one person found his or her tongue tied, brain drained of all conscious thought, unable to maintain coherency in the face of such an incredible contradiction. They made an impressive couple; Martin with his two and a half meters, Melody pressed against his side, both of them covered with heavy, healthy looking muscles (though it sure looked better on Melody than on her beau). Melody seemed unaware of the disturbance they were causing; Martin was merely indifferent.

The odd match up probably dominated the conversation over myriad dinner tables that evening, and crept into pillow talk later. Kelli brought it up at least three times, and I was pretty annoyed toward the last because she seemed more interested in speculating about it than in dealing with the business at hand. I was persistent though and soon enough she was too busy to gossip. I heard later that there was lively speculation at the ensuing get together of Edina Crowley's sewing circle, and I actually overheard some rather nasty comments made at the next council meeting while we were taking a break. Someone told a crude joke that involved unlikely variations in genetically engineered sexual organs one night at the tavern, and everyone present knew who was meant to be the object of the banter. I confess to feeling more than slightly curious about their relationship myself, but the vehemence I detected around me was bothersome and I tried to put the whole thing out of my mind.

The council meetings were growing more heated as well.

The Safehaven contingent, as led by Sobriety Carter, made no secret of their intention of being district capitol. In terms of head count, they made up thirty percent of the voting population, if you included all of the outlying farms including our own. They were already treated as a resource center by the company administration, and they had the most developed infrastructure. I didn't like Carter, obviously, but the only good argument against him was that the town was poorly situated to make use of water transport, and its expansion was circumscribed by the low quality of the land to its south.

Ned Grant didn't like the idea at all, but Gansett Village was at least three years behind Safehaven in development, and had only a fraction of the population. He'd been fighting a delaying tactic ever since the talks started, arguing that the choice of a district capitol was not a priority, that it was more important to codify the laws we wanted promulgated at the planetwide conferences that would make most of the big decisions. Trade laws, bankruptcy, credit lending, price supports, taxation, and civil rights were all at the top of his agenda and he was supported, unsurprisingly, by Aki Song, as well as, surprisingly, Karl Mancel, the Malcolm observer. Carter countered that it would improve our bargaining position if we were to make it clear that we had organized ourselves and were united behind a single district council with an established infrastructure. I hovered somewhere in between the two positions, as did Kuriel Nganda and one or two others, but for the most part we were polarized on the issue, with no one showing any sign of movement.

The situation grew even less predictable when Ned decided to stir the pot. There were about twenty of us assembled that day in the town's new meeting house. It was Tami Pakarang's turn to provide the refreshments and she'd outdone herself. We usually had a variety of pastries, some bearfruit and spongemelon, and the inevitable caffee. I always wake up with a growling stomach, so I'd already eaten when I arrived that morning, but the smell of fried jackalope strips and scrambled crab eggs made me hungry all over again. I filled a plate and sat down next to Cindy Aguilar, who seemed the most reasonable of Carter's faction.

It was Ned Grant's turn to chair and he called us to order and led us in a round of applause for the refreshments. The meeting started as always with a summary of the minutes from the last. Technically, our council consisted of forty two persons, but we never managed to get everybody together at once, and averaged about twenty five. Safehaven was disproportionately represented most of the time simply because it was easier for their delegates to attend, although the membership as a whole was pretty closely tied to population. And technically speaking, I was part of the Safehaven delegation, although no one, myself least of all, thought of the Baxters as part of the town.

"Before we get to the first item on today's agenda, we have a couple of announcements to make." He glanced down at Aki Song, who looked mighty pleased with herself. "First one's personal, but I wanted you all to know that Aki and I have decided to sign a marriage contract and raise a family." It had been an open secret that the two community leaders were romantically involved, but no one had expected them to marry. At least I hadn't. There was another round of applause, hesitant at first but because people were startled, not disapproving. It had grown to be pretty enthusiastic when Ned finally waved us down.

"Our second announcement is kind of similar, and it's more relevant to this meeting. As you know, our two communities face each other across the upper Jackknife. Over on the west side, they have better land than we do, but not as much as they'd like in proportion to their population. In Gansett Village, we've got more real estate and ancillary facilities, but the soil isn't as rich or accessible and it takes a lot more effort to cultivate and harvest. Aki's people have hired themselves out," he nodded toward me, "and provided good labor, so we've been talking about making a similar arrangement. We were working out the details when an alternate plan suggested itself, and this past week we've convinced the majority of both communities to endorse our proposal."

He paused and looked around the room, making sure that he had everyone's attention. I think Sobriety Carter must have some kind of sixth sense, because I could see where his hand gripped the back of his chair so hard that his knuckles had turned white. He didn't know what was coming, but he knew he wouldn't like it, and he was absolutely right. Ned licked his lips and cleared his throat and made no effort at all to conceal his gloating. "The Managuan community and Gansett Village are formally merging into a single township, which we are planning to call Managansett."

I was caught as much by surprise as everyone else, and it was only afterward that I started thinking about the reactions around me. Most of the audience was relatively quiet, a few clapping their hands, some calling out questions, others silent and thoughtful. Like everyone else in the room I was trying to figure out what this meant in larger terms, and it didn't take long for me to do the relevant math. Ned's new town would have a population larger than that of Safehaven even with all of the farms included. It wasn't a fatal blow, but he'd neatly taken away one of Carter's best arguments for being district capitol. And with the joint community straddling the upper Jackknife, they were in an ideal position to take commercial advantage of the lower Jackknife and the Swift. I still wasn't fond of the maneuvering that is the basis of all politics, but I have to admit to feeling a spike of admiration for Ned's resourcefulness that day.

It wasn't until a couple of months later that I found out the whole idea had been Aki's.

My social life was starting to grow crowded. Kelli Nganda and I were seeing each other often enough now that Jill Garner started to wonder if she was missing something, and our previous casual relationship became more intense. More time consuming were the endless meetings with council members and their supporters outside of the formal gatherings. There was some pretty intense lobbying going on, and tempers were rising. Carter was smart enough not to approach me himself, but he sent each of his lieutenants in turn to cajole me into throwing my weight toward Safehaven's priorities. Needham, the banker, gave me a short course in banking law and won my support for a lot of his proposals. Kani Shikuro led a small faction that wanted to push for restrictive immigration and homesteading laws, but they seemed designed primarily to increase the personal wealth of the present generation and its descendants at the expense of slowing the inflow of talented and industrious newcomers. I said so, and Shikuro argued, and when he left we were both unsatisfied.

I commed home every two or three days and brought the family up to date. Mom and Dad made suggestions, and Cille asked a lot of questions. Mom was particularly good at pointing out some of the complex interpersonal relationships and the effects they had on the alignment of supporters, while Dad's understanding of the impact various policies would have on our own interests and those of our neighbors far exceeded my own. Cille was our legal expert, had been studying company and Concourse law, and she helped clarify a lot of issues that I hadn't completely understood. Dad came down to attend sessions from time to time, and I was impressed by the degree of respect he was awarded by most of the others, and a bit miffed that they didn't treat me similarly. After all, I was the one doing the day to day work.

The proposed merger of Gansett and Managua dominated local gossip for several days, but was soon displaced. There were persistent rumors of troubles within the Malcolm Cooperative, and Karl Mancel admitted in guarded tones that there were some differences of opinion among the members. He missed three consecutive meetings, and when he returned for the one following, he was even less forthcoming than usual, no mean feat in itself.

And the buzz about Melody Miller had never completely subsided.

If her dalliance with Martin Harwell had been just an isolated occurrence, the conversation might have died out. Those genuinely not interested - there were a few - would have been joined by the overwhelming majority, who preferred to consider it an anomaly, an aberration, or even a misrecollection. But their relationship continued, and grew increasingly difficult to ignore.

Melody and Martin were spotted at the Andromeda Café in Aladdin by Anselm Rohm, who was already telling people about it back in Safehaven before letting his wife know he was home three days early after negotiating a license to import limited artificial intelligence modules. Jeri Kaplan, an elderly woman who lived directly across from Melody, reluctantly admitted that Martin had in fact visited her there on at least two occasions, and the Wilber kids reported that Melody's single seat sports flitter had been making regular trips up and down the dirt road leading to the Harwell farm. Melody and her bright red body suit were still seen around town in the mornings, but with decreasing frequency.

Their relationship was for a while the talk of the community, and then, by the end of low summer, the Subject No One Spoke About.

"Sometimes people get strange notions in their head for a while, but eventually they pass." Ruth Brock's oblique comment summed up the community's hopes. Jill Garner's reaction was more pointed. "Assuming that everything is properly proportioned, he's probably great in bed."

Teddy Wilber saw Melody jogging through one of the Harwell fields that bordered the Carter farm, her red suit unmistakable even from a considerable distance, bright and early one morning. More than one person noted that her lights were rarely on in the evenings, and that no one really saw her regularly any more. No one except Martin Harwell. When Melody casually mentioned to Kani Shikuro that she was more or less living on the Harwell farm now, he was so shocked that he closed up early. Word spread through Safehaven like a brushfire.

Reaction to Melody in the weeks that followed was bipolar. When she was alone, she found people as receptive as ever, and if she noticed that no mention was ever made of her change in living conditions or her steady companion, she gave no hint of it. On the other hand, when Martin accompanied her, people remained correct, polite, even helpful, but it was the difference between the old flat style vids and the new trivideos, an absent depth of response.

She gave no indication of noticing that either, but Martin picked up on it right away. It was one of the few things that made him smile.

To be fair, Melody contributed to Martin's socialization. He washed more regularly and wore clean clothing when venturing into town, the complaints about rancid odors emanating from his property diminished and finally ceased altogether, and he replaced the aging, noisy turfcrawler with a used but serviceable, and mercifully quiet, sandshifter brought in from Aladdin. On those rare occasions when Martin ventured off his property without escort, people even remembered having seen him, though they rarely spoke of it to each other. But Safehaven refused to be mollified, recognizing correctly that his concessions were for Melody's sake and not its own.

My own interest in Melody had waned now that I was comfortably situated with Kelli and Jill, although Jill's increasingly demanding disposition was starting to annoy me. And another issue had risen to intrude into everyone's thoughts. Fayid Souk, the company representative, told the council that we would need to accelerate things. "The company wishes to reallocate resources from this area into more profitable regions." He would later tell me privately that the company had had two large exploratory ships go missing in this sector and that there were growing rumors of a hostile force operating nearby, presumably not human. The Concourse had limited contact with two space traveling races far from Aragon, but the only known sentients in this region were a primitive people on a protected planet in the Celanasian system.

The company's desire to move to safer and more profitable areas meant that the calendar for independence was going to be shortened, and that meant that we had to start thinking about who would represent us at the planetary convention. There was a complex formula for this. The council would appoint a portion of our delegation, and there were requirements that the separate communities be reasonably fairly represented. The balance would be chosen through a general election, although the company could also appoint two local citizens to our delegation if they felt any individual interest group had been overlooked. Our district was entitled to send a total of ten representatives, of which the council would choose four.

There was an interesting provision to the rule. The council's appointments had to be made before the general election. Those appointed could not, therefore, be candidates for the elected offices. Sobriety Carter and Ned Grant were particularly ambitious and they had a choice to make. Either man could have an appointment simply by asking, and that would make it absolutely certain that they'd be on the Planetary Council. But both the local and planet wide bodies would be dissolved once the process ended, giving way to the new government of Aragon, which would necessarily be an elective body. The delegates who ran campaigns now would have much more public exposure, and would be better positioned to compete in the final elections. Appointees would start at a disadvantage.

Ten days after Fayid's announcement, the council chose its four appointees. Sobriety Carter had taken the safe route, but it was obvious that he wasn't entirely happy with his decision. I thought it was a smart move on his part. His support in Safehaven was largely on the surface; I suspect that in a secret ballot, he'd have seen large scale defections. It was his personality that played against him. He was intolerant of variant opinions, arrogant, and tactless. Ned Grant declined to accept a nomination, preferring to stand for election. Aki accepted, but Karl Mancel declined, and indicated that no one in the Cooperative would be participating in the Planetary Council, although they would vote in the general election. I proposed Needham, and the fourth spot was filled by Tasha Janigian, who sat in Ned Grant's place when he was unable to attend council meetings.

It was about that time that Jill Garner and I parted ways. The split had been coming for a while and I think both of us knew it. The sex was still good, but everything else was turning sour and if we continued much longer we wouldn't even be able to salvage our friendship. Kelli and I had only slept together a couple of times, but it felt more intimate with her than with Jill. I'm not ready to say that we were falling in love with one another at that point, but I certainly felt a degree of affection for her that was not the case with Jill. When Jill and I first started seeing each other, she had warned me up front that she had no intention of getting involved on a long term basis, but that she found me attractive and thought we might have some fun together. I blame myself for not realizing sooner when she started feeling differently, and for not acting more quickly once it became obvious.

I never did anything as bad as call her by the wrong name in a moment of passion, but that last night together I was thinking of Kelli and how much I'd rather be with her, and something must have told Jill that I wasn't concentrating on the matter at hand because she rolled off me unexpectedly and sat on the edge of the bed.

"Is something wrong?" My voice was hoarse and I felt a twinge of formless guilt.

"Yes." When she didn't say anything else I sat up, tentatively touched her back. She flinched away from me, then stood and retrieved her clothing from the recliner onto which she'd thrown it. "I can't do this anymore, Ennis."

I was in this strange state where I both did and didn't understand what she meant. I watched her dress and found myself thinking about Kelli again, and guessed what the problem was. "I'm sorry," I said softly, meaning it but not sure that made things any better.

"No need." Her voice sounded tired. "This was supposed to be a temporary thing, remember? I warned you not to get too attached. I was always better at giving advice than taking it."

I wanted to say something about us remaining friends, but every string of words that came up in my mind sounded either patronizing or insincere so I stayed silent instead. Then she left and I felt an enormous wave of relief, and that made me feel even guiltier.

"Looks like Melody's put on a little weight." Fayid sipped at his barley beer, letting his eyes follow Melody as she walked past the front window of the tavern and out of sight.

Abe Chandler nodded agreement. "Don't see her out there jogging any more. Maybe she's getting out of shape. Of course, I'm sure she and Martin get plenty of exercise other ways."

"It'd be quite a run to get here from...from where she's living now." Fayid deliberately ignored Chandler's crude reference. He was from one of the planets dominated by Islamic Reformists, but his family had been very conservative.

"Sure is a shame. She looked real good in that body suit of hers." Chandler's eyes were lost in contemplation of a memory.

"It is that," I agreed, and changed the subject. The four of us constituted a special subcommittee tasked with drafting a new homesteading law. The others grudgingly got back to work, but I could tell we weren't going to get much more done that day.

Dr. Fortunato was scrupulous about patient confidentiality, but when Elsie Brenner's daughter saw Melody leaving his mobile clinic the day he flew up on one of his periodic visits, she jumped to the correct conclusion.

"Melody's with child! I could see it in her face." She chortled. "Can you believe it?"

Few did, at first, but as low summer progressed to high, Melody switched to maternity clothes and something small died within the hearts of many of Safehaven's male residents.

She miscarried the same day the council had set as the deadline for nominating candidates to the Planetary Council, reportedly after falling down a rickety flight of steps to the root basement at Harwell's farm.

I wasn't in Safehaven at the time. I'd only been home on one brief trip since the council had been formed, and when Sobriety Carter proposed that we take a ten day break to get the current harvest wound up, I seconded his motion. There was no doubt in my mind that Dad had everything well in hand back at the farm, but he did things slightly differently than I would have done, and I wanted to see firsthand how he'd dealt with the rustgrass infection.

We still didn't have a direct land connection to Safehaven, but we'd built a narrow road out to the lower Jackknife as well as to the Swift. I hitched a ride with Ned Grant and Zai Kreller was waiting for me with the new flitter that Dad had ordered. It would fit four if you didn't mind being close to your neighbor, but was quite comfortable for two, and it was certainly faster and easier than walking all the way back to the house. Dad was out when we got there, but Mom and Cille were both standing on the porch, alerted by the low hum of the flitter. I hugged them both with more enthusiasm than I expected, and realized how much I missed home.

When Dad came in a little while later we were sitting in the kitchen, drinking caffee while I deflected questions about my sex life and stoutly defended the short beard I'd started growing. When Dad had come down to Safehaven to address the council, he always seemed as much bigger than life as always, but back in a familiar context, he seemed physically smaller than I remembered, which probably had something to do with the fact that I'd added some muscle mass and even a bit of height during the months I'd been living away from home.

He seemed a trifle distant but it wasn't till some time later when we were out walking alone, watching the suns go down, that he said anything. "Now what in the hell possessed you to nominate me to go to Aladdin?"

"We've got the biggest farm in the district, bigger than the next two combined." It was true; most of the original settlers had claimed their land in a relatively tight cluster north and west of Safehaven. They'd lacked foresight, because while their kids could certainly claim new land of their own when they came of age, there was no contiguous land available. Mom and Dad had been criticized for isolating themselves so far to the north, but Dad had his eye on access to both forks of the Jackknife, and Mom was already carrying me and planning for Jesper and Cille.

"All the more reason for me to stay home. We've got twice as much work to do as anyone else."

"We've also got twice the hands, more if we need it."

"I'm not the politician type, Ennis. If the Baxters need to send someone, it ought to be you. You're doing all the scutwork now; you should reap the glory for it." He made "glory" sound like a bad word.

"It wouldn't work. Sobriety Carter is a council appointee and a farmer, so only one of us can be elected as a general candidate. The company won't accept a third because it would leave someone else under represented. Tami Pakarang was talking about running, and she has a strong following, but she'll sit things out with you in the race. If I'm the candidate instead, she'd mount her own campaign and win handily. Most people think I'm too young and inexperienced."

Dad sighed, but he didn't look surprised. I'm pretty sure he had figured this out all by himself and that his protest was more form than substance. I brought him up to date on the latest round of deliberations. Carter's group was no longer the united front it had been at the beginning; the farmers had a different agenda than the shopkeepers and service providers, particularly with regard to interest rates, loan security, and other issues. We'd worked out compromises on most of the more contentious questions, but we were still just one comparatively small portion of the Planetary Council.

Our current hot issue was river transport. Without exception, the people of Safehaven wanted both the Jackknife and the Swift to remain open to everyone. Ned Grant wanted the right to regulate or even charge fees for traffic passing along the upper Jackknife, since the newly united community included facing shores. Ned had expected me to back him, since we Baxters hold all the land south of the fork for a considerable distance along both banks, but after consulting with the family, I'd sided with Safehaven.

"The rivers are a common resource like the air," Dad insisted. "They don't belong to anyone, and no one should be denied free access to them. If Ned Grant wants to charge a landing fee to anyone who puts up at one of his piers, that's his right, but the Baxter facilities will remain free to anyone who doesn't abuse the privilege." Dad also pointed out that other forms of transportation would inevitably replace the river in time. There was already talk of building a land route from Managansett up north through the Sleeping Lady Valley to tie in with the major east-west road currently under construction. The company had undertaken this major project to link the mining district directly with Aladdin because even though they would no longer be directly involved on Aragon by the time it was finished, they had negotiated a long term repayment contract with the mine owners and a consortium of investors in Aladdin.

We talked about the farm then, and Dad brought me up to date on a few things we hadn't discussed over the com. He praised

Zai once or twice, mildly, but for Dad that was the mark of strong approval. She was unofficially his second in command now. "Your sister still does her share of the work," he told me, "but she really doesn't take much interest in the farm."

"She still studying like crazy?"

"Yes, but she doesn't seem to be concentrating on any one thing. I think she's looking for something to do with her life, but hasn't found anything yet that can hold her interest."

"She will eventually." I was right, but it wasn't going to be anything like what I imagined.

CHAPTER SIX

The elections were held during first autumn. Dad refused to campaign but still won easily. Ned Grant was the only one to carry a larger percentage of his constituents. The Managuan side would also send Adrian Mercuriopolous, whom I had never met although his brother ran a tavern in Safehaven, and Safehaven itself chose Jill Garner by a narrow margin. Vikki Portman would be representing the Malcolm people, none of whom would run themselves. She lived in town, but supported herself as the Cooperative's business agent and the company had agreed to waive its usual rules.

The first meeting of the Planetary Council was scheduled for the following spring. Farming was a year round project on Aragon. We had bio-engineered crops which were hardy enough to survive in the colder weather, although our climate was very moderate and didn't change drastically as it did on most other worlds. It did require some additional labor to maintain the accelerated harvesting and planting schedule, however, and Dad was reasonably happy with the timing, which left just enough leeway to get the spring crops established before he'd have to travel up to Aladdin. The first round of meetings was scheduled to run twelve days and would mostly serve to allow the delegates to meet one another and exchange their various proposals. The serious negotiating wouldn't start until the second round.

Our district council had done better than I had expected. We'd developed a fairly comprehensive list of proposals, and we were all still talking to one another, except for Sobriety Carter and I, and that had nothing to do with the council. For the most part, I thought we'd done a good job. There were a few controversial provisions that I doubted would stand up. The wholesalers in Aladdin weren't going to like an artificial limit on their fees, and the more influential importers weren't likely to accept a cap on their profits, even if we did phase it out over twenty years. Ned Grant had pointed out that we needed to include a few things we were willing to give up in trade for concessions from the other parties.

We decided to continue to meet every fifteen days or so to discuss strategy and address issues that we might originally have overlooked. That meant it was no longer important for me to actually reside in Safehaven, so I packed up my belongings and moved back home. It felt good getting back there, although for the first few days I felt like a stranger. Jeb Booker and Zai Kreller were managing so many of the everyday activities of the farm that there was little for me to do, although Dad took pity and let me fill in for him from time to time.

The worst part was being separated from Kelli Nganda. Once Jill and I had gone our separate ways, I'd found myself more attracted to Kelli than ever, and I had even started thinking about raising the subject of a marriage contract. Cille kidded me about it from time to time, usually when we were alone. The first few days I was back, she fussed over me quite a bit, but after that she retreated to her room and her com and continued her endless studying. Then Mom tore something in her right knee and was immobilized for a while, and Cille took over the housework without a word of complaint. I was worried about her, but it was a formless kind of worry. She seemed content if not joyously happy, had grown less dependent upon her medication, and had even fleshed out some. I couldn't help thinking how attractive she might be now if it hadn't been for that terrible accident.

We made a substantial profit that season. The pseudowheat was thriving along the banks of the Swift and the yield was a full thirty percent better than we'd ever previously harvested. There was a major bluebug infestation west of Aladdin and the wholesale prices for cornfruit and some of our other crops jumped startlingly high. There had also been a fresh wave of settlers from offworld coming to claim their homestead before independence day, so there were more mouths to feed. We could have sold everything we grew, but Dad suggested that we hold back some. "We have storage capacity and if we're able to send some to the wholesalers during the winter when no one else has warm weather crops available, they'll be more likely to come to us first in the future."

It was a particularly fierce prime winter all over Aragon that year. There wasn't a lot of snow accumulation, but there were flurries every day or two, the winds were savage and constant, it remained quite chilly if not bitterly cold throughout, and a truncated second autumn had left many of our neighbors scrambling to get fresh seed into the ground.

I was spending three days in Safehaven, one day for the

council, one to arrange some purchases of seeds and soil supplements and other business issues, and one day to visit with Kelli. We talked to each other every day on the com, and she'd come up to visit the farm a couple of times since I'd moved back. It was a great relief to see how well she got on with the family. She had never met Cille before, but as far as I could tell, she hadn't so much as flinched when they shook hands. Our relationship had gone from casual to compulsive to comfortable, and now even Mom was asking when I was going to stop wasting my time and propose.

The council meeting was perfunctory; we didn't even have a quorum, and the only issues pending were of little consequence. We managed to stretch things out for half a day before adjourning, and afterwards I wandered over to the magistrate's office. Someone had vandalized one of our piers and the adjacent storage shed on the lower Jackknife and I wanted to see if Colson had had any luck tracking down the culprit or culprits, most likely kids..

Grant Colson was in a foul mood when I arrived, although he treated me quite civilly. The company had sent him to Safehaven with no help and a limited budget, enough to maintain a small office and hire two locals as part time security officers. Khalkri and Vallencourt were both down with the green flu and he'd been listening to petty complaints for most of the morning. "Most likely it was Evan Carter and the Brodie brothers, but they're not talking. I think I scared 'em some, but unless one of them brags to the wrong person, I don't think we're ever going to officially close this one."

It was pretty much the answer I expected. I'd lived in Safehaven long enough to know who the hellraisers were. I asked after Colson's wife and we exchanged some minor gossip, and then I was getting ready to leave when Betty Wilber showed up with the twins, insisting that Martin Harwell had killed himself by jumping into Satan's Throat. The magistrate was understandably skeptical.

"Grant, my boys don't tell lies." Betty Wilber definitely had her feathers ruffled. "If they say they saw him do it, then he did it."

Colson bit back what he wanted to say, a reference to Teddy and Eddy's malleable definition of truth as demonstrated by the fact that he'd found some stolen game packs in their possession even after they'd insisted they had nothing to do with their disappearance from the rec center. But the thirteen year-olds looked genuinely upset this time. "Well, maybe that's what they think they saw, but maybe he just went for a swim." Satan's Throat wasn't the safest spot, and most bathers used Wallaby Pond instead, but it wasn't uncommon to find the more adventurous diving into the rougher water where the lower Jackknife narrowed and went underground to feed the swampland beyond.

"No, sir!" They erupted in chorus, then exchanged glances. The one with the red shirt – I couldn't tell them apart for sure but I thought he was Teddy - resumed, speaking for both of them.

"It was up on the foot bridge, sir, the part where we're not supposed to go." He dropped his eyes, realizing he'd just admitted to a minor sin, then rushed on, hoping to cover his tracks. "We didn't mean to go out so far but we kind of forgot. Anyway, Mr. Harwell, he was standing up near the big Judas tree on the far side, real quiet so we didn't see him until he moved. It was like he was waiting for something, and when he saw us, he walked straight to the edge and just sort of flopped in without even taking off his clothes."

"The far side across from the bridge, you say? Well, that wouldn't be my favorite spot for a swim, but it's safe enough if you watch what you're doing. The Throat's a ways further down." The point where the Jackknife disappeared into the ground had been dubbed Satan's Throat when the town was first settled. Violent waters, sharp rocks, and a torturously convoluted course made it our most notable natural danger. On two occasions, careless swimmers had been sucked in, and only fragments of their bodies had emerged at the other end of the funnel.

"But we saw him go into the Throat!" Eddy took over from his brother. "He only swam for a few seconds, then he kind of shook in the water and just floated after that. Never even tried to swim back."

Not a suicide maybe, but a heart attack? I considered that a more plausible explanation, although as a Decant, Martin should have had little susceptibility to common physical defects at his age. "I suppose I'd better check it out." Grant sighed, toggled the com, and tried to raise someone at the Harwell farm. The screen remained stubbornly blank. He sighed and resigned himself to a trip. "All right, I'll look into it right away. Appreciate your bringing the kids in, Mrs. Wilber. I'll get back to you as soon as I know something worth telling."

"All right, Grant." She half turned, hesitated. "One other

thing. Tell them about the clothes you saw."

Teddy's eyes widened. "Oh, yeah. Forgot. We saw Miss Miller's stuff there. You know, that bright red thing she wears when she goes running."

"The body suit?"

"Yeah, that thing. It was on the ground behind some bushes. We looked around and called her name but she never answered."

As soon as they were out the door, Grant sighed and ran his hand through his hair, which was starting to thin. He tried calling the Harwell farm again, but there was still no answer. "Just what I needed, a long walk for what's probably just kids letting their imagination run away with them."

I had no plans for the afternoon, Kelli was working, and I was curious, so I offered to go along with him. "I'd be glad to have you, Ennis. Unless Martin's sitting there sunning himself, I'm going to have to make at least a cursory search along the riverbank. It'll go a lot faster with help. We can try calling direct, but Martin's never been very good about carrying his personal com around with him."

We didn't find anything to substantiate the boys' story. No body parts, although they would have been sucked into the Throat. No clothing along the shore, on the footbridge or at either end. There was no sign of Melody's red body suit either, which meant either she'd been there and gone, or that the boys had made up that part of their story, if not the entire thing.

"Have to search below the Throat to be sure, but if those boys weren't lying, I'd say they fooled themselves into thinking they saw something they didn't."

When we got back to Safehaven, Grant thanked me and said he was going to run out to the Harwell place personally if they didn't answer the com this time. I waited outside and it wasn't long before he reappeared, looking more pissed than ever. "Still no answer," he growled and headed for the aging company flitter.

"Mind if I come along?" I'd never actually seen the Harwell farm and I was curious about it, as well as the current mystery.

"Suit yourself."

Several dozen crabhens were chattering happily in their run when we arrived at the farm, finishing up the last of some carrion that had been dumped there for them. Crabhens are omnivorous scavengers, and they had a highly adaptive DNA structure that made them ideal for introduction to new colonies. They were also low maintenance, and were far enough down on the food chain to be profitable both for their eggs and their meat. The farm was in better condition than I'd expected after hearing the town gossip, the porch was swept, the yard relatively cleaned up, the corrugated plasticote freshly painted.

Melody answered the door. "Grant! Ennis! What are you two doing way out here?"

"Morning, Melody. Is Martin home?"

"No, he went out before I got up this morning. Is something wrong?"

Grant sighed. "Maybe, maybe not. Mind if we come in for a minute?"

Melody took it well enough, but she'd always been a strong person. "It could be, I suppose. I know he did swim there from time to time. I've been there with him, but I didn't like it much. Too rough and noisy."

"Well, we don't know for sure that anything happened, or if it did, that it was really Martin it happened to."

"Is there any chance it was someone else?"

I couldn't see how anyone could be mistaken for Martin Harwell, given his size, but Grant didn't have the heart to cut her off without a hope. "There's always a chance."

Then he somewhat awkwardly brought up the subject of Melody's red body suit. "The kids say they saw it up there, but we couldn't find it ourselves when we looked."

She shook her head. "It's packed away somewhere. I couldn't wear it while I was pregnant. I could go look for it if you'd like."

Grant assured her it wasn't necessary. "The boys were most likely mistaken. And if they're mistaken about that, they might just as well be wrong about the other thing. Chances are Martin is perfectly fine."

But Martin didn't come home that night, and even though no body parts were ever recovered downstream, Grant reluctantly acknowledged that the twins had probably told the truth.

"The body must be hung up underground some place. Might work loose eventually. Harwell didn't seem the type to kill himself, though. I still think it was some kind of accident."

The day I was supposed to go home, I walked up to the Harwell place and visited with Melody for a while. She was obviously distraught, but she kept herself under control. Martin had no heirs, so his farm was open to claim once he was officially dead. I suggested that she might want to take part of it for herself, but she wasn't interested. "I wouldn't want to profit from Martin's death. I'd feel guilty for the rest of my life."

Melody told me she thought Martin had committed suicide. "He wasn't the kind to have an accident, and he was strong enough to swim right up to the Throat and back. I know it's hard to believe that he had a sensitive side, but he was really upset when I lost the baby. I guess it was the first thing he ever really loved. I tried to help him get over it, told him we could try again, but it was like he just didn't hear me anymore."

We made small talk for a bit longer and then I left for home, feeling as though I'd just witnessed the second major tragedy of my life.

Cille seemed like almost a different person to me. She'd always been self confident in a childish way but now she was a formidable young woman and she knew it. After my stint in Safehaven, I think I acquired a somewhat inflated opinion of my own maturity, because one evening while Mom and Dad were gone on one of their rare trips to Aladdin, I decided to play the big brother and give her some advice.

"You know, Cille, one of these days you're going to have to decide just what you want to do with your life."

We'd just finished watching the trivideo and were sitting there drinking the last of a bottle of wine I'd brought back from Safehaven. It was expensive, an offworld import, but the vineyards on Aragon had yet to produce an acceptable fruit. Cille emptied her glass and set it down carefully before answering.

"What makes you think I haven't?"

"Well, all you do is sit around and study one thing or another. You're not really interested in the farm or…" I let my voice trail off.

"Or raising a family? That's what you were going to say, wasn't it?"

It was, but I wasn't about to admit it. "I just don't like seeing you cut yourself off from things like this."

She nodded her head, to herself and not me, and I knew I'd put my foot in it. "Do you remember the controversy a few months ago when the company tried to extend its mineral royalty limits?"

"Vaguely. Some local legal experts request an advisory from the Concourse and the company backed down."

"More or less. The legal experts involved were Cille Baxter and two associates from Tyrada." That caught me by surprise, but before I could react she asked another question. "Have you ever heard of Lake Lilith?"

"Of course I have." Lake Lilith was east of Aladdin, a wilderness area where the native Aragonian plantlife still thrived. The company had planned to reseed it until a group of investors incorporated themselves and purchased the development rights so that it could be turned into a park and resort area.

"I own thirty percent of the Lilith Development Corporation."

"But how? You've never drawn anything major from your credit account." Cille received one fifth of the farm's profit every year, just like the rest of us, even Jesper, wherever he might be, although his just accumulated in his account. She used her income to pay her com bills and other incidentals, but otherwise it just sat there drawing interest.

"I have another account." Cille had the grace to look a bit shamefaced. "I do legal consultations, specializing in trade law. You do remember that I received a degree a while back?"

"But you've never practiced!"

Her eyes were laughing at me. "Ninety percent of legal activity takes place over a com, Ennis. I've successfully sued the company twice, failed once, and negotiated eight settlements. I have two people working for me part time, one in Aladdin and one in Tyrada, and I'm on the waiting list for an AI secretarial system once the embargo is lifted."

"I didn't know," I said weakly. "Mom and Dad?"

She shrugged her head. "Mom knows most of it and I imagine she's told Dad. It's a different world from theirs, and I think Dad's a little bit disappointed that I'm not more interested in the farm, but there it is. I'm not."

"Are you planning to leave then?" The idea of Cille leaving the farm dismayed me. I didn't want her to go because she was my sister, but also because I still thought of her as a fragile young thing with a horribly scarred face who would attract unwelcome stares wherever she went.

"Not in the immediate future. I told you, I do most of my work over the com." She reached over and patted my knee. "Don't worry, Ennis. I won't steal away in the night; you'll have lots of warning. I will have to start traveling soon though. When the company leaves Aragon, we're going to need to have a judicial system in place, and I might even end up being a judge someday."

Dr. Paul Fortunato's mobile clinic landed on our newly constructed airpad a couple of weeks later. We'd had a couple of cases of fire rash, Jeb Booker being one of them, and he'd brought enough vaccine for everyone. It took most of the day to get everyone inoculated, and Mom talked the doctor into staying the night. We all sat up talking until pretty late, late for farmers anyway, and then everyone went to bed except the doctor and I.

We were sitting out on the back porch, swapping stories about people we knew in Safehaven, gossiping mostly. Then he caught me by surprise and asked about Melody Miller.

"Melody quit her job and moved out of Safehaven, determined, as she put it, 'to put the past to rest'. There was talk she might change her mind and take over the Harwell place but nothing came of it. Sobriety Carter claimed most of the fields for his kids, and the rest, including the farmhouse and barn, is back in the public trust."

He was quiet for a while. "Ennis. I'm an honorable man, aren't I? I mean, I never violate a patient's confidence."

"Not that I know of, Paul." There was something odd in his tone that made me swivel my head and watch him closely.

"And I wouldn't do that, would I? It would be unethical to tell someone what went on between myself and a patient."

"No, no, I don't believe you would. Everyone trusts you, Paul."

"Well, you're wrong. I'm going to say something now that I have no right to say."

"You are?" I might have thought this was the buildup to some elaborate joke except that Fortunato seemed almost painfully serious.

"Remember at the inquest how she said Martin was upset on account of the baby died?"

I must have looked pretty dumb right then because I wasn't following what the doctor was trying to say. "Melody, you mean? Sure. Hard to believe it about the bastard, but I guess he had some feeling somewhere."

"That's a load of crap! He never gave a fuck for anything or anyone." Anger cut through the haze of alcohol. "She didn't fall down any staircase either. The bastard beat her up, punched her in the belly so much he cracked two ribs. Didn't want some brat to come along and spoil things for him so he killed it. Might have killed her too; she was bleeding inside pretty bad for a while."

I was stunned, and a fugitive thought scampered through my consciousness at that moment, whispering that I'd seen something a while back that was out of place, something that my subconscious had been working at quietly all this time without my even knowing it. This should mean something, I thought, but I couldn't figure what it was. The silence stretched and Paul stood up and stretched his arms.

"I'd appreciate it if you kept that to yourself, Ennis, but I had to tell someone before it burst right out of my skull. I know someone in my line of work is supposed to value human life, but I've got to tell you that I smiled when I heard that Martin Harwell was dead. And now I'm going to bed."

He did exactly that, but I sat there a long time, using my mental tongue to probe at an aching tooth of memory that I hadn't even noticed was there. And then I experienced a moment of terrible clarity that troubled my sleep so badly that I had trouble rising on time the next morning.

Grant Colson probably would have been more successful on a more settled world. He was a fair records administrator, and most of the time he got along well with people, but he didn't have a knack for problem solving and, frankly, not much imagination either. In Safehaven, a quiet, backwater town on a mostly rural planet, he was able to fit in pretty well because most crime was juvenile, and he spent more time negotiating compromises between outraged parties than actually apprehending criminals. There'd been a few assaults in Safehaven over the years, but no homicides.

I made a special trip in to see him, but I didn't really know what I was going to say until I got there. He still remembered the vandalism we'd experienced, but I told him not to worry about it.

"I understand Melody Miller's left."

"Sure did. Not too surprising. She's living over in Linden Township now, working for the company."

"Do you remember the day you and I went out to talk to her?"

"Sure. What's going on, Ennis?" Grant was sharp enough to realize I wasn't making casual conversation.

"When we got there, the crabhens were gorging themselves in the feed trough."

"If you say so. Wouldn't surprise me."

"They were eating entrails, Grant."

His face twisted in puzzlement. "So? Maybe Martin slaughtered a choat." About half the farmers kept choats, a durable grazing animal that yielded tough but nourishing steaks and hams. I'd never acquired a fondness for the taste myself, but we kept a few in a small pasture.

"Martin sold off all the choats when the old man died. He never ate meat."

"So maybe he bought one for Melody from one of his neighbors. What are you getting at, Ennis?"

I sighed. This was much more difficult than I'd anticipated, and if I was wrong, I was going to look like a complete fool. But I was pretty sure I was right.

"Melody's a strong girl, isn't she?"

"Sure is. Doctor Fortunato said she nearly died when she had her accident, would have if she hadn't been in such good shape."

He waited and I floundered and finally burst out with the whole thing, telling him what I thought had happened to Martin Harwell. Grant's eyes changed expression along the way. Angry first, then puzzled, finally unhappy.

When I had finished, he was thoughtful for a while, then asked his only question. "Then why was that red suit of hers lying up there?"

"Well, I guess after she untangled herself from Harwell's hollowed out body and swam to shore, she wore that for the run back to the farm. She must have waited for the kids to arrive so there'd be a witness but she wouldn't want anyone to see her out there naked."

"So what you're saying is, she exchanged one body suit for another."

"More or less."

"So what do we do about it?"

That caught me up. Grant was the representative of justice here, not me. It looked pretty certain to me that Melody Miller killed her lover in revenge for the death of her unborn child, gutted his body, climbed inside and walked it down to the Jackknife.

"She killed a man, Grant."

He nodded. "So did I once. Back on Veruscant, I was working security when the Carolists were trying to bring down the government. Spotted a terrorist planting a minibomb and killed him when he tried to run. That bomb would've killed thirty or forty people."

"He deserved to die then."

"So did Martin Harwell, to my way of thinking."

I didn't have a response to that, but I was uncomfortable.

Grant stood up and started walking slowly around the office with his hands clasped behind his back. "You know, when I was training for this post, they made me do a lot of studying, even some old fashioned live classes with a hologram teacher and an AI to field questions. They said a whole lot about the law, company law, Concourse law. I don't recall them ever mentioning anything about justice though. But I do remember learning that sometimes the law had to be flexible, particularly on a newly settled world where people and institutions hadn't completely adapted."

"This isn't quite the same thing," I argued. "We're talking murder here, not land disputes or survival policy."

"All right then, I need you to make a formal statement and accusation. Once I have that, I contact my counterpart in Linden, and he arranges for the company to send in an arresting officer and a team of investigators. Most likely the trial will be held in Aladdin, so you'll have to travel up there to testify."

I squirmed in my seat. "Why me? I may have figured this out, but you're the company's legal hand here."

"The law says there must be an accusing party, and besides, you're the only one who saw, or at least remembers seeing, what had been dumped in that feeding trough."

"Why couldn't you be the accusing party?"

"I could, but I won't." He was facing me now and met my eyes without blinking. "Dying was the best thing Martin Harwell ever did for Safehaven, Ennis. Melody had no right to end his life, but she did. If I could reverse that, I would, but for her sake, not his. She's not the kind of person who's going to find that easy to live with, no matter how much he deserved it. But I don't feel any sympathy for Martin Harwell. So if you press me, I'll take official action, but if you don't, I'll be damned if I'll pursue it on my own."

So I went home, troubled, so preoccupied in fact that Cille noticed and cajoled and bullied me into telling her what was wrong. Not surprisingly, she felt sympathy for everyone concerned.

"We all try to make our lives into things of beauty, Ennis. Even Martin Harwell must have been looking for some kind of happiness, and maybe the greatest tragedy of this whole thing is that he had it right in his hands and didn't know it. He closed his fist and crushed his own future. My guess is that he never really felt any emotional attachment to anyone, not even Melody, and it never occurred to him the effect it would have on her to lose her child. He probably wanted things to go on as they had before and would never have understood why they could not."

I didn't understand how that was possible and said so.

"We each look at a different world, Ennis, and we all try to make it over into what we want."

"So what do I do, Cille? Do I tell Colson to pursue things or just leave them alone?"

"I can't tell you how to shape your world, Ennis." She smiled, a mixture of sympathy and amusement. "You're going to have to make your own decision."

And I did. I put Melody Miller out of my mind and went back to work, assuming that the issue was closed forever, at least insofar as I was concerned.

Things didn't work out that way. They rarely do. But it was a long time before I ever saw Melody Miller again, and two days later a new and unexpected crisis drove thoughts of the death of Martin Harwell completely out of my mind.

Dad collapsed while he was inventorying supplies out in the barn.

CHAPTER SEVEN

Jeb found him when he went in to pick up a spare powerpack and immediately called for help. Somone had already fashioned a stretcher by the time I arrived. "There's no sign of injury," Jeb told me, "but he's feverish, his pupils are dilated, and his fingernails are discolored."

I shot him a look and he met my eyes, then turned away. We both knew what that meant. Wegman's Disease. Jeb had already put in an emergency call and Dr. Fortunato was on his way. Fortunately, he'd been visiting patients at Goodhost and would be with us within minutes. We brought Dad to the house. Mom was clearly upset but she managed to stay calm, although it was Cille who supervised as we got him into his bed. The doctor arrived a few minutes later and we waited while he completed his examination.

When he emerged from the bedroom, I already knew the answer. Actually, I'd guessed the truth from the outset, but I was hoping that there might be some less serious condition I didn't know about that would exhibit the same symptoms. For the most part, humans were immune to the quasi-viruses native to Aragon. There were a few exceptions, most of them trivial, a couple of them not. Wegman's was not; it was invariably fatal. Children and young adults were not at risk, but occasionally older people contracted it, possibly because of changes in their immune system connected with aging. Its most distinguishing characteristic was a light blue discoloration which appeared initially in the nails and hair, later in the skin, gradually darkening until the infected individual died.

Mom, Cille, and I sat at the kitchen table with the doctor, and he told us calmly and unemotionally what to expect. "His fever is down now and he's resting comfortably, and I've given him something to keep him asleep until morning. It's definitely Wegman's, and I'm sorry to say there's still no cure, not even a likely prospect." Mom was staring at him expressionlessly, but I could tell from the position of her shoulders that she had her hands clenched out of sight in her lap. Cille was more animated and couldn't seem to sit still, but she also seemed to be in control of herself. I was the one who got angry and shouted that the company should have devoted more effort to finding a cure.

Paul waited for me to get it all out of my system, then continued in the same quiet manner. "The news isn't all bad. We have learned a lot about how the disease works and we can make your father reasonably comfortable. There are boosters we can use to support his immune system and retard the advance of the quasi-virus. At one time, Wegman's claimed its victims within weeks. Today we can do much better. Your father is otherwise healthy and you can afford the best treatment."

"How long?" It was Mom, and her voice trembled ever so slightly.

He hesitated. "That's hard to predict, Maryam. One or two years almost certainly, possibly four. And during that period, we may well find a cure, or at least a more effective palliative."

"Will he have to stay at the clinic in Aladdin?" Cille's voice was brittle, almost unrecognizable. "I think he'd rather die than be confined to a hospital bed."

The doctor shook his head. "There are two known strains of Wegman's. Your father has the less destructive variety and won't require around the clock monitoring. Most of the time he'll feel fine, although his energy level will be low. He won't be able to maintain his usual workload, he'll sleep a lot and will have to take a great deal of medication, but he'll remain mobile and feel reasonably well right up until the terminal stage. I'd recommend that he wear a life signs monitor from now on, and we'll check him out every few weeks." He glanced around the table. "Jon's mental attitude is very important. If you treat him like an invalid, he'll feel like one and won't fight as hard. It's important that you act as normal as possible, and that you keep him active and alert. I know you Baxters are strong minded people and don't quit when the going gets tough." He didn't look at Cille as he said this, but the way he didn't look at her told me that he was thinking about her. "If I ever met a man strong enough to defeat Wegman's, he's the one sleeping in that room."

Dad didn't beat Wegman's, of course. There's still no cure. He lasted long enough to see Aragon become independent, and that was good, but he didn't last long enough to see us lose our independence only eighty eight days later, and maybe that was good as well.

The next few days were very difficult for me. For all of us, I guess, although we didn't talk about it among ourselves, even in Dad's absence. He seemed almost his normal self that first morning, though a bit haggard. He'd regained consciousness while the doctor was with him and he knew that he had Wegman's. There was no danger of infection by contact. The quasi-virus was everywhere. Those who became susceptible contracted it, those who retained their immunity did not. Vikki Portman's brother, who had died of it a year earlier, had continued his chiropractic practice even after his hair had turned bright blue. We discussed it for about an hour, calmly, almost clinically, then called in Zai Kreller, Jeb Booker, and Garner Elsevier, who had replaced Flo Balcombe a few months earlier. They were our three top employees, and we wanted to tell them officially what they already knew.

We reassigned some of Dad's duties on the spot. For the most part, we had a good crew working for us, and not just because we paid better than the other farmers. Zai and Jeb were both intensely loyal to Dad, and that morning was the first time I saw Zai betraying her emotions physically. Her voice was scratchy and a muscle twitched in her left cheek, and on a couple of occasions she turned away from the rest of us and stared into the corner of the room. Dad closed by thanking them all for their loyalty. Jeb looked uncomprehending and Garner kept saying how sorry he was to hear the news, repeating the same phrase over and over like a mantra.

"I've come to think of you all as an unofficial branch of the Baxter family. I want you to know that whatever happens today, tomorrow, or a year from now, won't change that, and even after I'm gone, you'll be provided for." We'd discussed this earlier and decided now was the time to reveal the broad outlines of the new family trust we'd created. Zai was already a junior partner because of the land she'd claimed for us, but we'd quietly incorporated a year earlier to take advantage of the prevailing company policy rather than risk waiting until the Planetary Council codified its own rules. Zai's share had been doubled without her knowledge, and Jeb and Garner had become stockholders, although Garner's share wasn't much more than a gesture at this point. All three were stunned when we told them, and I think their protests were genuine. We hadn't made them rich by any means, but Zai and Jeb were now drawing an income close to that of most of the smaller farmers in Safehaven, and Garner could see the same in his future if he stayed with us.

Dad had one more announcement to make, but he waited until Zai and the others were gone. "It's not going to be possible for me to serve as a delegate to the Planetary Council. That's a long term commitment that I may not be able to fulfill and," his face crinkled into one of his rare smiles, "since I never really wanted the job, this is a perfect excuse to bow out."

I opened my mouth to object, then closed it. I didn't want Dad going off to Aladdin for large chunks of whatever remained of his life.

"Under the provisions of the election, I'm entitled to appoint a representative in my place if I'm unable to attend a session. I don't think it was intended that I use that privilege for my complete term of office, but since my replacement is a family member and fully qualified to serve, I don't think anyone will object."

I was on my feet, telling myself to calm down, but my voice was strained. "No! There's no way you can send me away from the farm again, not now! We have to redesign the irrigation system from the Swift, the north wharf needs to be rebuilt, there's a yield problem in the east field, and we're behind schedule with the soil revitalization project."

Perfectly composed, Dad turned to me with raised eyebrows. "Are you saying that Zai, Jeb, Garner, your mother, and I are all incapable of handling these things?"

"No, but…" My voice trailed off as Dad waved his hand at me.

"It's all right, Ennis. I know what you meant. Don't worry, I'm not planning to send you off to Aladdin in my place. Cille is going. She's more qualified than any of us to deal with the legal issues, and I was planning to take her with me in any case."

I glanced at Cille and Mom and from the expressions on their faces, I knew that I was the only one surprised by the announcement. I think I was hurt for a few seconds, felt left out, but then I started thinking about all of the studying Cille had been doing, law and history and economics and such, and remembered how Dad had subtly encouraged her, shifting chores that she would ordinarily have done to others, building the addition to her room to house more sophisticated communications and computing equipment, and I realized that all the pieces had been there for me to assemble into a complete picture long ago.

"I think that's a great idea," I said at last, and meant it. "Congratulations, Cille. Maybe you'll end up being Senator Baxter."

"The hell with that, Ennis. I intend to be Planetary Governor."

I had to face another crisis a few weeks later, a more personal one. I was still seeing Kelli Nganda as often as I could, but Dad's illness and a series of minor but time consuming problems made it increasingly difficult to travel to Safehaven for more than a very brief visit. She'd come out to the farm a few times, but she worked long and uncertain hours as an apprentice veterinarian, and it was becoming increasingly difficult for us to be with each other on a regular basis. I'd noticed that she had become rather withdrawn when we were together and felt some hesitation myself. It was a clear case of negative feedback; the more aware of the problem we became, the more pronounced was our reaction, which made us even more aware that our relationship had hit a downturn.

By mutual agreement, we decided to take a vacation from each other. I sulked around the farm the first couple of days, but then I spotted Dad vomiting out behind the new rubbage silo where he thought no one would see him, probably a reaction to the medication he was taking rather than the disease itself. I sneaked off so he wouldn't know he'd been observed, but it gave me some perspective about my own comparatively minor personal problems and my attitude improved considerably after that.

Jeb and Zai proposed that we lay some new roads. "We're big enough now that it's more efficient to bring in supplies overland than by air or water. We need a roadway to the north wharf and another one in to Safehaven." I was skeptical at first, but Zai showed us how much we were spending for the air shipments – flitters were practical on the surface but horrendously expensive to operate in the air – and Jeb already had estimates for the construction costs.

"Worst case, it takes us three years to recoup the investment. The route I've marked takes us through unclaimed land except for one little corner of the Chandler farm, and I think we can convince Abe to go along with us since it works to his advantage as well. The route's not as direct as I'd like but," he smiled, "it provides access to six of the biggest farms in Safehaven. If we pay for it, no one's going to voice any objection. And we can probably cut the cost by at least a third if we do some of the work with our own hired help when they're not busy."

"Are you saying we have too much hired help, Jeb?" I already knew the answer. I wanted to know if he did. When Jeb first came to work for us, he'd found it very difficult to organize complex projects. Maturity had changed that.

"Not at all. In fact we'll need to add some temporary field hands for the second spongemelon harvest this year. But we have scheduling problems all the time. We waste a few work hours almost every day, and sometimes a lot of them all at once, because it takes so long to move people from one place to another. If we shift that labor to clearing land, it'll be practically free and our efficiency will improve as transit times shrink."

I played devil's advocate a while longer, but their plan was approved without reservation. And to be honest, I had an ulterior motive for agreeing. A direct overland route between our holdings and Safehaven would make it much easier to travel back and forth regularly. I was already missing Kelli.

We'd already had more bad news that year than I liked, and there was no end in sight. We had another wormswell under a cultivated field – not a big one admittedly and the crop loss was insignificant, but it gave us some uncomfortable moments, and part of the irrigation system had to be temporarily re-routed. Then we had an another outbreak of rustgrass that cost us so much in treatment costs that we barely broke even on that season's crop. Dad had his good days and his bad ones, and we never really knew how many of the latter there were because he concealed how he was feeling. And on top of everything else, there was some very disturbing news from offworld.

Patrols in the region had been beefed up significantly and there was still talk of a major military buildup in preparation. The incidence of missing ships had dropped dramatically, but only because the commercial exploration ships had largely moved to less uncertain sectors. The universe is really big, and there's no reason to invest time in a questionable area when there are so many others that remain unexplored. But when the heavily armed cruiser *Daedalus* failed to return from a routine patrol, a determined effort was made to find out why. With almost no publicity, a good sized expedition was sent to retrace its route, led by the battleship *Ichiyo* and numbering more than a dozen warships with half that many again support craft.

They found the *Daedalus*, or what remained of it, in an unnamed star system one of whose planets was nearly earthlike and had been marked for potential development. They also found an indeterminate number of alien ships of a design previously unknown. Even today it's not certain who fired first, but if the task force didn't initiate hostilities, it would in all probability have been attacked anyway, so the question is moot. Weaponry was surprisingly similar except that the human ships were marginally better armored. The aliens were more numerous, however, and their attack so tightly coordinated that the task force fled back to friendly space with the *Ichiyo* badly damaged along with six other warships and two support craft. The remaining ships were presumed destroyed.

It wasn't close to Aragon as these things are measured, but it was close enough to discourage some of the independent traders, which meant the price of imported items jumped and the volume of exports dropped dramatically. Aragon's economy faltered, staggered, and limped onward. Since our farm produced food primarily for domestic consumption, we weren't directly affected. People still had to eat. But they were more selective and had less credit to spend, so the specialty crops we had been experimenting with ended up costing more than they brought in, and even some of our staples took some price hits. The season following the encounter, the farm barely broke even overall, and we had a marginal loss the season after that. Fortunately we had a very large credit reserve, but some of the smaller farms were in serious trouble, and a couple of them only survived by obtaining loans from the Virtual Surety, a new investment group whose board of trustees included Cille. One of those saved was Sobriety Carter, but Cille made me promise not to tell him that she was involved. Needham's bank in Safehaven had not been healthy since the Gansett Trust opened, and had little capital to lend to its neighbors.

There was considerable clamor in Aladdin for a beefed up military presence, and in fact two companies of marines were landed and housed just outside the city. It was just a placatory gesture, however. There were rumors that a major fleet was being assembled at Balinor, but nothing was ever officially confirmed. As the months passed and nothing happened, people on Aragon largely forgot the aliens, but very few of the merchant ships returned.

The schedule for Aragon's independence had to be changed again. If anything, the company was more anxious than ever to wind things up and move their resources to less risky areas, but a precondition of autonomy was a certain degree of self sufficiency, and the worsening of our trade situation forced the company to use its own vessels to make up the difference. We fell below the critical threshold very quickly.

Which is not to say that the legislative work was put on hold. Cille spent more time in Aladdin than at home, and she was in fact our best source of reliable information about the unrest in the capitol. For the first time in its history, Aragon had a visible number of unemployed workers. The spaceport commission had reduced its staff by almost a third, the fledgling manufacturing industry was hard hit by the fall off of exports, and some newer enterprises failed completely. The Lilith resort project in which Cille was heavily invested suspended operations indefinitely, although they retained control of the property. A handful of immigrants who had adequate credit resources filed for and were eventually transported to other colony worlds. The company had already agreed to limit the number of new settlers, but suddenly that wasn't a problem because very few people wanted to risk being close to a hostile alien power. Reassurances that adequate military protection would soon be available convinced no one.

The economic situation may have hastened the collapse of the Malcolm Cooperative, but it was probably inevitable. Very little of what happened reached outside ears until later, and then from partisans of one side or another and therefore suspect, but apparently disagreements about various aspects of the cooperative management system led to polarization into two distinct and approximately equal groups, with a block of uncommitted members almost as large who were drawn one way or the other singly and en masse. Instead of treating problems as challenges to be solved as a single community, the two factions began blaming each other for everything that went wrong. One animosity fed another, followed by recriminations, sabotage, and a rash of shouting matches and sporadic physical violence.

Mom had made some friends on the inside, so she was one of the first to know. Approximately one fourth of the residents suddenly put their shares up for sale. Most planned to relocate to Goodhost or elsewhere on Aragon; a few wanted to emigrate offworld. The remainder split into three factions, two of whom petitioned the company to support their interpretation of the bylaws of the community. The third and smallest faction couldn't decide what they wanted to do, and tried to pretend that everything was going to proceed as it had in the past.

The company refused to intercede except in an advisory capacity, and after that the dissolution accelerated. Grant Colson had to call in the Colonial Police to suppress rioting. Karl Mancel, who had tried to remain aloof from the controversy, was attacked by unknown parties one evening and suffered a serious concussion. One of the storage silos burned to the ground, fortunately an empty one, and there was a less successful attempt to burn down one of the communal living facilities. Reluctantly, the company purchased the holdings of the smaller of the two main factions, and there was another exodus before things settled down. Those remaining were too small a number to maintain the elaborate agricultural and social system of the Cooperative, and one season later the Cooperative was for all practical purposes a satellite village of Safehaven.

We Baxters weathered it all reasonably well, even turned a small profit. Some of the other farmers fared badly. Abe Chandler threw up his hands and sold his farm to the Tonobis, although he stayed on as foreman for the first year before eventually relocating to Willow, a new settlement north of Casper. Most of the other small holdings built credit deficits that seemed likely to cripple the economic growth of Safehaven for some time to come. You could feel the change in mood just walking through its streets. People looked down at their feet, and they didn't greet each other in passing, and the constant flow of social events had slowed to a trickle. On more than one occasion, I caught someone glaring at me while I was there, and Kelli told me there'd been complaints that we were making a fortune while everyone else suffered.

"We've been luckier than most," I conceded, "but our profit this year is down more than ninety percent. That's not much of a fortune. I could show you the figures if you want."

"I believe you, Ennis. But it wouldn't matter even if you were losing money. When people are angry, you can sometimes reason with them, but they're not just angry any more. They're frightened. They're afraid that they're going to lose their homes and they're worried about the Cranes."

The Cranes were the mysterious aliens whose presence had cast a shadow over our economy. For the most part, it was impossible to know which if any of the countless rumors of encounters with them were true. The military had by now recovered some of their dead, though no living prisoners. Our troublesome neighbors were humanoid, averaging a bit more than two meters tall but with about the same average body mass as a human. They had recognizable faces, although the eyes were more widely separated and the horny ridge that looked like a nose wasn't one. They breathed through the sides of their head. Most of their additional height resulted from what appeared to human eyes to be disproportionately long legs, hence the nickname. Their skin was considerably tougher than ours, but their bones were more fragile. Cille speculated that they originated on a lower gravity world where they had no significant competition from other animal forms, but possibly one with inimical plantlife. "Their skin would protect them from barbs and toxins, but hit one with your fist and you'll likely break a bone or three." As it turned out, they weren't quite that fragile, although her speculation about their homeworld was surprisingly accurate.

The most disturbing rumor was that the Cranes had raided a fledgling colony world and made off with some of the local inhabitants. If true, it was undoubtedly to gather intelligence, but scaremongers had already created elaborate stories of vivisection and other atrocities. The official word was that no such incident could be confirmed, but the weakness of the denial only made it sound more credible.

The next season was exceptionally good in terms of yield, which flooded a somewhat shrunken market with produce, lowering prices and worsening the situation locally. Zai had suggested increasing the amount of land we'd set aside for specialty crops, despite the bad experience we'd had the previous year, and that decision made the difference between a profit and a loss because unaccountably the demand for luxury foods went up as the demand for staples declined. The grumbling from Safehaven grew louder – even Dad was hearing it. Kelli lost some clients because she was involved with me.

"Do you want to break things off, at least for a while?" She had told me about the drop off in her business while we were walking along a path above Satan's Throat, and I decided to make the offer, painful though it might be.

"No, of course not. You know me better than that." Actually I did. She was as stubborn as they come. Her older sister had moved out and had recently left Aragon rather than stay under the thumb of their autocratic father, but Kelli just dug in her heels when their wills crossed and more often than not it was her father who abandoned the contest. "I've been thinking about closing down the office though. If I was catering to a clientele with exotic pets, they could come to me for treatment. With farm stock, I spend almost all of my time in someone's barn or out in a pasture. All I really need is a place to store my equipment and supplies."

We talked about that for a while, and I mentioned the surveyor's shelter we'd built along Baxter Road , which now linked us to Safehaven. "It's not fancy, but it has power hookups and there's plenty of space and it wouldn't take much to turn it into living space." Kelli seemed interested, but the shelter was closer to us than to the town which meant she'd still have a lot of traveling to do, and then we found a shady place to sit down and eventually lie down, and there was no talking for a while, and after that a perfectly logical solution came to both of us.

I'm not sure I ever really understood Kuriel Nganda's feelings about my engagement to his daughter. The expression of stolid neutrality remained on his face throughout our announcement and he shook my hand properly if not cordially and gave us the formal permission we had not intended to ask for. My family was considerably more enthusiastic, I'm happy to say. Kelli and Cille had always gotten along well, and they threw their arms around each other and disappeared to plot against me while Mom and Dad and I worked out logistics.

"You could build yourselves a place down near the Swift," Dad suggested. "There's some pretty country there."

I may have given the impression that we'd turned the entire countryside into cultivated meadows, but that wasn't the case. About two thirds of our joint holdings had been cleared. We methodically identified areas which were to remain untouched, some native growth, some imported stock. There was a local tree, colloquially called squatters, that made excellent windbreaks, and we'd actually planted them in strategically placed lines along the borders of individual fields. Squatters didn't grow as fast as the poplar variant that had been designed for Aragon, but they branched more thickly, and they never grew more than ten feet tall, which minimized the amount of shadefall on the fields.

The Baxter farm was roughly triangular. The northern tip consisted of gently rolling hills on the tallest of which we'd built our house. The eastern side was much flatter, all the way to the Jackknife, and the western side grew progressively rougher the further south one traveled. Some of the fields in that southwest corner, the Rollers, were unprofitable even when times were good, but we'd cleared them in order to establish our claim and prevent the road from Safehaven from undercutting our position. The road between us and town passed through fields and forest, crossed two good sized brooks, and at its southernmost part threaded through a narrow strip of marshland just before it reached the Tonobi farm and veered off toward Safehaven. The prettiest country was in the Rollers, particularly along the river, but that would put us a good distance from the main house as well as from Safehaven.

"We were thinking about the little meadow above South Brook."

Dad nodded. "It's pretty enough there, and practical as well." Then Mom wanted to know about wedding plans and Kelli was summoned back and much of the rest of that day remains a blur. We were married at the end of the season, and if the farmers in Safehaven resented the Baxters, it certainly didn't prevent them from coming in force to the ceremony and the gala party that followed. It was one of Dad's good days – they were coming less frequently by now – and he greeted each of our guests by name and made them all feel welcome, even Sobriety Carter. Our new house wasn't quite finished, but we moved in anyway, and even though we'd been intimate for some time before the wedding, it seemed to take on an entirely new flavor afterward, and I confess that for several days I was less attentive to what was going on around me than I would normally have been.

What I missed was the rising controversy about the company's plan for our independence. Rumors of encounters with the Cranes had begun to decline, but no one knew whether this reflected the actual state of affairs or simply that the military had clamped down more effectively on communications. Then the company announced that it was accelerating the independence project after all, supposedly so that it could redirect its assets into more promising emerging sectors. Some of the same people who had been complaining about the company's paternalism in the past now protested against being abandoned unprepared, but Cille thought that the majority of the delegates agreed with the company's decision. They had already ratified a basic constitutional structure for Aragon, and there were at least skeletal agreements for commercial and credit laws, immigration policy, social services, taxation, and most other branches of government and public law. There had been some bumps in the road, but it looked like Aragon would be independent in less than a local year, and plans for the first election of a formal legislature were already being developed. The legislature, to be called the Assembly, would govern exclusively for the first year, with two executive positions to be filled by general election during the second. Cille was considering running for one of the two postings, and I often wonder what would have happened if we'd ever gotten that far.

But of course we didn't.

CHAPTER EIGHT

Two incidents brought Kelli and I roughly back to the real world. I hadn't been neglecting my responsibilities on the farm, but as soon as they were done each day, I rushed back to the house, waiting impatiently if Kelli was out curing a teracalf's cholic or spraying crabhen nests for dust molt. I have no reason to doubt that Kelli was similarly single minded. It was almost by chance that one evening we turned on the newslink and heard about the disastrous battle near Dorking's Star.

There were probably efforts made to suppress this story as well, but the results of the second full scale encounter with the Cranes were too widely known and terrible to be concealed. Officially it was a skirmish involving four of our biggest ships, with at least a dozen cruisers and twice that many smaller vessels. A scoutship had reported an enemy presence in the uninhabited Dorking system and the squadron commander gave the order to attack what appeared to be a much smaller force. The navy claimed to have destroyed all the target ships, so they probably did manage to get the majority of them, but then a much larger Crane force appeared and turned the tables. Whether it was a fortuitous arrival on their part or an elaborate trap was open to conjecture. The results were the loss of nine capital ships and twelve smaller vessels, with heavy damage to virtually every other ship in the squadron. There were no credible figures about damage inflicted on the Cranes. The survivors had scattered and limped into orbit around eight different colony worlds, including Aragon. Live coverage from Aladdin was sobering. A steady stream of injured were carried out of the landing craft. At least one news agency had a monitor in orbit, because an inset on the screen showed a damaged cruiser with huge tears in one side and scorch marks all across its hull.

My immediate and admittedly selfish reaction was concern that this would further depress the prices we could charge for our produce. A family meeting seemed wise, so Kelli and I climbed into our new flitter and headed north, arriving at dusk. The house was all alight and several figures moved behind the windows. Jeb came out to meet us, his face tense. "We were just about to call you. Your father collapsed a few minutes ago and we can't rouse him."

Dr. Fortunato was way up north so another physician filled in for him. I was so numb I never even got his name. He and a meditech were in my father's room until late that evening, and when they emerged, the doctor looked grave. My mother insisted that he sit down and brought both men something to drink before settling to hear what they had to say.

"Your husband's sleeping normally now and his vital signs have improved. I suspect that he'll be up and about in a day or so." He licked his lips in a nervous habit that I found irrationally annoying at the time. Kelli sensed my irritability and put her hand over mine. "I'm sure you're aware of the seriousness of his condition, and this is obviously not a good sign. He's a strong man, but his own body is working against him now. You can expect more incidents like this, and they'll become increasingly frequent until he's used up all his strength." He left the next sentence unspoken.

"How long?" My mother's voice seemed perfectly calm.

"Another season, probably two. But not much more than that. I'm sorry."

Mom called Cille in Aladdin after the doctor left and she flew home the following morning. Dad was conscious and appeared cheerful by the time she arrived, but he was clearly weak and drifted off to sleep while she was talking to him. She and Mom went off together to compare notes and I tidied up the guest room where Kelli and I had spent the night. Kelli had gone over to the Aguilar farm to treat a sickly choat and I had tried to occupy myself redesigning the fertilization program until Zai and Jeb tactfully told me I was making things unnecessarily difficult.

I walked around aimlessly for a while and then Cille came out and joined me. Neither of us wanted to talk about Dad just then, or at least I didn't and Cille recognized that fact.

"So how are things going in the big city?"

"They were fine up until a few days ago. We tried to meet yesterday, but most people were too preoccupied to get any real work done."

"The Cranes?"

She nodded. "Things are worse than we're being told. The problem with telling people that everything's fine when the opposite is true is that they panic when the truth starts to slip out, because they don't know how much has been concealed."

"What we heard this time was pretty bad."

"Have the rumors about Urku reached this far?"

I frowned. "Wasn't that the planet where the Cranes supposedly abducted some farmers?"

"Not farmers. They attacked a naval intelligence post with ground troops. Killed about half the station's complement, a hundred or so, and took the rest away. I had dinner the other night with Admiral Halleck's daughter. She's being evacuated to Presidia for safety."

"Do they expect an attack here then?" I had thought myself immune to the contagious fear I felt in Safehaven but apparently I'd been fooling myself. I could feel my pulse quicken.

"They don't know what to expect. Not enough data for meaningful analysis. The incidents have been tentative, from both sides, or at least they were until Dorking." She reached over and grabbed my arm. "Ennis, I think we should transfer all of our reserve credit offworld, back to Presidia or even further."

It was a few seconds before I could answer. "You think the war will touch here then?"

"I think it would be prudent to be cautious. I moved most of my personal accounts a few days ago."

There was a long, awkward silence, and I realized Cille was waiting for me to break it. I still didn't want to talk about Dad. "Do you think this will affect the self rule date?"

She shook her head. "There's enough momentum to keep us rolling now, and the company is desperate to disengage and move their resources a little further from the fire, if not entirely out of the frying pan. Less than a hundred days to go." She sighed. "Sometimes I doubted we'd ever get this far."

"You enjoy it though. The politics, I mean."

She looked at me oddly, as though I'd pointed out something she'd never realized herself. "Yeah, I guess I do. Hell, I know I do. A lot of it is frustrating and tiresome, of course, but sometimes I find myself caught among people with wildly divergent opinions, all of them sure that they're right, all of them honestly trying to do what's best, and I figure out what the common threads are and use those as the basis for a compromise. Sometimes I fail. Quite often, actually.

But I've had some successes as well, and there's nothing that feels quite so good."

"From out here, it all looks pretty chaotic up in the capitol. I've heard people calling it the human wormdance – a very pretty way to suck up energy."

She laughed. "I hadn't heard that before. I like it. The Assembly sounds so boring; maybe we should have called it the Wormdance. Maybe I'll suggest that. I wouldn't mind being First Speaker of the Wormdance." We walked silently for a few moments. "How are things going? With you and Kelli, I mean."

"Things are great." I meant it too. "I was a little worried that we'd lose some of our edge once we were actually married. Hasn't happened yet though."

"I really like her, you know. She sees the people we hide inside ourselves. Do you know she's the only one outside the family and my doctors who has ever been able to talk to me about how I look?"

I flushed. It was dark enough that she couldn't see my reaction but I'm sure she was aware of it. I still had difficulty discussing the accident and its aftermath. "I guess people are embarrassed. Have you talked to the specialists lately?"

"I saw Doctor Pollar last month. There's a new version of syntheskin that's virtually indistinguishable from the real thing. It has to be replaced periodically and there are some other minor drawbacks, but it's a big improvement over what's been available before now. It's rather expensive, of course."

I turned on her impatiently. "Listen, Cille, I don't want that to stop you. I know that we're not turning a big profit right now, but our credit reserves are very comfortable and we're not actually losing money. I think it's time to do something."

Her eyes flashed in the moonlight. "I AM doing something, Ennis."

"You know what I mean."

This time her voice softened. "Yes, I do know. I'm sorry I snapped, but that's exactly what Pollar said to me. Three times."

"Well, maybe he's right. If we don't have enough credit, we can borrow."

"Oh, Ennis, it's not the cost. The cost of the entire treatment wouldn't even make much of a dent in my personal funds. I don't need to draw on the family account." It would be several years before she told me that her investment account at the time was already larger than the Baxter Family Trust. "It's the timing. There's so much to do right now. I can't take time out for personal issues. And I'm not sure that I would if I could."

"Why not? If it helps you lead a more normal life...."

"I DO lead a normal life, Ennis, thank you very much."

"You know what I mean, Cille."

She relaxed, but only a little. "Yes, I think I do, but I'm not so sure you understand me. First of all, negotiations are at too important a point right now for me to take time off for personal reasons. But second, and in some ways more important, is the question of image. Do you remember the trouble you had as a council member because of how young you were?"

"And the fact that I wasn't Dad. Yes, I remember."

"Well, I'm a lot younger than you. I'm the youngest and physically the smallest delegate. The same will be true when I'm a candidate. As enlightened as we might want to think ourselves, the fact is that when many people decide among the choices offered, they're going to prefer a square jawed, powerful looking man or woman to a comparatively dainty young girl. Well, right now they don't look at me as a dainty young girl. In fact, many of my colleagues have trouble looking at me in the first place. But they all respect me, Ennis. They respect what I stand for and what I do rather than what I appear to be."

"Are you saying that your appearance is an...an asset to your career?" I was appalled at the idea.

"At this point in my life, yes, I think it is. And I will not endanger my career, and the contribution that I have to make to our future, for cosmetic reasons."

There was something in her tone then that I recognized, the same resolution and self assurance that colored my father's voice when he wanted to control a situation. Something flickered in my mind, perhaps realization that my little sister wasn't depending on her big brother any more, that if anything she had become the dominant half of our relationship. It felt disorienting and annoying and a bit frightening. I couldn't think of anything to say, and after an awkward pause, she punched me playfully in the shoulder.

"It's too dark to see your face clearly, but I think I've shocked you a bit."

"Yes," I admitted. "You're right about that."

"Oh, Ennis, listen. I will deal with the syntheskin issue eventually, I promise. But not right now. Things are moving too fast and they're too complicated. I've lived like this for a long time and I'm used to it. If I wait another year, I'll have a constituency and a power base. It won't matter if I wait till then to change the way I look."

She was wrong about that, but there was no way that any of us could have known what was coming.

The furor over Dorking subsided but never went away. Traffic from offworld dropped off again, and many of those who did arrive were military personnel. The garrison in Aladdin increased in size and there were new restrictions placed on ships requesting permission to orbit the planet. Cille and the other delegates were informed rather than consulted, but since the colony was still technically under company control, there was little weight to their protests. Thanks to falling prices, the Baxter Farm was unprofitable that season, and we had a lot of company..

Dad had two more attacks, less frightening now that we were prepared, but still unsettling. In both cases he regained his good humor very quickly, but he lost some weight, slept much longer than usual, and occasionally had troubled following a conversation if it went on for more than a few minutes.

There were reports of several more sightings and another significant clash with the Cranes, but this time luck or weight of arms was on our side, and the enemy was driven off with heavy losses. Rumor had it that several survivors were taken prisoner, but no one would officially confirm the story. Tension ran high in anticipation of a counter strike, but in the weeks that followed, there were no sightings of the Cranes at all, and there was even public speculation that their defeat had frightened them off. The effort to find planets with Crane colonies accelerated despite the risk of clashes, but no trace of them was found, and after several weeks there was a sudden surge of optimism. Perhaps they'd abandoned this sector altogether.

The company took advantage of the relaxation of tension to push for disengagement. The delegates – now officially known as the Constitutional Assembly – was of a like mind. The local military commander objected publicly, decrying any instability while there was still a military emergency. Representatives of both the company and the Assembly pointed out that no such military emergency had been declared, and the commander withdrew his objections somewhat gracelessly. A few days after that, Aragon was officially a free world rather than a managed colony, authorized to send an observer to the Concourse when it next met to begin the application process for full membership. We all traveled to Aladdin for the ceremony, Dad included, and he looked almost his old self as he watched Cille being introduced as a member of the interim Assembly. Most, though not all, of the delegates were declared candidates for the election to be held one hundred and twenty days following independence, and Cille was running against Sobriety Carter.

Less than an hour after we returned to the farm, Dad collapsed again. His vital signs were so low that Mom used the emergency pack while I commed Dr. Fortunato. This time his examination didn't take nearly as long and the news wasn't good.

"He's stable now, but the deterioration is advancing steadily and he'll be weak and often disoriented from now on. Let him get out of bed if he feels up to it, but keep an eye on him. I'm sorry, but this is the terminal stage." He gave us a list of instructions, things we could do to make him more comfortable, how to respond to potential problems, what to expect. "He may experience some transitory mental problems – trouble sleeping, forgetfulness, hallucinations, things like that. Fortunately, it's unlikely that he will feel any significant physical discomfort."

I wanted to com Cille and let her know what happened, but Mom talked me out of it. "Tomorrow will be soon enough. There's nothing she can do right now. Let her have her day of glory first."

The next several weeks were very painful for me, watching my father's rapid decline. Much of the time he remained alert and, as far as I could tell, cheerful. Cille called almost every day but at Dad's insistence we discouraged her from coming home. "She's got important work to do right where she is." He talked to me about Cille a lot, and Jesper a little, and told me how proud he was of the man I'd become. There were a few memory lapses, but otherwise his state of mind seemed unchanged. Then one morning he sent a chill down my spine.

"Jesper was here last night."

I'd just finished outlining the new crop rotation scheme we'd worked out, and he caught me completely unawares.

"He came after you were all asleep. Sat on the bed and talked to me for a while."

"Dad..." I didn't know what to say. Or even if I should say anything. It seemed a harmless delusion, and if it comforted him, it would be cruel to challenge it.

"He's grown into quite a man. Taller than you, believe it or not, and heavier through the shoulders. I almost didn't recognize him, because of the beard. He's let it grow down to his chest." He chuckled. "Your mother would not approve."

I settled back into my chair. "I'm glad to hear he's well."

"He didn't want me to tell anyone else he'd been here, says he's not worthy of being a Baxter again just yet, that he has to accomplish some task he's set himself first. But he knew he would have to come now if he was going to see me at all, and I want someone in the family to know what happened after I'm gone. Your mother has enough on her mind right now, so I'm telling you. You'll have to decide for yourself when it's best to tell her and Cille."

'I'll make sure they know," I promised.

He died the next day, the 86th day of Aragon's independence, peacefully, while my mother was reading to him. On the 88th day, Aragon lost its freedom.

Cille was at the farm when the Cranes attacked. At daybreak, we had spread Dad's ashes in the north field, accompanied by a very small group of friends that included Paul Fortunato, Ned Grant, and Aki Song. We had a buffet breakfast back at the house, after which they left us alone with our grief. Mom was a rock, but she excused herself and went to lie down, so Cille, Kelli, and I took a walk, not talking much but too restless to sit. We were on our way back to the house when Cille's com beeped in emergency mode.

We could hear the strained voice quite clearly. "Cille, the capital is being attacked."

"Attacked? What are you talking about?" Cille asked the question but I think we all knew the answer well in advance.

"The Cranes!" The man's voice sounded strained, frightened. "They blew up the barracks and the power station, and they're all over Constitution Hall. Most of the other members were inside and they're either dead or captured. Their landers are everywhere, at the port, on the outskirts of the city. I saw two of them come down in the park."

"Are you safe, Evan?"

"I don't know. I'm going to try to get out of the city. There are fires burning all over the place, but I've only heard a few explosions. They caught us completely by surprise. I'll try to call you again later." The signal died.

We all stood looking at each other for a few seconds, then bolted back to the house.

News was almost impossible to come by. All of the standard feeds had been cut, possibly because the power was out in Aladdin and, presumably, other urban centers, more likely because the attackers had destroyed or deactivated the comsats. There were small military garrisons in Tyrada and Casper, and they were almost certain to have been targeted, but we had no way of finding out if there had been any successful resistance. Cille tried to reach anyone she knew in Aladdin by means of the slower comnet service, but the only person who picked up was another member of the Assembly who happened to have gone home on a visit at a fortuitous time. The fact that the comnet was still working meant that the Cranes had not knocked out all of the installations, but we were limited to planetary communications only.

"What happened to our orbital defenses?" Kelli's voice crackled with tension.

Cille just shook her head. "I don't know. The *Bludgeon* was supposed to be there. It should have had time to warn us at least."

We started receiving coms from people we knew, all hoping we had more information than they did. Over the course of the next two days, we pieced together a reasonably coherent, though sometimes contradictory account of what had happened and was still happening. Some things seemed certain. The Cranes had landed troops in every urban center larger than Safehaven, killing or capturing our small garrisons. Power stations and communications centers were seized or disabled. Government Center was specifically targeted, indicating that they had excellent intelligence. We heard some reports that the Cranes were firing indiscriminately at civilians, but other accounts indicated that they were brisk and efficient and didn't fire except defensively. They didn't interfere with efforts to fight the fires, and in fact in at least one case they cleared traffic to allow emergency vehicles to pass. All communication offworld had ceased, but the planetary com lines were all restored within hours.

A town meeting was called in Safehaven, and we all went, Mom included. It was chaotic, loud and unorganized, and you could taste the fear in the air. Tami Pakarang and Kani Shikuro tried to impose some order, but they were unsuccessful until Cille joined them. Her calm demeanor and recognizable face seemed to help, and the din subsided enough that a reasoned discussion followed. Unfortunately, no one knew enough to make any meaningful suggestion. Armed resistance was out of the question. We had a few personal weapons scattered among us, mostly used to keep down Aragon's sparse but destructive native vermin, but not enough to matter, particularly given the ease with which the invaders had overwhelmed the professional garrisons.

"I think it's clear we need more information before we can make any intelligent decisions." Cille had become de facto moderator of the discussion. "For the time being, it's probably best if we conduct business as usual, or at least as close to that as we can manage."

"And what happens if they show up here tomorrow?" Someone had shouted it from the crowd.

"That depends on how they act. We have heard nothing to indicate that they're waging war against the population at large. Most of you have talked to people from Aladdin and elsewhere, so you know they're not killing indiscriminately and are in fact restoring power where it was interrupted. We still can't communicate off planet, but that's really not surprising. I'm not suggesting we let our guard down, but we shouldn't panic either."

"What happened to the navy?" someone called out.

Cille shook her head. "I don't know. But I'm sure by now that they know something's happened here and it's only a matter of time until they react. If we keep our heads down until they arrive, we'll have a better chance to live through this." What Cille didn't know, and what none of us would learn until much later, was that the Cranes had attacked and occupied four other colony worlds as well, and had been driven back from three more. The military had suspected something and quietly repositioned its ships – stripping us of the *Bludgeon* without our knowledge – but had underestimated the breadth of the enemy attack.

Reaction was divided, chaotic, and often senseless. A few people had already closed up their homes and headed out into the wilderness, planning to hide out from the "monsters". Others, mostly young people, wanted to organize an armed resistance movement, overt or covert, but their ideas were more romantic than practical. There had been a trickle of refugees from Aladdin, most of whom gave contradictory accounts of what had taken place there.

A communications specialist named Lang was the most plausible witness to arrive in Safehaven. "A few of them know our language. They keep urging people to stay calm, and they're scattering their troops all through the city. They kill anyone who attacks them, but they haven't been interfering otherwise." That confirmed some of the reports we'd been receiving, but she also told us that she'd heard that a large number of patients at Aladdin's main hospital had been summarily executed. "I didn't see it myself, but I spent one night hiding in a culvert with a meditech who said he'd been there when it happened."

The meeting had mixed results. Some people seemed calmer, others more anxious than before. A few announced their intention to join the exodus into the countryside. The militants quieted and became more conspiratorial and I was frankly a bit concerned about what they would do. Many of Safehaven's less savory young people, including those I believed responsible for a series of vandalisms of Baxter equipment and facilities, were among their number. It seemed unlikely they could do much more than protest loudly, however, given the limited number of weapons available.

Cille was unusually silent during the ride back to the farm. Kelli and I stayed for dinner, then returned to our own place. We slept fitfully, and were both up and about when Mom commed us shortly after daybreak.

"We have visitors," she said calmly. It wasn't necessary to be more explicit. "They want to speak to you, Ennis. Apparently their analysis of our customs tells them they need to deal with the oldest male member of the family."

Kelli and I ate hurriedly and took the flitter up to the farm. There was a human military lifter in the meadow, guarded by at least four of the Cranes, whom we would later know as Lysandrans. It was the first time I'd seen them in the flesh, of course, and even in that moment of stress I noticed how graceful they appeared. They were slightly taller than most humans, and their legs seemed disproportionately long and thin. When they weren't actually using their arms, they kept them pressed against their sides, and the contour of their bodies often made it appear that they had merged into the trunk. Each had a fairly deep chest, containing their lungs and a resonating chamber that gave their voices a deep, tremulous tone. A long thin neck held the head, which was unusually long, sweeping up to a bony crest that gave the appearance of feathers. They were not avian though, no actual feathers, and very little body hair, none of it visible under ordinary circumstances. The ones that we saw that first day were predominantly silver in color or in some cases gray. I would later discover that they came in several other colors as well – gold, yellow, beige, even a very faint rust red.

The guards looked in our direction but stayed at their posts as we climbed out of the flitter and walked up to the house. Another guard was stationed there, and I imagine he was watching us closely, although Lysandran eyes are hard for humans to follow. Mother and Cille were inside, sitting in the main room, and in the chair opposite was a silvery gray Lysandran with one of Mom's best china cups in his six fingered hand. Two others of his kind stood unobtrusively in corners of the room.

"Come in, Ennis. This is Sylandris, a liaison officer for the Lysandrans. He will be visiting with us for a while." Her voice was outwardly serene, but I knew her well enough to sense the anger that lay beneath it. "His guards are taking the guest cottage, so I've had his things put in your old room."

Sylandris rose and nodded in my direction but did not offer his hand. I'm not sure if I would have taken it, but I'll never know for sure. "It is my pleasure to meet you, Ennis Baxter. Please excuse this intrusion into your holdings." His mastery of the language was excellent, but the Lysandran resonating chambers gave the words a constant vibration that slightly blurred the individual sounds. When they grew excited, there was an intermittent booming as well, but Sylandris was perfectly relaxed that first day.

I nodded back, not trusting myself to speak, while Mom introduced Kelli. Sylandris gave her a bow as well, but even my unpracticed eye noticed that it was more cursory. First impressions are often misleading. The Lysandrans were not biased about gender, but they believed that all life was arranged in a series of interlocking hierarchies. While greeting Cille upon first arriving, Sylandris had remained inclined forward until she spoke, acknowledging her as his superior. She was, after all, a member of our government, whatever that might mean under the present circumstances.

"Please seat yourselves. I am sorry that it is necessary to impose but it is unavoidable. First, I would like to reassure you. We wish you to continue your lives as before. Your property will not be confiscated, you are in no danger from us unless you engage in hostile acts, and we will do whatever lies within our power to restore normal commerce."

I digested that and the countless questions I wanted to ask all rose up at once and left me fumbling for words. Cille came to the rescue. "Sylandris has explained his people's mission here. The Lysandrans have assimilated a number of other races already and they feel confident that the situation will normalize quickly." Her anger was well concealed except to those who knew her well.

"Please be assured that we do not wish to force our ways upon you. We recognize that different conditions are required for each people. Like your Concourse, we have certain minimum standards which you must address, but in all other ways the people of Aragon and the other human worlds which have now joined us will determine their own laws and customs."

"But not specifically Aragonian laws and customs," said Cille pointedly.

Sylandris emitted a low thrum for a second. "As I have explained, Cille Baxter, we are seekers after perfection, even if we always fall short of our goal. There exists an unknowable optimal form of society for each species. We will help you and the other worlds to choose the best from each and meld them into a single system which you will then be free to modify to meet your own needs. But we recognize that the standards of our own race are not necessarily appropriate to your kind. We do not," he hesitated as though searching for a word, "we do not proselytize. You are free to continue with your existing social structure or to change it. This will be an entirely human decision."

"So long as we and the other conquered worlds make the changes universally."

"Certainly. Why would you wish to do otherwise? Any innovation which benefits one world should be shared with all, should it not?"

I finally found my tongue. "If your people are so altruistic, why have you attacked us? Why not leave us to manage our own lives?"

He thrummed again. "Societies like individuals must be tested again and again if they are to move forward toward the ideal. It is also necessary to achieve clarity about the relative strengths of others, cultural, aesthetic, and military. We have learned something about ourselves from every race which we have encountered, and we believe that in each case we have given as well as received."

"What do you want from us? From the Baxter family, I mean."

"Yours is the dominant family in this area. We ask only that you act as our agents."

My back stiffened immediately. "We will not take your side against our own people. If that's what you've come for, you might as well leave right now."

Sylandris gave a short, low pitched whistle. "I have perhaps missed a nuance of your language. We are not asking that you work against your people. We desire that you announce our presence and our intention of establishing ourselves in this area. Our previous experience has been that this reduces the chance of unpleasant incidents during the transitional period."

I wasn't sure that I understood him, but Cille filled the gap. "You'll be establishing a garrison locally?"

"It will not be a military mission, although we will of course provide protection for our representatives until assimilation has reached an acceptable level. Our goal is to educate your people concerning our intentions, even to provide some technical help."

"Missionaries," said Kelli, almost under her breath.

Again the low whistle. "You misunderstand. Your supernatural beliefs and customs are not our concern unless they interfere with your progress as a species, and we have in the past made great efforts to accommodate such complications. I have a very limited understanding of this aspect of your culture, but I have been told by those who have studied it more closely that there does not appear to be any significant conflict."

"So what precisely is it that you want us to do?" I had grown impatient with this circumlocutious conversation, and wondered if Sylandris could interpret human emotions.

"We consider it important to maintain contact with dominant individuals. For this reason, I have requested domiciling within your home on a temporary basis. " I doubted that it was a request, but I let it go. "It would be helpful if you were to meet with whomever you deem advisable from the surrounding communities. Reassure them that we are not here to pillage and destroy. Inform them that some of our number will be coming to live among them for a period, that we wish to minimize the disturbance this may cause, and ask that quarters be prepared for those who will follow."

Cille spoke up before I could, but we'd had the same thought. "There are some among our people who might harbor hostile intentions toward your kind. They won't change their opinions just because we tell them you're peaceful, particularly since you've attacked us without provocation and killed many of our people."

Sylandris thrummed. I was starting to see a pattern, whistles for mild alarm, thrums for…what? Impatience?

"We have only killed where necessary to establish dominance. Conflict between our two species was inevitable. It costs fewer lives to strike early and with great force to compel peace than to delay and encourage unrealistic expectations. But to answer your question, we recognize that in certain individuals matters of dominance may lead to irrational behavior. If we are attacked, we will defend ourselves, and will do our best to limit the violence to those directly involved. In time I believe you will come to recognize that we are benevolent guides rather than oppressors. But make no mistake about the order of things. Lysandra IS dominant on this world now, and our patience and tolerance for those who refuse to accept the truth is finite."

CHAPTER NINE

We talked for most of the rest of that day. Sylandris seemed perfectly relaxed, but I noticed that his guards watched us closely the entire time. On one occasion he dropped his head to his chest and took a small tube into his mouth, the other end of which disappeared into a noticeably lumpy portion of his cloak. I wondered if our atmosphere wasn't completely to his liking, and some clandestine spying out of the corner of my eye confirmed that the guards were also fitted with the tubes. The Lysandrans all wore billowing cloaks around their upper bodies, and I wondered what else might be concealed inside. I was also uncertain how much of what Sylandris was telling me was the truth. It would be some time before I realized that he never told a single lie, although he didn't tell us all the truth either.

"You are the sixth race we have encountered," he told me, "and you are by far the most numerous."

"Have you conquered the other six as well?" I wondered if Sylandris was sensitive to the tones in human voices. His grasp of our language was excellent.

"Dominance has been established in each case. One race chose to extinguish itself rather than accept the order of things, but the others are now members of our community." He had leaned forward at this point in a very human gesture of concern. "But we do not 'conquer' others in the sense that humans mean. Customs, laws, government, and other values are very different among the Phylaxians than among the Drune, for example. As I have told you previously, we do not impose ourselves except in the most minimal fashion. For most of your people, the alteration of the chain of dominance will have no effect."

"That's not necessarily true," objected Cille. "Onerat is a constitutional monarchy. Pastel has a minimalist representative government. Of the worlds you claim to have conquered, or dominated if you'd prefer that term, only Laertes has a representative government similar to our own. You're telling us that we must all adopt the same form of government, an identical code of laws. Which form must we accept, and who's going to make that decision?"

Sylandris thrummed impatiently. "Some variations in laws are acceptable to accommodate local conditions. The uncertain weather conditions on Laertes, for example, require the construction of shelters and other emergency facilities which are unnecessary elsewhere, and these must be commonly supported. But the broader answer is that, yes, you will all adopt an optimal social structure. The decision will be made by your own people, however, not us, although we will assist if that seems advisable. Why would you want it otherwise? Surely humans are rational enough to want to live under the best possible conditions. You must recognize the advantages of not having to learn an entirely new set of behaviors just because you have traveled to a neighboring world. Conflicting systems will inevitably lead to recurring dominance struggles. I am familiar enough with human history to know that you have fought among yourselves over this issue almost from the onset of intelligence."

"And I suppose you've never fought among yourselves? Never had to resolve your own issues of dominance?" I felt offended at this indictment of humankind, particularly coming from a representative of an occupying army.

"No, Ennis Baxter. In all the recorded history of my people, there has never been a war among us. There are individual struggles for dominance, of course, as these are necessary in the establishment of order and authority. All societal differences were decided rationally, by comparing the varying sides of an issue and choosing the dominant, the optimal one. Sometimes these decisions required resolution of personal questions of dominance, but there was never a time in which numbers of our people took arms against each other."

'Let me understand this," said Cille after an unusually long silence. "Lysandran culture was shaped by the outcome of a series of personal duels."

Sylandris whistled and thrummed simultaneously this time. "The parallels are not exact. Human duels were usually to the death. In our case, it was only necessary to establish dominance. Tell me, if you were commanding the human fleet at the system you call Dorking's Star, and the commander of our forces had offered to surrender his command, would you have accepted or would you have sought to destroy your vanquished foe?"

"We are not barbaric, Sylandris. We do not kill just for the joy of it."

The thrum disappeared. "Then we are not so different after all, are we? "

We talked for most of the rest of that day, and my active distrust cooled to a determined wariness. If Sylandris was telling the truth, Aragon would largely govern itself once we and the other captive worlds agreed on a common governmental structure. And if we couldn't agree, the Lysandrans would impose one, but it would be some variation of what already existed. When Cille asked how the Lysandrans governed themselves, Sylandris responded with a lengthy, complicated description that seemed unwieldy and unworkable to me. Cille told me later that I was oversimplifying by calling it rule by interlocking commissions, pointing out that the emphasis on personal dominance in their culture meant that there had to be a handful of highly placed individuals who actually gave the orders, but it was apparently very rare for them to overrule the decisions of their subordinates. One very distinct difference between Lysandrans and humans is that in their case, once the pecking order was established, there was no need for the dominant party to reaffirm his authority with any regularity. A newcomer might challenge the status quo, but those once vanquished were forever subordinate barring gross incompetence at the top. Senior Lysandrans who felt their grasp slipping invariably resigned and retired before they could be challenged.

"Humans don't work like that," I protested. "We don't have an innate respect for authority; in fact, we enjoy a healthy skepticism about our leaders."

I couldn't read Lysandran body language but Sylandris shifted his position in what I suspected might be exasperation. "That is only because you persist in choosing your leaders for reasons other than their ability and integrity. If you elevated those who were best suited for the job, there would be no reason to distrust them."

"And you're going to decide who those best suited are, I suppose?"

"Not at all. It will be generations before we understand your culture enough to have an intelligent opinion on the matter, but it is irrelevant. If your species prefers to be guided by flawed leaders, we will not interfere."

"So long as the process is the same everywhere," interposed Cille thoughtfully.

"Yes," Sylandris agreed. "When we first came upon the Drune, they existed in four star systems. Each of the four was governed in a different fashion, and each government insisted that their way should be the dominant one for all of the others. Our observers expected them to meet and mutually determine which was the superior form, perhaps by blending some elements from each. It is what we would have done had Lysandra ever developed competing cultures."

I doubted that, but there was no point in arguing with him.

"We were horrified then when the Drune began fighting among themselves, using weapons which would destroy their opponents rather than subdue them. We sent forces immediately, long before we had intended, but it was already too late for one world whose orbital defenses failed. Almost the entire population died. All that potential was lost because the Drune could not resolve the question of dominance in a civilized manner. As a species we have vowed that we will not allow this to happen again. Do you understand now why we must insist on this step?"

I saw more than that. I understood that we had not been conquered by just an ordinary army. We were at the mercy of an army of missionaries.

Involuntary hosts though they might be, Mom and Cille made every effort to accommodate the newcomers. Sylandris was accompanied by four guards, who were given two rooms in the guest cottage adjacent to the main house. Jeb and Zai had each built themselves a small place elsewhere on the farm, but Garner and some of the steady help still lived in the common barracks building that stood next to the cottage. A military style lifter clearly of Lysandran design dropped off a considerable stock of supplies just before high sunset. Only one of the soldiers spoke a limited amount of our language well enough to be understood.

"We will of course compensate you for the use of your facilities," Lysandris assured us.

"That won't be necessary." I could tell Mom was offended. "You said that you can eat human food. What will you want and how often?"

There was a faint whistle when Sylandris answered. "With some few exceptions, yes, we can tolerate human foods. You have the closest metabolism to our own that we have encountered. It is only necessary to provide some minor supplements from time to time. But I do not wish to impose upon you or your family. We have brought sufficient to sustain us." He paused, and I sensed somehow that he was suddenly less certain of himself.

"If, on the other hand, it would be unmannerly of me to dine apart, I would be honored to share meals with my hosts."

"Invited or not, you're a guest in our house. There will be a place available for you at every meal. Whether or not you use it is up to you."

Kelli and I decided to stay at the farm that evening. She fell asleep almost immediately, but I tossed and turned so much that I was afraid I'd wake her, so I slipped out of bed, padded through the house on bare feet, and stepped out onto the porch. It was a clear, cool night and I could smell the bearfruit blossoms in the distance, with a slight undercurrent of bitter grass. Sylandris was so motionless that it was several minutes before I noticed him standing at the far end of the porch. I retreated involuntarily, instinctively reacting to the proximity of an alien lifeform in the darkness.

"Please do not be alarmed." His pronunciation was not as precise as it had been earlier. "I did not wish to intrude upon your privacy."

"I couldn't sleep," I said finally, feeling vaguely defensive. "You've given me a lot to think about."

"I too have had much to think of. You humans have strange dominance patterns. I noticed, for example, that you defer to your mother much of the time, as does your sister. And she is a member of your government, but she defers to you."

"It depends upon the issue. Are your leaders so talented that no one else commands respect?"

"Of course not. That is why we have the...what you would call committees...to advise them. Our leaders have demonstrated a superior ability to make decisions, but they still require the talents of the rest of us to provide them with the knowledge that enables them to choose among options. From what I have learned of your history, it is not so different with your people, when they are at their best."

"Under some circumstances, yes. But why not allow the committees, or the individuals, who are closer to the issue make their own decisions? My mother runs the house and the family finances but she and I jointly administer the farm and delegate the day to day decisions to those we trust."

"And what happens if two of your subordinates disagree about a course of action?"

"Then one of us makes the decision for them, after listening to both sides. But we try to let them work it out between themselves first."

"Do they resent you for doing this?"

"No, of course not." I hesitated. "Perhaps sometimes, but it's a passing resentment. They realize that the farm is our responsibility and that we have the final say."

Sylandris moved a step toward me. "Would it not be simpler if you stepped in as soon as the question arose? If this was the established way of doing things, would you still be resented for interposing yourself?"

"Possibly not, but by depriving my people of the chance to make any decisions, I would stifle their initiative. Why should they think for themselves if they're never going to have the authority to shape the outcome?"

There was a short pause. "There perhaps is the essential difference between our two races, Ennis Baxter. If you and I were the only two humans in the world, one of us would be dominant, however informally. Is that not true?"

After a moment, I nodded. "Yes, I suppose so."

"At every decision point, there would be two possible situations. We would both agree on a course of action, or we would both disagree. Is this not also true?"

I nodded again, wondering if he understood the gesture.

"In all these occasions, the choice of the dominant partner would be the one adopted. This might be the right choice in the majority of cases, but not in every individual case. "

I wasn't so sure about that, but again I nodded. "Theoretically, assuming that dominance wasn't established simply because one of us could physically overpower the other."

"Assuming that I were the dominant one, and that I overruled you on every occasion where we disagreed, would you continue to make suggestions?"

Once again I hesitated. "Yes, but only if I thought there was a chance of convincing you that I was right."

Sylandris' voice thrummed slightly. "Now assume that we are the only two Lysandrans on this world, and that you are dominant. The same rules apply. It is you who makes the decision whenever we disagree, because you have achieved dominance by proving that you have a superior decision making capacity."

"All right. Are you saying that a Lysandran would continue offering choices that he knew would be overruled?"

"Yes, that is precisely what I am saying. Because you would only have achieved dominance by demonstrating that your decisions are more likely to achieve the desired result."

I thought about that for a while. "But what if I started making more wrong decisions than right ones? What if it turned out that your judgments were more valid than mine?"

"Then I would have established dominance, and you would thenceforth defer to me."

I laughed. "I find it hard to believe that your leaders would willingly relinquish power just because they guessed wrong a few times."

"They would not need to relinquish power. Dominance would shift independent of their will. One of our kind who recognized that his dominance was shifting would resign his position voluntarily." The thrum vanished and he turned away from me. "The human unwillingness to accept this is why you have so many different governments and cultural forms. You are constantly fighting your own best interests because you don't understand the role of dominance."

"So you're going to force us to change, whether or not we want to?"

"No, we cannot and would not change your essential natures. As I said before, we will allow humans to choose the structure under which you shall all live, just as we have done in the past with other races. We will not force ours upon you., even though we are dominant, because no sentient being has sufficient knowledge to make these decisions for those of another species. Our goal is to help you reach your own ideal, not force you to conform to ours."

"Perhaps our ideal is to be just as we are, chaotic, unfocused, variegated."

"That is not an ideal, Ennis Baxter. It is despair."

We remained silent for a long time, and I was thinking about returning to bed when Sylandris broke the silence.

"Your sibling, Cille, displays features of a type with which I am not familiar."

My jaws clenched and I had to force myself to relax. "There was an accident when she was younger. A fire. She was very badly burned."

"As I thought then, her appearance is not natural."

My hands closed on the fence rail until my fingers hurt. It was unlikely that Sylandris meant to be offensive, but I was enraged that he'd brought the subject up.

"She needs some further medical treatment to compensate for the effects of the accident." I felt a moment of despair wondering how this new situation was going to affect her ability to acquire syntheskin.

"And Cille has become a person of considerable dominance, a member of your government, despite this misfortune."

"She has a great deal of influence, yes."

"This accident must have been a very great tragedy for all of you."

My anger surged just under the surface. "It was a difficult time, but we're past it."

"Not entirely, I think. You humans cling to the past so tightly. It is important to remember your history, certainly, but you cannot let it lessen the present."

I wasn't in the mood to be lectured to by an alien being about my family's emotional entanglements. "I'm very tired. I'll see you again in the morning." And I went inside without waiting for an answer, hoping that Sylandris would have the good sense not to bring up the subject again. This time I fell asleep almost immediately, something I would not have been able to accomplish had I know how significant that brief exchange really was.

The following morning Kelli, Cille, and I drove into Safehaven. Cille and I had commed a few influential people and they had spread the word. Almost everybody in the community was assembled at the fairgrounds when we arrived. People were used to listening to Cille now, so she did most of the talking. She summarized what we'd been told by Sylandris, then her interpretation. "It's way too soon to know how much of an impact this is going to make, or how long it will take the Concourse to retake the system." She wisely didn't mention the possibility that they wouldn't be able to do so. For all we knew, the rest of the Concourse would fall to the Lysandrans as easily as had we, although we were talking hundreds of planets, most of them far more advanced than we were. "They seem to want us to go on pretty much as before. I'm not sure what the future of the Assembly may be, but they understand commerce and want us to be as self sufficient as possible on a local level. One of their officials has required us to house him at the farm and several others of their kind will be coming to Safehaven in a few days."

There was a lot of murmuring at this, some fearful, some angry. Cille raised her arms and waited for it to die down.

"Most of those who come will be soldiers but they insist that they are only here to observe and learn. The soldiers are there to protect the civilians." This was an oversimplification. Sylandris had not been able to make clear to us the distinction between soldier and civilian among his kind, individuals seemed to shift back and forth between the two categories, or perhaps all Lysandrans were automatically enrolled in their military. "Ennis tells me that the Harwell house is still vacant so I've suggested that the bulk of their party establish themselves there. A few, perhaps as many as half a dozen, may require rooms within the town proper later on." There was another murmuring, louder than before, and it took longer to die down.

"Obviously, we don't know much more than you do, but the ones at the farm seem reasonable enough. They can eat our food, even use our sanitary facilities." That got an uneasy laugh. "It's not going to be pleasant having them among us, but it could have been much worse."

There was another angry shout from the crowd and this time I identified the source, young Brodie Bors. "Maybe you want to suck up to the Cranes, but we don't want them here!" A few others, mostly young people, shouted in support.

Cille hesitated, and I stood up. "You weren't so brave when Jeb Booker caught you stealing power packs from our barn last year." I was staring right at him and saw his expression switch from pugnacity to embarrassment. He opened his mouth to shout something back, but I pushed on before he had the chance. "No one likes having the Lysandrans here. Maybe we can do something about that, maybe not. It's too soon to tell. Right now they're in control. The five of them out at the farm probably have more weapons than all of us combined, and there are at least several thousand of them on Aragon." I actually didn't know that, but it made sense.

"Are you saying we should just surrender without a fight?" It was one of the Tonobi twins; I couldn't tell them apart. Her tone wasn't belligerent, just puzzled.

"No, I'm not saying that. I'm saying we should choose where to fight so that we have a chance to win. Right now, we don't know whether the Navy is going to show up tomorrow and throw them off the planet, or whether we're going to have to wait for them to regroup, maybe even re-arm. We don't have enough information right now to decide anything like that." I couldn't help wondering how a Lysandran dominant would react in this situation. Presumably he or she – I didn't know whether female Lysandrans could be dominant – would just make the decision for the community and inform them without having to listen to objections, complaints, or angry outbursts. "They're coming here to study us, but that should give us a chance to study them as well. What I think we should do is form a committee to deal with them. As far as the Lysandrans are concerned, the committee's purpose will be to handle housing and other practical issues, and to make it easier for them to complete their mission and leave. They'll expect we don't want them around, so there's no point in hiding it. But while they're watching us, we should be watching them, gathering all the information we can and pooling it so that when the time comes to do something, we can do the right thing, and with the best chance of success."

I turned and looked at Brodie Bors. "What we don't need is some hero attacking the first Lysandran to step off a flitter. The hero will most likely be dead, which deprives us of one set of eyes and ears, and the Lysandrans will be even less inclined to trust us. They might even send in a bigger military force and make life more difficult for everyone."

At that point, I ran out of words, but Cille stepped in as if on cue. "We're not suggesting that you collaborate with the enemy. Our goal must be to regain our freedom. We are urging that you don't expend lives and efforts prematurely and needlessly."

There were a few more questions after that, but none of consequence, and people began to drift away, somber, sullen, and despite our reassurances, frightened. Kelli and I went to visit briefly with her father and brother while Cille talked individually to Needham and a few others whom she thought might best constitute the formal liaison with the Lysandran contingent. The double shadows of dusk were starting to come together when we finally started back to the farm.

That evening I had a brief, puzzling conversation with Sylandris. He was, I suspect, sulking a bit following our dinner conversation. After admitting that he was functionally male in a double gendered race, Cille had asked him point blank about the status of female Lysandrans. "You will be pleased to learn that in that respect, we resemble most of your historic human cultures."

"That depends upon which human cultures you're talking about. Do your females have the same rights as the males?"

"They have equivalent rights, yes." Our guest's grasp of the English language was so thorough that I knew this wasn't a slip.

"Equivalent, but not the same?" Cille pressed the issue.

There was a thrum in his voice now, and it wasn't a faint one either. "Our two genders pursue more variant lifestyles than among humans. Most of our females bear young with considerable regularity so they are, naturally, excused from most other activities during their fertile years. You must understand that reproduction is physically somewhat different with our kind. Human women evolved to remain mobile while carrying young so that they could escape predators and enemy tribes, and hunt for food. We had neither predators nor other tribes to contend with. Lysandrans were at the dominant end of the food chain even in our own prehistory, and since we spread gradually and cooperatively from a single source, we never had the concept of an 'enemy' until we ventured into space and ran into the Voluskans. Our females are rather fragile and virtually immobile for most of the time they are with young. But once past child bearing age, they perform the same services and are granted the same privileges as males."

"Can your females be dominant?"

"Ah, I see your intent. The answer is yes, they can be dominant, even over our males. But I must admit that they rarely achieve the highest positions in our hierarchy simply because they must begin their career so late in life and are therefore at a disadvantage. But at least one of the vessels orbiting your world has a female as primary officer, what you would call captain. And no, we have no intention of restricting the roles of females in human society in any way, although if your people chose such a structure, we would not oppose it. As I told you, the difference in our case is the result of evolutionary necessity. It would be inappropriate to apply it to others. Your planetary Assembly will remain as it is, slightly skewed in favor of females, if I remember correctly."

I saw Cille's interest intensify immediately. "Then the Assembly will not be abolished."

"Not unless in the course of time you decide to do so yourselves. Most members chose to return to their homes once the city was secured, and we allowed them to do so. But they will be requested to return in a few days to prepare for the negotiations with the other human worlds."

"Then I should be prepared to leave at any time?"

Sylandris let a few seconds pass. "There is no hurry. Please do not change your habits prematurely."

Pleading fatigue, he excused himself a moment later to take one of his frequent naps. Lysandrans did not sleep for prolonged periods as humans do, but rested frequently for much shorter intervals. But in this particular case, I thought he was making an excuse, that he just wanted to absent himself from us for a while, and that disturbed me because I couldn't think what might possibly have unnerved him.

Kelli and I went home that evening. I was worried about leaving Mom and Cille alone with the Lysandrans, but Mom pointed out that they weren't alone. Several farmhands were living nearby.

"They'll be fine," said Kelli. "Jeb Booker was teaching one of the guards to play hookball the other day. And even if there was trouble, your mother and Cille are two of the most formidable people I know."

"But they're not human, Kelli. We can't expect them to behave the way humans would."

"No, we can't. But they're an intelligent, rational species. From all accounts, they've restored order and public services everywhere, and responded violently only when they were threatened." We'd had a com from one of Cille's friends in Casper. A band of self styled resistance fighters had tried to ambush a Lysandran flitter convoy. Only a couple of the two dozen lightly armed men had survived the encounter. There had been a few other incidents elsewhere, none on the same scale. Surprisingly, there had been no reprisals.

I was still uneasy with the situation, and promised to return in a day or so, sooner if they called. We spent that evening at home, then took the flitter in to Safehaven. The first contingent of Lysandran observers was to arrive that day, and I felt obligated to meet them. Cille had offered to come as well, but Sylandris had requested that she remain at the farm, to consult with him before the restoration of the Assembly.

The meeting was strained and awkward, but all things considered, it came off pretty well. Savoril was some kind of sociologist specializing in alien contact, and he spoke almost as fluently as Sylandris. Fossicker, who spoke only a few words, was apparently dominant to Savoril. Lysandrans soldiers and civilians all dressed similarly, assuming that Sylandris and Savoril were in fact civilians, but there was a brisk sense of purpose about Fossicker that reminded me of career military officers I'd seen in Aladdin. I introduced the Lysandrans to the three committee representatives. Tami Pakarang looked nervous but interested, Kani Shikuro looked dour and disapproving – but that was his normal expression, and only Jill Garner seemed to be openly angry. Melody Miller's place was vacant and had been set aside for their use in town and Dan Kater, who actually grinned and tried to shake hands before realizing his error, was detailed to take them out to the Harwell farm and show them around.

The Lysandrans all carried weapons, even Savoril, but they were unobtrusive. Even years later I have trouble reading Lysandran body language, but even then it seemed to me that the entire party, save Fossicker, looked around curiously rather than warily. A mostly unfriendly crowd had gathered and there were some angry words spoken quietly, but the calm attitude of the aliens somewhat disarmed the onlookers. It didn't hurt any that the Lysandrans were physically quite attractive, a point which I probably should have made earlier. Their bodies were finely sculpted, with smooth, gradual curves and no sharp edges. By no stretch of the imagination could they be described physically as monsters. They were graceful looking both at rest and in motion, and their body types varied very little except for coloration. There were no fat Lysandrans, no thin ones, none with crooked limbs or cleft palates or any other disfigurement that I could recognize. Savoril was yellowish gold, Fossicker a silvery grey. There were six others in their party, none of whom were introduced by name, two of them silver although not as glossy as Fossicker, one a rich gold, one so pale he might have been albino, and the last a chalky rusty red. They had two flitters of Lysandran design, both obviously armored.

Once the formalities were taken care of, I met privately with the committee, which was much larger than we had let on to the Lysandrans, and reinforced the need to gather information and not exacerbate things. I was particularly concerned about provocative incidents. Brodie Bors wasn't likely to have the nerve to do anything on his own, but there were other hotheads in Safehaven who might. Grant Colson told me he had already briefed his people to be on the lookout for any trouble that might be brewing. I felt a nagging sense of responsibility for the entire situation which I couldn't shake, even though it was clearly illogical, and finally forced myself to return to the house.

Days passed and then weeks and life slowly seemed to be returning to some warped form of normality. That's when I came home one night to discover we had a visitor.

Kelli came outside as I parked the flitter, her face serious. "Sylandris is inside, waiting for you," she told me.

CHAPTER TEN

Sylandris apologized immediately for intruding without invitation, which I found rather ironic given the circumstances under which the Lysandrans had arrived on Aragon in the first place. There seemed to be something odd about his demeanor, however, and I was thoughtful as we exchanged the preliminary meaningless pleasantries that seem to be a universal shortcoming of sentient life in the universe. It was while we were arranging ourselves comfortably in the small room that Kelli and I called our den that I realized what was different. It hadn't been difficult to identify the more obvious tonal qualities of Lysandran voices – the thrum of impatience, the whistle of alarm, the mild booming that accompanied excitement or surprise. But I was hearing something new today, a thready, barely perceptible vibration.

"I assume your people will have no problems adjusting to the townspeople."

"No more than the townspeople will have adjusting to our presence." There was a prolonged silence, and since I felt no particular urge to make things easier for him, I let it continue until he stirred and spoke.

"Your sibling is a remarkable individual."

Cautiously, I agreed with him. "She has overcome a great many obstacles in her life. She has more courage than anyone I know."

"It is different among my people. It is considered selfish to ask others to endure the burden required to care for one who has limited functionality."

"Cille is no burden to us. She has always done her share of the work."

"As I have said, she is a remarkable person. Such an achievement would not be possible for one of us. The shame of it would have caused the individual so deformed to have ended its own life."

This time I was the one who rearranged my limbs, but it was anger, not restlessness that made me move. "There is no question of shame, Sylandris. What happened to Cille was not her fault. If anyone was to blame, it was my father, my brother, and I."

He replied hastily and this time with the whistle of alarm. "Please, my friend, I have no wish to offend. I am sometimes clumsy with your language." Which wasn't true; he spoke more clearly and precisely than most humans. "It is simply that I wish to convey to you how extraordinary the situation is. It is unprecedented in our experience to find an individual who has overcome such a handicap and become a member of a government. We have not encountered such an extraordinary thing among any of the other races we have enlightened."

I allowed myself to be mollified, but remained wary. "All right. So what's the purpose of this conversation, Sylandris? You didn't come out here just to tell me how unusual Cille is. I knew that already."

The thready sound was back and I could have sworn that his eyes shifted away from me, although they came right back. It was such a "human" act that I found myself suddenly disoriented and missed a few words.

"In such cases, we have taken the task upon ourselves until the logic of such a path is clear to those we teach. It is a sometimes painful transition, but pain is best accepted and dealt with in the present so that the individual is free of it in the future."

"I'm not sure I'm following you." I tried to bring back the words that I missed, something about reshaping cultural norms to more productive ends.

He hesitated, and the flesh covering his throat was visibly vibrating, almost certainly the source of the thready sound. "It is sometimes necessary to teach a child self discipline in your culture, is it not? Even if the experience is not entirely pleasant for the child."

"Yes, it is," I said slowly, perceiving for the first time that there was some kind of danger here. Sylandris wasn't threatening me, not openly; in fact, I had the distinct impression that he'd come here to warn me. But what was he warning me about?

"Your people also value the concept of self sacrifice, the individual good exchanged for the greater good of the whole."

"Within reason, yes. Sylandris, if there is something you want to tell me, why don't you just come out and say it."

"One's official functions must sometimes take precedence over personal preferences." I may have imagined it, but he sounded a bit stiff. "My role here is to ease the transition from the old way of doing things to the new. We have made and will continue to make some concessions to the prejudices of your kind, but there are some areas in which we expect a degree of cooperation greater than that which we have already requested."

"Such as?"

"Those elements of society which retard the advance of a people as a whole must be removed. If you find unhealthy plants in one of your fields, you remove them to make way for those that will provide a better yield, do you not?"

I'm not so obtuse that I didn't understand what he was getting at. "There's a big difference between a cornfruit and a human being, or a Lysandran for that matter."

"On a personal level, that is of course true. That is why we have sometimes taken it upon ourselves to relieve others of the responsibility."

I didn't speak for a long time. My first reaction was shock and anger, and I had to repress a desire to physically attack Sylandris. If I was understanding him correctly, and I was reasonably certain that I did, the Lysandrans culled what they considered defective individuals from among themselves and their subject people. The defectives presumably included those who were handicapped by accident or by hereditary problems. I suddenly remembered the stories about the murder of patients in the hospital in Aladdin, and wondered what had happened to those humans who had been seriously injured in the fighting. Had they all been killed, presumably along with any Lysandran soldiers who had been irreversibly maimed? The fury made me physically ill, and the only reason that I didn't act upon it was the realization that Sylandris could only have had one purpose in telling me at this particular time.

It was a warning.

"Cille's injuries have been addressed. She has had a highly successful career and she's a member of the planetary government."

The thready sound had almost disappeared. Sylandris seemed more at ease, perhaps having realized that I understood what he was not saying. "She is an exceptional being, and has caused some consternation among my superiors. They do not like anomalies."

"Then perhaps they need to revise their preconceptions."

There was a brief thrum. Impatience with me, or perhaps frustration with his own kind. I never did find out which, but I suspect the latter. Sylandris had devoted his career to understanding other species, and that necessarily forced him to examine other ways of thinking. I had already noticed that he rarely spent time in the company of his fellows, and I had thought that a function of his rank. In the days to come, it would seem to me that it was he who was the outsider, that the others considered him and his kind as tainted by foreign ideas.

"Our peoples are not as different as you might think. It is often easier to eliminate an anomaly than to broaden one's understanding, particularly when established plans are not proceeding as rapidly as was predicted."

I nodded, more to myself than to him. "How much longer do you think they will be willing to tolerate the problem?"

"There has been trouble in the communities of Casper and Linden. Some of your people have been less willing to accept the small changes that have been requested. Lysandran lives have been lost unnecessarily. Human lives as well. In the past, we have always reacted to such a development by accelerating the process of incorporation. There are no voices suggesting that this would not be equally effective here. I believe that a decision in this matter is imminent. Once such a course has been agreed to, there is no purpose in delaying its implementation, and certainly no room to make exceptions for possibly extraordinary circumstances."

I stood up, and my voice was shaking with fury. "I appreciate the effort you have made to explain the situation to me," I said formally. I should probably have thanked him for the warning, but at that moment, I detested him along with all of his kind, and what I desired most was that he would leave so that I could pass on the information as quickly as possible. Even now after all the years which have passed, when I look back on that day, I am still puzzled by Sylandris. Lysandran culture and the psychology of its people is far more homogeneous than that of humans, and the fact that he engaged in even this trivial act of dissent must have caused him great distress.

He rose and gave a very human nod, and moments later he was gone.

His flitter wasn't even out of sight before I was on the com to Cille. She answered promptly, but audio only. I didn't even know whether she was at the farm or back in Aladdin.

"Cille, where are you?" I was unpleasantly surprised to hear my voice shaking.

"En route to the capitol. Is something wrong? You sound worried."

The Lysandrans insisted that they didn't listen in on the com links, but no one really believed them. "How soon can you get back here. We need to talk. Family business." Kelli had come into the room and she read my mood instantly, stood nervously waiting for me to explain.

"We're supposed to pick up passengers at Junction. I could get off there and try to get a ride back on one of the barges."

"I'll send Jeb to get you. Or I'll come myself."

"All right. I'll be at the Exchange." She didn't ask any more questions. Cille knew I wouldn't be asking if it wasn't necessary, and she shared my distrust of the security of the com.

I closed the connection, then hastily explained things to Kelli.

"Do you really think they'll kill everyone who doesn't reach some minimum level of physical perfection?"

"Yes, I do. Have you ever noticed how hard it is to distinguish among our liberators? The only reason I can identify Sylandris from a distance is because of his distinctive coloring. I think they've selectively bred themselves to conform to a very narrowly defined set of criteria." I remembered something else. One of Cille's friends from Aladdin had told her that he'd been to the main Lysandran encampment in Aladdin and that he had been dismayed to see that the only injuries we'd inflicted on the invaders had been minor wounds. "Kelli, I think they even finish off their own kind if they're seriously wounded."

"But that's inhuman," she protested, and then laughed nervously at her own words. "So what do we do?"

"First we get Cille out of their clutches before they decide she's not up to their standards."

"But what about Lemmie? Or Ruth Brock?"

"Damn!" I'd forgotten that her brother had Fagin's Syndrome, which would prevent him from ever growing emotionally beyond his early teens. And Ruth Brock had a prosthetic arm. "Scottie Wilber has epilepsy, and there's probably half a dozen people with artificial organs. I have no idea where they'll drop the boundary between those who live and those who die. We have to warn them all."

Kelli bit her lip. "What are we going to do? Your sister and some of the others can hide out in the wilds, but Lemmie has to have constant care."

"We'll work something out, but for the time being, we need to pass the word – and quietly so our visitors don't realize what's going on – and get them out of the Lysandrans' reach. And I don't trust the coms. Take the flitter. Tell your father and have him pass it on to the others in town, but by direct contact only. Take as much time as you can, then join us at the farm."

"What are you going to do?"

"I'm going after Cille. She's going to have to go into hiding, and she's not going to like it one bit."

I commed Jeb and he picked me up in the flitter. He knew me well enough to recognize that I was disturbed, but I wasn't ready to take him into my confidence yet. The truth was, I had no idea what to do and was hoping that Cille would be better equipped to deal with the situation. It seemed more in her line than mine. If a swarm of bluebugs threatened a crop, if there were complaints about work assignments from our Managuan hires, if the autotillers developed mechanical problems, or the irrigation system got clogged up and overflowed, I could deal with the problem, and damned well, if I do say so myself. But this was beyond me. This was something that could cost lives if it wasn't handled right, and I felt suddenly uncertain and incompetent. I wanted to talk to Dad about it, because despite his protestations to the contrary he'd always been politically savvy, but Dad wasn't around anymore, and the most competent person I could think of was my kid sister. Somehow, at that moment, she seemed a lot older to me.

The trip to Junction took almost two hours even traveling by air but it seemed to take much longer. For much of that time, I was caught up in my own thoughts so completely that I was rather surprised when the small trading town emerged from between two gently rolling hills. I hadn't said more than a handful of words to Jeb during the entire trip, so it must have been obvious that I was worried about something, but Jeb had known me long enough to keep his own peace and let me work things out in my mind. He brought us to the landing field behind the Exchange Building and I wasn't a third of the way to the entrance before Cille emerged, moving purposefully in my direction, her carryall banging against her back.

"What's going on, Ennis?"

"I'll tell you on the way back. Let's get out of here."

She and Jeb listened quietly and intently as I described my conversation with Sylandris. Jeb looked shocked and concerned, but not panicky and his grip on the controls never wavered. Cille looked grim and even slightly angry, but not nearly as surprised as I had expected.

"That fits in with some of the intelligence I've been seeing. You're right; the Lysandrans don't appear to have any seriously wounded, even though there's been some guerilla activity up north. They're either slightly hurt and sure to recover or they're dead. We don't have a definitive description of what happened at the hospital in Aladdin. There was a lot of fighting there and our own side caused some of the damage, but it's entirely possible that there were some summary executions." She touched my arm. "We have to get this information out, and quickly."

"How? I know they say they don't monitor the coms, but I don't want to bet people's lives on their word."

"No, I'll have to go to the capitol and tell the other delegates. They can get the word back to their constituents."

I shook my head. "You're not going anyplace except into hiding. Cille, I don't think Sylandris would have told me this if action hadn't been imminent. He more than hinted that the occupation forces are becoming impatient with the pace, though I can't imagine why. It's only been a few weeks since they invaded."

She looked thoughtful. "There have been some rumors that they've had a few reversals elsewhere. Nothing specific, but a large number of troops and crew were shuttled into orbit on very short notice a few days ago, and there are only about half as many ships in the system now as there were initially. But I have to take the risk, Ennis. There are too many lives at stake."

"Including your own. Look, why can't you just make a recording and let someone else take it to the capitol. You can contact whoever you trust and let them know it's coming and that it's important. Then you and whoever else might be at risk go into hiding."

"But where?"

It was Jeb who came up with the answer to that one. There were numerous caves in the serrated hills, some of them quite extensive and quite hard to find. I could only think of half a dozen people from Safehaven who had serious physical defects and they could be concealed there quite easily. We could move food and other supplies there in a matter of days, and clandestinely support them for as long as was necessary.

"What do you suppose the Lysandrans will do when they find out we're missing?"

I shrugged my shoulders. "Your guess is as good as mine. We'll deal with that when the time comes."

The time came sooner than any of us expected.

Zai flagged us down as we approached the north pier. She had been concealed from sight behind a stand of trees, emerging only when we were close enough that she could recognize the flitter.

"There's trouble. A Crane patrol landed at the farm, looking for you, Cille. They didn't say why. A couple of them stayed behind when the others left." She paused, glanced around nervously. "Ray Stickens came in from town. He says they've been searching houses and arresting people in Safehaven. Ennis, Kelli and her father were both arrested. I don't know why or where they've been taken."

My heart seemed to stop for a few seconds. "All right, we'll deal with that later." I turned to Cille. "I think you'd better get out here. If one of their patrols spots us, we're out of luck. Stay away from the farm and the town. We don't know what kind of surveillance methods they use. Do you remember the cave where we used to play dungeon when we were kids?"

Cille nodded. "I'll have to go through the Rollers though." She glanced at the two suns overhead. "It'll be dark by the time I get there, but I can find my way."

I opened the storage compartment and took out the survival pack. "You'll have to rough it tonight, but tomorrow I'll have someone drop off some supplies in that little gully north of Wallaby Pond. Wait till second dusk before going after them."

"All right. What are you going to do?"

"Go into town and find out where Kelli is. I'll get a message to you as soon as I can."

We waited until she'd disappeared into the woods with Zai, then set off on our own. "Drop me off in Safehaven, then head back to the farm and get someone you trust to bring a few days supplies up to Wallaby Pond."

"All right. Let me know if you need any help."

"We all need help, Jeb. I have a feeling the Lysandrans have more surprises in store for us."

Safehaven was in an uproar. It looked as though the entire population was in the streets, some shouting angrily, others moving about aimlessly, still others arguing with one another, and the rest standing sullenly about, angry and scared or both but not sure how to express what they were feeling. There was no sign of the Lysandrans. I found Grant Colson without too much difficulty. He was gamely trying to restore order and convince people to go home, but without noticeable success. I'm not sure if he was actually pleased to see me, but I really didn't care.

"What's going on, Grant? Jeb told me the Lysandrans arrested Kelli and her father."

"Them and a few others. Kuriel's got a broken arm but Kelli's all right. They're being held in the old grain warehouse." He gestured back over his shoulder toward the Jackknife. "The Crane military commander says they'll be let go in the morning."

"Why were they arrested? And how did Kuriel break his arm?"

"They came for Lemayel and Kuriel and Kelli tried to stop them. There was a scuffle. One of the Cranes pulled a weapon, but he didn't use it. Kelli hit one of them in the head with a shovel." He let a brief smile twist his lips. "Knocked him cold. They hustled them both into one of those personnel carriers they use, along with a few others who gave them trouble. But it looks like they just wanted to get them out of the way. The others have already been flown out of town."

"What others?"

"Lemayel Nganda. Ruth Brock. Selim Fahd. Scottie Wilber. Old Man Castro. Those are the ones I know of."

I nodded. I'd forgotten about Selim Fahd's artificial eyes, and had no idea what part of Abraham Castro was defective. There were a couple of others I thought might be included, and I mentioned them to Colson.

"No, so far as I know, they're still here."

"It might be a good idea to get them into hiding for at least a few days."

He gave me a funny look. "You know what this is about, don't you?"

"I think so." I gave him a very brief summary of my conversation with Sylandris. For a few seconds he looked as angry as anyone else in town, but then his face returned to its usual impassive blankness. Then he asked about Cille.

"She's covered, at least for now. Can I get in to see Kelli?"

"I doubt it. The Cranes guarding the place don't rate language lessons, and their officer headed off with most of his troops toward the southwest."

"Goodhost," I said quietly. "My guess is they're on the move all over the planet today. Helping us to get through the pain as quickly as possible, as they see it." I made a disgusted sound.

"This is going to play right into the hands of Evan Carter and Brodie Bors."

"Are they still talking about a guerilla war?" Colson nodded, and I scratched my head. "Can't say I'm entirely unsympathetic at the moment, but the logistics are still against us. We don't have the weapons we need for armed attacks. Our best bet is to still to bide our time and learn what we can about their weaknesses, wait for them to lower their guard a little and think we've given up. And we need to be able to communicate securely with Aladdin and Casper and the other settlements." Cille had quietly approached a few people whose business involved significant travel and the skeleton of a communications network was beginning to form. Osker Needham thought he could eventually figure a way to conceal coded messages among electronic financial transactions.

"They talk loudly and foolishly but haven't done anything yet. I hope this isn't the stimulus that'll push them over the edge."

"Maybe you could convince them to cool it for a while."

He shrugged. "I'll probably end up talking at them instead of to them. They didn't listen to me much when they were youngsters, and now that they're mostly grown, they don't want to see me either." He sighed. "Look, chances are they'll let Kelli go in the morning. If you want to stay here in town for the night, why don't you use the Nganda place. I closed it up, but the front door lock is broken."

"Maybe. But I think I'll go over and see if there's any chance of getting Kelli out of there tonight."

"Try it if you want to. Just don't go getting yourself locked up as well."

I did end up sleeping at the Nganda house, though not very well, and only after a strained conversation over the com with my mother, who informed me that Sylandris was staying out of sight, leaving her to deal with Lysandran soldiers who could barely communicate with her. She told me they were looking for Cille, asked if I knew where she was, but there was something oddly indifferent in her tone, and I guessed correctly that Jeb or Zai had told her what was going on.

Just after sunrise, the Lysandrans guarding the warehouse were picked up by a military vehicle. There were about a dozen people inside, most of them with minor injuries. Kelli hugged me so tight it hurt, but her eyes were glazed and she seemed to have aged a few years overnight. Her father was in considerable pain and we dropped him off at the med station before trying to find out where they'd taken Lemayel and the others.

We never did find out.

Several weeks later I asked Sylandris, and he insisted that he didn't know either. "Our practice in the past has always been to ensure that the break is complete, that nothing remains to trigger undesirable emotions." But we were determined to find out whatever we could. Along with Cindy Aguilar, Grant Colson, and Kani Shikuro, we went out to the Harwell place and spoke to Savoril, under the watchful eye of his armed and unusually vigilant guards. His command of our language had never been as good as that of Sylandris, but that day he seemed deliberately obtuse, insisting over and over again that "those individuals are no longer members of this community" and "we intend only to help your culture free itself of barbaric traditions". Even Colson was beginning to fume by the time we finally abandoned it as a lost cause and returned to Safehaven.

My father-in-law's arm had been tended to, but Kelli wanted to stay with him until he was better able to take care of himself. Kuriel had always seemed self possessed and unemotional to me, but it was clear that the loss of his son had been a devastating blow. With Mara gone off planet and her fate unknown, Kelli was the last of his family, and he was suddenly so dependent that I hardly recognized him. I made her promise to com me if she needed anything and assured her in turn that I would let her know what was going on. We exchanged a few simple code words so that we could pass on news over the coms without giving anything away, then sat quietly together until Jeb arrived with the flitter to take me to the farm.

Mom was waiting when we arrived, met us outside the house. She was outwardly calm but I knew from the way she curled and uncurled her fingers that she was tense. We talked in low voices as we walked toward the house, and I explained what had happened in Safehaven and why Kelli wasn't with me. One of the Lysandrans was standing alertly on the porch, watching us.

"Avram went back today and checked on the supplies. They're gone. I assume you know where she's hiding."

"In one of the caves. It was the best we could think of on such short notice."

"We'll have to think of something better for the longer term. I assume you've heard about the fighting."

I hadn't checked the public com channel since before the trouble started so I didn't know what she was talking about. There had been riots in Aladdin, Tyrada, Casper, probably all of the cities and some of the smaller townships. Someone had managed to bring down a Lysandran flitter in Linden by attaching a bomb to its hull. "They sent in a large force and searched the town from one end to the other, seized anything even remotely resembling a weapon. There were a couple of deaths. Human ones, I mean."

We fell silent as we neared the house. The Lysandran guard watched us closely, but if there was any visible emotion being displayed, I still didn't know how to read it. Mom and I went inside. "Where's Sylandris?"

"In his room. He hasn't come out yet today. The other one is out in the cottage. Zai is keeping an eye on him."

"All right. I'm going to talk to Sylandris."

Sylandris came out when I knocked, and his voice thrummed with concern, but only slightly. I tried to convince him that he needed to talk to his superiors, that humans valued all life equally and that we were if anything more protective of those who were physically impaired than those who were not.

"I have already drawn that conclusion from my studies," he replied. "But I must tell you, Ennis Baxter, that it is an attitude which most of my people will never accept. One of my siblings was born disfigured and was culled immediately, and it is an act which neither I nor the rest of my family regretted then or now. The sense of loss was intense but it could only then begin to heal. The willingness of your species to endure such prolonged punishment is irrational and counterproductive and can only increase your pain."

I glanced around the room, just to be certain neither of the soldiers was present. "But you warned me for Cille's sake."

His whistle of alarm was so strong that I had difficulty understanding his speech. "I did not warn you of anything, Ennis Baxter. We simply discussed the differences in attitudes between our cultures, as part of my duty to understand your people and assist in their transition to a more rational social system. If you remember, I referred to your sibling as a troublesome anomaly, but I neither suggested then nor condone now that you or she engage in any specific course of action."

He had done us a good turn and I should have been grateful, but I wasn't. If he and his kind had minded their own business, the crisis which required his warning would not have arisen in the first place. But I held my temper because I knew that Sylandris was a weak link among our conquerors. Perhaps his career as a xenologist had forced him to become more flexible in his beliefs, or perhaps Lysandran society wasn't as monolithic as we'd been told, or perhaps he was just mentally unstable. Whatever the reason, he was a potential asset, and I couldn't afford to alienate him.

"Well, the anomaly is no longer among us. How much effort is likely to be exerted to locate her?" I didn't know if he'd answer that, or if the answer would be truthful, but I had to try.

"If there were no other distractions, further measures might be taken. But as I'm sure you know, there have been several violent outbreaks in the past few hours, and we have not tried to burden your people with an overly large garrison." I took that last as a rationalization of the large scale movement of troops off Aragon in recent days. "Under the circumstances, and assuming that the anomalous situation does not draw attention to itself, further efforts at apprehension will be confined to those areas where its presence might destabilize your culture."

In other words, if Cille tried to return to the Assembly, she'd be taken, but the Lysandrans were not about to expend resources searching for her if she stayed out of sight. I must have given some physical interpretation of relief, something that Sylandris could recognize, because he added a warning.

"Do not think, however, that this is a phase which will end at some future date. The removal of deficient individuals will continue rigorously now that it has been imposed. Certain heroic medical procedures will be discontinued, all birthings will be monitored, and other steps will be taken to maintain the desired minimum level of fitness. We are flexible in most aspects of our administration of your culture, but in this we will not bend. To do so would be to condemn your people to perpetual suffering, and that would be an ethical crime that would undermine our own beliefs."

I nodded, message received, and left him without another word.

CHAPTER ELEVEN

The next few weeks were more traumatic for the people of Aragon than the invasion itself. The Lysandrans had overwhelmed our defensive forces so quickly and so easily that for most of the population, it hadn't really seemed like a war, particularly since the invaders had not initially interfered significantly with our day to day existence. We really hadn't gotten used to governing ourselves before that status was lost, and in many ways the Lysandrans seemed to be just another manifestation of the company that had developed Aragon in the first place.

All that changed when they decided to "help" us by weeding out the unfit. There was sporadic fighting in Linden and Tyrada for several days, and at least a score of people were killed, mostly members of a group of young people who holed up in the Tyradan mines and raided the nearby military encampment at night. The Lysandran authorities might have been puzzled by our stubborn refusal to admit we'd been conquered, but it wasn't long before they took precautions and ambushed a large party of raiders. Many others were wounded, and those with significant injuries also disappeared. It would be many years before a team of botanists stumbled across the remote island where the Lysandrans disposed of the remains of those they took away, hopefully after euthanizing their victims as painlessly as possible.

There was trouble in Safehaven as well, though we were mercifully spared the worst of the violence. It consisted mostly of petty sabotage. One of the two Lysandran personnel carriers was disabled when someone poured synthfuel into a vent and set fire to it while it was parked and unaccountably unguarded. Shots were occasionally fired at Harwell house, even though there were round the clock patrols protecting it. A distraught woman assaulted Fossicker on one of his rare forays into town, but she was dragged off by two of Colson's deputies and no serious harm was done.

Although I could see no evidence that I was under surveillance, I didn't dare go to see Cille myself. We sent bedding and other supplies via hands we could trust, and I recorded messages to her and received some back. She remained in the cave only ten days before sending me a detailed list of supplies she wanted, along with a recorded message. "I can't stay here, Ennis. There's nothing I can accomplish sitting in a cave. I think I know a place where I can go and be relatively safe. I'll try to get messages back to you once I've reached it."

I recorded a lengthy list of reasons she should stay, and almost went to see her in person, but then I replayed her recording before erasing it and realized that she had made up her mind. There was no point in arguing with her. We gathered all the materials she'd asked for, and two days later she was gone. It would be weeks before we heard anything from her again.

The Lysandran plan to restore at least the face of our planetary government collapsed when the elected delegates all resigned in protest, forcing the authorities to deal with various municipal groups instead. They weren't particularly happy about that and the public comline was full of exhortations to accept the new state of affairs and cooperate in order to help shape our future. Sylandris even approached me about representing the region. "Each community will be encouraged to elect new delegates to replace those who refuse to serve.

"Our representative is Cille Baxter," I told him coldly.

"No such person exists," he replied. "Your people persist in rejecting the real world, Ennis Baxter. There can be no gain from this."

"You told us that we would be allowed to govern ourselves, within certain limits. If we cannot choose our representatives freely, then you rule us directly no matter how much you protest to the contrary. The people of Safehaven trust my sister to do what's best for them, and they're not likely to change their mind just because you don't care for their choice."

"I confess that I still do not understand you humans. You cling to pointless symbols rather than accept reality, even when doing so works against your best interests."

"Cille is not a pointless symbol," I answered with some heat.

"Cille Baxter no longer exists," he said quietly, "regardless of whether or not she still lives."

They went ahead with the elections. Less than ten percent of the eligible voters in Safehaven participated, and Sobriety Carter was elected even though he vowed not to serve. Managansett chose someone named Hobson with a similar lack of enthusiasm. When the time came to leave for Aladdin, Carter went after all, but he was plainly not comfortable with his decision. Ted Vallencourt caught Brodie Bors setting up a primitive shrapnel bomb near the Harwell ranch and Grant Colson locked the boy up for a few days mostly to keep him out of trouble. Evan Carter announced his intention to join some unspecified rebel underground, postured around town for a few days, and then disappeared.

After the initial unrest, Aragon settled back into sullen quiet. Fossicker and his people started coming into Safehaven again, and sometimes they were even treated politely. The new Assembly dealt with some minor administrative issues and codified a few existing laws but did nothing either satisfying or offensive. There was still occasional trouble from Tyrada. A group of drunken miners ambushed and killed three Lysandran soldiers, losing nine of their own in the process. That resulted in a work stoppage, a tactic apparently new to the Lysandran military, who were so totally ineffectual responding to it that the miners finally went back to work on their own.

But beneath the calm there were rumors, rumors of a more sophisticated underground that was biding its time, stockpiling information and weapons, spying on the invaders, identifying collaborators, plotting a rebellion. Some of the stories were obviously apocryphal. Some were not. It seemed unlikely that they had offworld contacts, for example, and there were so many claims of secretive assassinations that if half of them were true, the Lysandrans would have to have reinforced themselves every few weeks. On the other hand, there really was an explosion at their military headquarters in Aladdin, though Sylandris insisted that it was an equipment malfunction. He may have been telling the truth; his voice was unaccompanied by whistles of alarm or the thrumming of concern, but I never did discover just how well informed he was, or whether he had acquired the human ability to lie..

We also starting hearing about a charismatic leader named Gaunt who supposedly headed the amorphous underground centered in Tyrada. Most of the more lurid and less credible exploits were attributed to this mysterious figure or his cohorts. He was described as a man about my own age with a thick, dark beard, unruly hair, and penetrating eyes. He was variously reportedly as operating from a secret cave complex near Tyrada, from a treehouse in the forest north of Casper, and from a secret underground Navy base somewhere in the northwest. Some stories said he was a colonial police officer, others that he was a survivor of the Naval contingent, an operative dropped onto the planet clandestinely after the invasion, or a hermit who had emerged from the wilderness after seeing a vision of the slaughter of the Lysandrans. There was never any mention of him on the public comlines, which the Lysandrans certainly monitored.

Kuriel Nganda's arm healed, but he was never quite the same. Kelli spent a great deal of time running back and forth between our two households, and I tried to be patient and understanding all the time, and usually succeeded. We received word from Cille at last and in intervals of several weeks thereafter, usually in the form of a recorded message delivered clandestinely. She had found what she thought was a safe refuge and assured us she was quite comfortable though her movements were restricted. Her appearance made it impossible for her to blend in with the general populace; even unsophisticated Lysandrans would recognize that she didn't look normal. Despite Cille's reassurances, Mom grew increasingly depressed and introspective, and although she remained polite and hospitable to Sylandris, responding to his every request, she no longer initiated any effort to make him feel more comfortable. She sat out on the porch a great deal, and each time I came to visit she seemed to have grown older.

Based on the pattern of the messages we received and some internal clues, we initially suspected Cille had found refuge somewhere in Aladdin. It made sense, since she knew many people there, and there was undoubtedly an organized if not particularly effective resistance movement in our capitol city. But as the weeks passed, I began to suspect otherwise. The background in one of the recordings was decidedly rural, and I thought I spotted the distinctive frondlike branches of one of the indigenous trees. I was pretty sure she'd taken refuge at Lake Lilith, the resort project of which she was still technically part owner. A few small buildings had been erected before the effort faltered. I never made any effort to confirm my suspicion, though. I was terrified that I might do something that would draw attention to her.

We passed the anniversary of our independence, which was quietly but unofficially celebrated all over Aragon. And then we passed the anniversary of the invasion, which was not celebrated at all. The new Assembly belatedly got down to codifying a lot of trade law and life went on. The farm made a modest but steady profit despite an increase in taxes and the general depression of the economy.

There was no further talk of appointing delegates to the offworld conference that was supposed to work out a uniform code for all the occupied worlds. I asked Sylandris about it once and it took him a long time to answer. "The incorporation of your species is the largest such endeavor that my people have undertaken. It is taking longer than anticipated to establish the proper mechanism for further integration." He was being more circumlocutious than normal and I chose to interpret his response as meaning they were having more trouble subduing some of the other worlds they'd invaded than they had had on Aragon. Not surprising, since most of them would have been more populous and more heavily developed. And I did not know until a couple of years later that they had underestimated the size of the Concourse, believing that humans occupied only a few dozen worlds rather than several hundred.

A few days later there was a raid on Aragon. No one knew exactly what had happened, but people in Casper saw the unmistakable signs of an orbital battle, and there were reports of frantic activity inside the Lysandran bases in Aladdin and Tyrada. The next day we all waited for news of our liberation, or at least of troop landings, but the news line said nothing about any military action, activity among the Lysandrans returned to normal, and there were no further signs of a human counterattack. Some people were elated in any case by the knowledge that we hadn't been forgotten and that there was still a human force at large, but others were depressed by their evident failure to achieve anything tangible. As the days passed with no further activity, the latter emotion became more predominant.

That's when the Aragon resistance movement began to accelerate its direct attacks on the Lysandrans, and in some cases on those humans who collaborated with them.

Kelli and I were in Safehaven when we first heard the news. We'd just visited her father, who seemed marginally improved, and were on our way to Shikuro's to pick up the order we'd commed in earlier. There was a sudden whirring sound from overhead and a Lysandran military transport landed right in the middle of the street, disgorging a dozen heavily armed soldiers. They moved to strategic positions from which they could keep the entire area under surveillance, roughly pushing aside a few people who were too slow to give way. Two more alighted a moment later, one wearing the elaborate cape of an officer, the other relatively nondescript, probably an interpreter. They headed directly for Grant Colson's office. He was watching from the window and met them at the doorway. All three disappeared inside.

The soldiers made no effort to interfere as people slowly resumed their business, but they carefully watched anyone who approached too closely. Their wariness was palpable, and I used my com to access the newsline, assuming that something serious must be going on. The stream of information was painfully dull, however, and I disengaged. "Let's go," I said. "Maybe Shikuro knows what's going on."

But he was just as puzzled as we when we found him standing in his doorway, his eyes blinking nervously. "What's happening?" he asked, before I could say a word. We confessed our ignorance and all three of us went inside. Our order was ready and the two of could easily carry it back to the flitter, but we hadn't made it out the door when the search party entered.

Colson was the only human, closely followed by the officer, the interpreter, and four soldiers. Our magistrate looked annoyed, but he was also clearly worried. "Kani, the Lysandrans want to search your store."

Shikuro blinked. "For what? I deal in seeds and grains and farming supplies."

"I know that, but they have orders to search the entire town." He turned to me and nodded. "There are a couple of other patrols out searching the farms."

I glanced at the interpreter, who was likely the only one who could understand what we were saying. "What's going on, Grant? We've given them no trouble here."

"I know. But there have been some incidents apparently. I gather it's not just us. This is happening all over Aragon."

Kani retrieved the keys to the store rooms. Kelli and I started to leave, but were held until they could look through the parcels we were carrying. Outside we realized that more Lysandran troops had arrived, that the town had been cordoned off into sectors.

"What's going on?" whispered Kelli. "This isn't like them at all."

"I don't know, but it really has them stirred up. Let's go by the farm before home. Maybe Sylandris will tell us something."

Mom was sitting on the porch when we arrived, looking smaller and more fragile than ever. I had confessed to Kelli my fear that she was physically ill, but she assured me that the changes I saw were subjective. "She misses your father, your sister, and your brother, Ennis, and sometimes she's very depressed. But she hasn't stopped fighting. It may look like Zai and Jeb and Garner are running the farm lately, but your mother stays right on top of things. She spotted some major problems in Garner's irrigation system for the Rollers that Zai had missed, and she was the one who convinced the others to speed up construction of the west dock and establish a trade contract with Goodhost."

Sylandris was in his room and he emerged with what appeared to me to be reluctance. I never did learn how to read emotions from a Lysandran face, if indeed that's possible at all. But on this occasion, Sylandris made no effort to greet us, and only followed us out into the common area when I specifically asked him if we could talk. He remained completely motionless as I told him what we'd seen in Safehaven, and didn't respond until I asked him directly if he knew what was going on.

"There have been certain incidents in the past few days which have made it necessary to respond in this fashion."

"What incidents? We've heard nothing unusual."

"No, you would not. It would seem that we have been even less successful in our efforts to aid your culture than we thought. Certain irrational activities have continued, even escalated."

"You mean the resistance movement. I warned you about that. Humans have a long tradition of rebellion against authority."

"But it is not rational!" His voice boomed with excitement. "We have clearly established our superiority. Further struggle will only result in unnecessary loss of life and adverse effects on your economy and your cultural development."

"The fact that you have won a battle, that you have occupied Aragon for the moment, does not mean that you will win the war. Perhaps dominance has not been decided yet after all." I waited a moment, wondering if I'd scored a point for a change. "Are you going to tell us what's been happening or not? People are going to want an explanation for the searches, the show of force, and if none is forthcoming, it's going to make their resentment even greater."

"We recognize that. It was predictable given your racial psychology. It is not a step that has been taken lightly. There have been violent incidents ever since our arrival, but they have been largely ineffectual and rare enough that the aberrances were tolerable. During the past three days, that has changed. A small group of humans attacked a barracks in Tyrada and killed a significant number of soldiers. They used weapons of an advanced type and the attack was skillfully planned. None of the intruders were killed or identified. A similar effort was made against several security stations near the spaceport in Aladdin. These were less successful, and one of the attackers was killed. This individual carried an advanced weapon as well. We don't believe this equipment was present on Aragon at the time of our arrival."

"So your blockade isn't as effective as you claimed it was."

"A small force penetrated this system recently and engaged our forces, as I'm sure you already know. They were repulsed with severe losses. It now seems likely that this was a ruse to mask the delivery of military equipment to those of your people who remain unreasonably disaffected."

"Which is most of the population," I said, but under my breath. "You do realize that if we did in fact have that kind of equipment here, it wouldn't be hidden where a search like this would find it."

"Yes, and I'm certain that my superiors feel the same way. But some of the recent incidents have been so extraordinarily irrational that they have decided to take nothing for granted."

"Surely you've run into resistance before? I can't believe that the previous peoples you've conquered have just rolled over and played dead for you."

"There have been isolated instances, but nothing on this scale. And the violence has always been open and direct, not clandestine and sporadic." He stirred restlessly, an oddly human movement. "One of your people, a female, managed to evade our security and penetrate into our most restricted command center. She killed two of the most superior officers on Aragon including the second in command."

My spine turned to ice. For no particular reason, I was convinced that he was talking about Cille. "Was she killed?"

"I am ashamed to say that she successfully escaped in the ensuing confusion. One of our soldiers claims to have wounded her but there has been no confirmation."

"I don't suppose you know who it was?"

"We have not identified the individual, although we have an adequate recording of her from our surveillance equipment."

"Have you seen the recording, Sylandris?"

He hesitated. "Yes, I have." And then he must have read my mind. "She is not someone I have met before. She is nearly as tall as you, with light colored hair, and quite solidly built. During her escape, she physically overpowered two soldiers who tried to intercept her."

So it wasn't Cille. I felt almost giddy with relief. We talked for a while longer. Kelli was better at getting him to relax than I was, and he filled in some additional details about the guerilla attacks. The Lysandrans were reducing the number of posts they occupied so that they could better defend the rest, but it was obvious that Sylandris considered this somewhat shameful, as though it were an admission that they had somehow failed in their duties. On the other hand, random searches and increased military patrols were going to be the order of the day, and he even hinted that more troops might be brought in from elsewhere.

I asked him if there were similar problems on the other planets the Lysandrans occupied, but he either didn't know or wouldn't tell us. "I cannot provide any information on that topic."

We stayed for dinner, a quiet affair even after Sylandris pleaded fatigue and retired to his room. The three of us visited for a while, but mostly without talking. I went out and talked to Zai and she brought me up to date on farm business. Jeb was in Managansett for the evening. "I think he has a lady friend, but he's very secretive about it."

I dropped Kelli off at our house and went out to inspect the east fields, not because they needed any particular attention, but just to allow myself to think in the absence of human company. Quite honestly, I was troubled by these new developments, and uncertain about what I should be doing personally. Up until now, I guess I'd been expecting the Navy to come to our rescue, and it hadn't really occurred to me that we on Aragon should be doing something to help ourselves. I'd argued with Sylandris, and hoped that some of what I told him filtered back to his superiors and moderated their actions, but I certainly couldn't claim that I'd done anything to make their occupation more difficult.

On the other hand, the theatrics of young troublemakers like Brodie Bors and Evan Carter weren't likely to help either. They were too disorganized, too impulsive, too immature to wage an effective campaign. I ran through the list of potential leaders in Safehaven, and realized just how few strong minded people were available. For all his faults, Sobriety Carter was a leader, though I didn't trust his judgment, and in any case, he was in Aladdin. Tami Pakarang was another, but she'd been having serious health problems this past year and had dropped out of public view, as had my father-in-law ever since Lemayel had been taken. The only other obvious candidate was Grant Colson, and I knew how reluctant he was to step into that role. That seemed to put the onus on me to do something. After all, I had a direct line to the Lysandrans living with my mother, I was head of the largest holding in the area, and I was pretty sure I was respected if not liked by most of the people who mattered. That being the case, did I have an obligation to do something more than I'd been doing up to now? Should I be organizing strikes or revolutionary cells? Was there some way that I could get in touch with the resistance movement in the north?

It was first dusk when I finally came back to the house, my mind even more unsettled than when I had set out. Kelli met me at the door, her face stiff. "We have company," she said tensely.

"Who is it?" I hadn't seen any other transport in the area, so I didn't think it could be a Lysandran search party, and it wasn't. It was a human, a complete stranger, a hand's width shorter than me but considerably heavier, almost blocky. He was wearing dark clothing, including a sweater with a hood that flapped where it dangled between his shoulderblades. He stepped out of the shadows behind Kelli and peered around before speaking.

"Mr. Baxter? I need to talk to you. It's very important."

"Do I know you?" I stood where I was. His posture was alert, wary, and that made me feel the same way.

"No. My name is," he hesitated for a second and I knew he was going to lie to me. "Sheffield, Paul Sheffield." He took a half step backward. "Please come inside. I didn't mean to keep you out of your own home."

I still didn't move and my eyes shifted to Kelli's face. She didn't seem frightened, but she did appear to be worried. I nodded to her and she turned and we all went inside.

We had been planning to add to our house ever since moving in, but other priorities had always seemed to take precedence. Our common area was small, but large enough for three.

"I don't want to appear rude, Mr. Sheffield, but would you mind stating your business. We've had a long day and I'm not feeling particularly sociable."

"No longer than mine," he answered, somewhat testily. "I'm just a messenger, Mr. Baxter. I've been sent here to present a situation to you, and then to take your answer back."

"Back to whom?"

"A gentleman by the name of Gaunt. You may have heard of him."

I settled into my chair, unnerved by this sudden echo of matters I'd just been considering. I no longer had to think of ways to contact the underground; they'd found me instead. Oddly enough, I felt suddenly more relaxed.

"I was wondering how long it would take you to get around to us. Things have been comparatively quiet here. There are only a handful of Lysandrans in the area."

"Yes, the Cranes have been concentrating their forces where they think we're more likely to strike. They don't seem to have had much experience dealing with guerilla warfare, but they learn quite quickly."

"There are plenty of people here who would like to help, but frankly we don't have a lot of resources."

"That's a constraint everywhere." Sheffield's voice seemed to have relaxed, become almost friendly.

"What would you want us to do?" asked Kelli. "We don't have anything except a couple of hand stunners we use to clear out vermin."

"I'm a messenger, not a tactician. My guess is that Gaunt wants just enough trouble that the Cranes will send more forces here. The more we spread them out, the easier it is to strike at them. We have a few weapons, but their price was heavier than we hoped to pay." He glanced toward the ceiling and I knew what he was talking out. "It would be almost as useful to force them to spread their forces as it would be to kill them."

"But won't they just bring in more troops?"

He shook his head before answering her. "We don't think so. Our eyes and ears in Aladdin tell us they've been slowly bleeding troops away rather than adding them. And word from offworld is that they're taking some heavy losses."

I leaned forward, my voice tense. "You have contact off Aragon?"

He made a vague gesture with his hands. "Not reliably. We can occasionally get some coded messages broadcast from the spaceport. Can't do it too often or they'd catch on to us. But a Navy spyship flashed through the system a few weeks ago and replied, also in code, setting up a weapons drop. And we got a little bit of intelligence along with it."

"So the orbital battle really was just a ruse?"

He nodded. "Unfortunately, an expensive one."

"Do you know what's happening elsewhere?" asked Kelli impatiently. "Is there any chance the Navy will help us?"

"We don't know a lot about it. The Cranes have taken at least a dozen planets and struck at many more. The Navy took a pretty heavy mauling, but they didn't go easily. Their ships are a lot faster than ours, in transit as well as in battle, but apparently we had a bigger force than they counted on. We think there's a kind of stalemate now. We have enough ships spread around to defend against further attacks, but they can move from system to system fast enough to counter the Navy if it tries to reclaim any lost territory."

"Any chance of striking at their own worlds?" I asked.

He shrugged. "I imagine it's being considered, if they've located any Crane worlds. We just don't know, and at the moment, it's not relevant to our situation."

"So what, precisely, do you want us to do?" Most of the stiffness had gone out of Kelli's voice. I was still wary though. It occurred to me that Sheffield might be in the employ of the Lysandrans, sent to find out how much they could or could not trust us.

"As I said, I'm just a messenger sent to evaluate the situation and report back. The question is, are you willing to become players or are you going to sit back and watch?"

Kelli opened her mouth to reply but I overrode her. If Sheffield was legitimate, I wanted him to know we were reliable, but I didn't want to stick our necks out unnecessarily. "We'd be interested in listening to a more specific course of action, and would hope to be able to support it. That's the best we can offer you at the moment."

He chuckled and clasped his hands in his lap. "Fair enough. A thoughtful rebel is preferable to a committed hothead. I'll pass on your guarded enthusiasm. And there is one specific thing you could do to assist us right now."

"What's that?"

"Invite me to dinner. I've been living out of my knapsack for the past four days. Came down the Jackknife hidden in a cargo hold and walked the rest of the way. And it's nippy enough outside that I wouldn't mind sleeping under a roof tonight."

"Well, that much we can certainly do for you."

Sheffield slept on a cot in our storage room that evening, after gorging himself on Kelli's cooking. He talked volubly and amiably throughout the meal, and it wasn't until after we'd all retired for the night that I realized how little content there had been despite the verbiage. We still didn't know where he actually came from, or if Sheffield really was his name, or what he'd done for a living before the invasion. He mentioned Gaunt a few times, but only in the most inconsequential way, even when I'd asked some roundabout questions.

"He's a quiet man, but he sees deep into you," he told us. "Scratches that long beard of his and talks in a voice so low you have to strain sometimes to hear it. Never betrays much emotion, even when things are tense; doesn't show much of a response to good news or bad. But he's got a sharp mind. He looks at problems and sees solutions."

Kelli and I lay in bed, not talking, not sleeping either. I was the one who finally broke the silence. "What do you think?"

She drew in a long breath. "I think he's being straight with us, but I don't think he's telling us everything."

"Would you if you were in his place?"

"No. And I noticed you weren't going out of your way to make a commitment either."

"Just being cautious," I said defensively.

"I wasn't being critical, just observant. I understand what we're risking."

"Do you want us to stay out of it?"

"No, of course not. They took Lemayel, Ennis. My brother is gone because of them. And all the others." She still hadn't accepted that he was dead, thought just possibly the Lysandrans were keeping him in a camp somewhere.

"We might get ourselves killed, you know."

"I know." Then she rolled in my direction and put her arms around me and I put mine around her, and the rest of what happened that night you don't need to know.

CHAPTER TWELVE

Our visitor left us very early the following morning, after giving us a series of code phrases by means of which we'd be contacted in the future. I confess that I felt a mild excitement at the prospect, not unmixed with worry, and during the next few days, I gave every strange face an appraising look. But as one week passed, and then another, and finally a month, the excitement faded, and if Kelli hadn't been around to confirm my memory, I might have thought that night a particularly convincing dream.

Things had returned pretty much to normal in Safehaven, but that wasn't the case everywhere. The Lysandrans continued to make random searches, and even arrested a number of people in the larger cities. There were work stoppages in Aladdin and Tyrada, and a brief but destructive riot in Casper. We heard rumors that a military patrol was ambushed near Linden and that someone successfully sabotaged a transport in Junction, but there was never any official confirmation. Fossicker and his entourage made regular visits to town, ostensibly studying human culture although most suspected that they were also keeping an eye out for any signs of the underground.

We received another innocuous, uninformative, but reassuring recording from Cille. I wondered if she was involved with Gaunt's rebels. She wasn't the type to sit around idly in hiding while things were happening. I hoped she was acting out of character and had concealed herself safely in the basement of some half finished tourist attraction at Lake Lilith, but it didn't seem likely. She was at particular risk because even though the Lysandrans were comparatively merciful conquerors, they wouldn't recognize her as fully human. She wouldn't even need to act against them to draw a death sentence; it had already been issued.

Sylandris continued to behave strangely. He was never overtly unfriendly, but he was far less inclined to talk, even to his own kind, and became very reclusive. Until recently, he had made frequent requests for me to come up to the house and talk with him, but now we only spoke if I happened to be there on other business or to visit with Mom, and she told me he often emerged only for meals. He'd also become querulous and less flexible in his arguments, as though he'd abandoned all hope of understanding human psychology and was now convinced the only solution was to win us over to their value system.

"I am beginning to wonder if there is a basic flaw in human psychology," he told me on one occasion. "You seem to glorify obstinacy rather than achievement. We have demonstrated repeatedly that we have no desire to prolong the confrontation between our peoples and that we wish to interfere only minimally in your efforts to shape your own destiny. I realize that the violence directed against our soldiers originates among a comparatively small group, but it seems that the majority of your people implicitly if not actively support them."

"I can't think of anything we humans value more than freedom, Sylandris. Perhaps it's not entirely rational, but that's the way we are."

"But your version of freedom is more like anarchy. It is irresponsible to seek anything other than the optimal course of action. If you were offered three paths through the mountains of varying difficulty, would you not choose the safest?"

I sighed, because I knew we were en route to our usual communication barrier. "Not necessarily. I might choose the fastest, or the most scenic, or I might just be in the mood for a challenge. We don't believe there is a single optimal course of action, or more properly, we don't believe that it is always possible to determine what is optimal and what isn't. So we often follow several different paths toward what we think is a common goal."

"And by doing so, you condemn generations of your own people to unnecessary error and hardship. You create divisions that breed animosity, which is why you war against one another." He reminded me that the Lysandrans had never battled among themselves.

"Perhaps it would have been better if you had. You've locked yourselves into a single path which you call optimal, but you have no idea what the benefits might have been had you chosen another."

Sylandris launched into a pointless catalog of Lysandran accomplishments, so I decided to change the subject. I asked him if there had been similar trouble on the other occupied worlds, but he could not or would not tell me. But I sensed from the tenor of his voice that his distress level was rising, which I interpreted as a positive answer. When I tried to press the issue, he insisted he had work to do and that we would have to continue the conversation at another time.

On a different occasion, he issued what seemed to me a veiled threat. There had been a wave of sabotage in Aladdin so widespread that even Fossicker and one of his aides who had become reasonably fluent were willing to speak of it openly. I had stopped by the farm to review the north pier expansion project with Zai and found Sylandris standing under a tree near the main house, staring off across the sweep of cultivated fields.

I took a circuitous course to reach him so that I would enter his field of view from a good distance. I had developed a degree of respect for our uninvited guest and thought that we might even have been friends under other circumstances. But I remained aware of the fact that he represented the enemy, that he was not human, and that his emotional reactions might not be predictable. Surprising him did not seem like a good idea, even though he rarely carried anything I could identify as a weapon. On the other hand, the two soldiers who still accompanied him were never unarmed, and although I didn't see them anywhere about, that didn't mean they weren't around.

I wasn't sure if he had noticed my approach, because he had not stirred since I'd first spotted him, but I was still a few meters distant when he spoke. "This is a beautiful place you have made here, Ennis Baxter. You have brought order out of chaos, you contribute to the support of your species, improve the lot of your family, and increase your own stature. In many ways you are very Lysandran."

I chose not to be insulted. "There are certain basic values that all sentient societies probably share." I came to a halt just beyond arm's length. Lysandrans were used to speaking to one another from quite close proximity, and it had become common knowledge that you could put them at a disadvantage by maintaining an unusual amount of personal space. Often they would slowly, perhaps even unconsciously, try to close the gap. If the human involved was inclined to play, a conversation could be turned into an elaborate, awkward dance. It frazzled their nerves and gave us numerous tiny, childish victories.

He turned away from me, which seemed out of character. Lysandrans were also big on eye contact. As with humans, perhaps even more so, they used it to establish levels of dominance. "I'm not so sure of that as once I was."

Intrigued, I relented, closing the gap until I was at what he would consider a comfortable distance. "The universe is an uncertain place. Humans have always been aware of that. Perhaps Lysandrans could learn something from us."

His voice betrayed no alarm, but it was somehow thinner as well as softer, and I wondered what blend of emotion this might reflect. "Some would say that we have already learned too much. Some might feel that those of us who have tried to gain a greater understanding have been corrupted by an insidiously flawed species."

"I gather things aren't going too well lately." I didn't expect him to reply to that. Sylandris invariably avoided commenting on the rebels, as though he could deny their existence, or at least their legitimacy, by excluding them from conversation. But today he broke that rule.

"What purpose can be served by these petty attacks? Why do you humans persist in violence against what is clearly a superior force?" He turned to face me, his voice actually rose in volume, and there was a hint of the boom of excitement. "The main power plant in Aladdin was badly damaged last night by intruders. Much of the city is without power. It causes some inconvenience to our commanders, but our base has its own power supply and is functioning normally. It is your kind who will suffer most." He turned to me, clearly expecting an answer.

"I'm not a member of the underground," I half lied. "I don't know what their specific objectives were. Possibly it was just to make the general populace more resentful of your presence."

"But that's precisely what I don't understand!" he complained. "If the majority of the population is content with the status quo, why do they not help us to identify and neutralize these aberrant individuals? It defies reason!"

I was still finding it difficult to believe that the Lysandrans hadn't encountered anything like this before. It seemed more likely to me that they had managed to control rebellions among their other subject people, and suppressed the knowledge because it contradicted their societal truisms. "Just because most people aren't fighting you in the streets doesn't mean they're content with things the way they are. Some are indifferent, some are frightened, and most lack the means to do anything. Maybe the rebels are prodding them, maybe they're just trying to keep your leaders guessing about what they'll do next. This isn't just happening on Aragon, is it?"

Sylandris always pleaded ignorance when I asked this question, but this time he made a concession. "I have no firsthand knowledge, but there have been indications that this sort of disturbance is common, yes. For a while, we had hoped that it was an isolated phenomenon, but that doesn't seem to be the case. Your entire species is irrational." He subsided and turned to stare out into the distance again. "There is some concern that those of us who have chosen to study your ways may have become infected, corrupted by your defect."

"Why would that be? I haven't heard of any Lysandrans switching sides."

"No, that would be unthinkable. One does not surrender dominance to an inferior. But our two species share another trait. We do not like to admit our mistakes. Sometimes it is necessary to take extraordinary measures to conceal these errors, and sometimes the innocent must suffer along with the guilty." There was a long pause and I was on the verge of taking my leave when he spoke again. "I may be recalled soon. I don't know for certain. If that is the case, I wish you to know Ennis Baxter that I have found much to admire in you and your family. Your mother has treated me with dignity and kindness even when it was obvious that she was uncomfortable in my presence. And you have always seemed to give me a fair hearing even when we could not agree. Your family is, I think, remarkable among your kind."

The compliment made me feel somehow that I had betrayed my duty as a human and I felt a spark of anger. "And did you find Cille also remarkable?" We had not mentioned her since the day she had gone into hiding. It was unfair of me to break that silence, since it was Sylandris who had warned us in time for her to escape.

"Your sibling was perhaps the most remarkable of you all."

"She was sentenced to death because of an accident over which she had no control, and you still wonder why we resent your presence on our world?"

"All of our lives are touched by tragedy at some point. You spread the pain of loss over long durations where we prefer to deal with it as a single event. There are, perhaps, things to be said for both approaches. I cannot deny that forfeiting your sibling's talents was a great loss." He continued to speak of Cille in the past tense, even though he certainly knew she had escaped, largely because of his timely warning. "The acts of sabotage and other violence have been increasing. There are some who believe that the problem lies in our failure to adequately prove our superiority. They feel that a further demonstration may be required and I have been asked to provide suggestions based on my reading of the history of your species. They wish it to be some single act that will establish the fact beyond question."

There was something ominous about that. "What kind of demonstration? What are they planning to do?"

He wouldn't answer, and I finally turned to go. Just before I was out of range, he said something, so faint that I barely heard it. "It would be best to remain at home for the next few days." When I looked back, his head was averted and I realized this was all that he would say.

We heard the news the following afternoon. Lysandran soldiers systematically destroyed one out of every ten residences in Aladdin, Linden, Casper, and most of the other settlements. Safehaven and Goodhost were spared because there had been no serious unrest in either community, but Managansett was included. They were very careful to evacuate the residents, and the only known fatality was a man from Linden who broke free and rushed back into his home while it was still burning. An automated message was sent to every com unit explaining that this was done to educate everyone about the consequences of supporting the rebels, even passively

"It is with great regret that we take such extreme and unfortunate measures, but it has become clear that a demonstration was required. All residents of Aragon are considered citizens of the Lysandran Comity with the rights of any other citizen. However, it is important to remember that with rights come responsibilities, and it is the obligation of each citizen to help us apprehend the deranged individuals who act against their own and the common interest." To the Lysandrans, the rebels were apparently insane. I wondered if that made them sufficiently aberrant that they could be killed with impunity if captured.

The reaction was, of course, just the opposite of what had been intended. I knew that Sylandris had studied human history, and I imagine he was no more surprised than the rest of us. There were riots all over the planet for the next several days, and an unspecified but not insignificant number of Lysandrans were killed or injured. Someone set fire to the barn at the Harwell place, but no one was injured. One of Fossicker's aides was struck by a stone thrown by parties unknown while he was visiting Safehaven. More seriously, someone shot and killed two Lysandrans in Managansett. The public comline was quiet, but through private messages we heard of dozens of incidents elsewhere.

On the third day, a young woman working on a freight barge approached me while we were loading it from the east pier. She said one of the code phrases under her breath, so casually that I almost didn't recognize it. Then it registered and I stiffened, and she put one hand on my arm and suggested we walk a ways along the river.

She was from Gaunt and, quite simply, she wanted me to make trouble. "We'll leave the details up to you. It doesn't have to be anything spectacular, but it needs to be persistent and annoying. The idea is to draw troops away from the big cities, which leaves holes in their defenses there. This area has been very quiet up till now. That has to change."

"Won't they just bring in more personnel from offworld?"

She shook her head. "We don't think they can. In fact, they've continued to send ground troops off planet in the last few weeks despite the trouble we've been causing. It's a safe guess that they're running into difficulties elsewhere."

I never did learn her name, but she was more inclined to talk than our previous contact, so I asked about the Navy. "We don't have many people in Aladdin, and that's where we'd have a better chance of finding out what's going on. There's still some kind of fighting though, because there are three new Crane ships in orbit, and we know they're all heavily damaged."

She also mentioned the attempted assassination of the Lysandran high command. "It was extremely well planned and executed, but not by us. Someone neutralized the automated security system in each sector as the assassin penetrated, reactivating the alarms behind her, and somehow masking the oversight program. During the escape, magnetic locks were overridden, trapping most of the Crane soldiers in isolated compartments until they were able to disable the doors."

"If not by you, then who was responsible?"

She shrugged. "We're not the only game in town. There's enough going on in and around Aladdin that we're sure there's an organized group there. The rest could be random or spontaneous, particularly in Tyrada. Lots of hotheads there."

We couldn't talk much longer. The loading was finished and she boarded the barge. I never saw her again.

Kelli and I had been thinking and talking about this for some time, and we'd even drawn up a list of people we thought we could trust. Zai and Jeb were high on the list, but Kelli had reservations about Garner so we omitted him. Her father was certainly trustworthy, but he seemed to have lost most of his will to live following Lemayel's presumed death, and in any case Kelli was reluctant to put him in harm's way. I trusted Dan Kater, Jill Garner, and Grant Colson, and Kelli added Suki North from the medstation. We ignored Brodie Bors, Evan Carter, and their friends as being too undisciplined and erratic.

We approached them singly or together over the course of the next few days. Jill was initially cool, but I think that was because of our personal history, and the day after I broached the idea, she tracked me down, apologized, and volunteered. Colson was the only problem.

"They watch me too closely. I'd be putting everyone at risk if I got directly involved. I'll keep my eyes and ears open, though, and see if I can mislead the Cranes if they start looking in the right direction."

We had our first clandestine meeting a few days later, hiding in plain sight. Dan had dated Suki a few times before they decided it wouldn't work, so it didn't raise any eyebrows, or the Lysandran equivalent, when we invited them out to our place as a couple. Mom knew what was going on, of course, and she kept tabs on Sylandris and his two guards, to make sure they didn't drop in on us unexpectedly.

That first evening we threw ideas at one another, some of them absurd, some unworkable, some too dangerous. Our problem was a lack of targets. Fossicker and the others at Harwell house numbered ten, six soldiers and four civilians. There were four more soldiers living in Safehaven now, quartered in the small hostel next door to the magistrate's office. There were occasional visitors, but we never knew when they were coming or going. The only other Lysandrans in the area were Sylandris and his two guards, and I declared them off limits. There was too much risk to Mom, and it would bring unwanted attention to the farm. What I didn't say was that I felt that I still owed Sylandris for having warned us about the threat to Cille.

We also catalogued our weapons, which didn't take long at all. Dan had a couple of hand weapons like those we used to hunt vermin, not much more than toys. Suki knew enough to fashion poisons and had access to the right chemicals, Jill had a laser torch, and I knew where to get explosives that wouldn't be missed. We had nothing that could damage a flitter, and Dan's hand weapons wouldn't penetrate Lysandran body armor.

Our first efforts were almost laughable. Suki and I planted a makeshift bomb behind the hostel, but we did something wrong because the brunt of the blast was away from the building, so all we gained were broken windows. The Lysandrans weren't even there at the time. The following evening Jill and Dan set fire to the untended field behind Harwell house. We hadn't had rain for a while and it spread so quickly they were lucky to get away themselves. Fossicker and the others evacuated the building, but the wind shifted and the fire eventually burned itself out. They might not even have realized the fire was set and not natural.

Kelli was the one who drew first blood, and it was completely unplanned.

She had gone into Safehaven to visit her father, whose mood swings had become increasingly severe. After convincing him to take the medication Suki had provided, she went for an extended walk, which took her out of the town and along the Jackknife. She was just above Satan's Throat when she heard some splashing, and a moment later she spotted a Lysandran wading, if not exactly swimming, in a shallow, quiet backwater. The Lysandran equivalent of an assault rifle stood propped up against a tree along with some other gear and the elaborate cloak and sash combination they habitually wore.

Kelli acted instinctively, moved through the underbrush so that she couldn't be seen until the last possible moment, then burst into a run as she crossed the open space. She had the weapon in her hand and was spinning to run back toward town when something twisted under her foot and she fell flat on her face, hard enough to stun her. It took her a few seconds to draw a breath and roll over onto her back, and by then the soldier was out of the water and coming toward her.

Lysandran hands aren't all that different from those of humans and their weapons functioned in much the same fashion, although theirs were much quieter than ours. More through luck than intent, she fired and hit the soldier in the head. He toppled backward into the water without uttering a sound and never moved again. Kelli wrapped the weapon in the Lysandran's cloak and hid it in a hollow tree half a mile upstream before returning to town and taking the flitter back to the house.

She was dry eyed and seemingly calm when I came home later that day, but her hands were shaking, her eyes red and cheeks swollen. I don't think she slept very well that night.

There was considerable commotion the next day. I found an excuse to visit Safehaven because I wanted to gauge the Lysandran reaction, and got more than I bargained for. There were four military transports in the center of town and more of the aliens than I had ever seen in one place before. I was stopped and searched twice, once rather roughly, before I reached Colson's office. He was there with his deputy, Vallencourt, and six Lysandrans, one of whom was clearly an officer.

"What's going on, Grant?"

"Who is this person?" The speaker was a shorter than average Lysandran whom I didn't believe I'd ever seen before. He spoke fluently but with a tendency to clip off the ends of his words as though he couldn't wait for them to be out of his mouth.

Colson identified me and the interpreter consulted a hand held electronic device of some sort. "What is your purpose here at this time?"

"We've had some vandalism at the farm." True enough, after a fashion. Jeb and I had spray painted some anti-Lysandran slogans on the sides of two barns as camouflage. Everyone knew that Sylandris was living at the farm. We had decided to make a token effort against him to avoid suspicion.

"That'll have to wait, Ennis. We have bigger problems. A Lysandran soldier has been killed." The interpreter gave Colson what I suspected was a dirty look, but didn't interrupt him. "His weapon was stolen as well, but it's been recovered."

The interpreter's voice thrummed with anger. "It is not necessary to explain in such detail at the present time." Colson blinked at me and I guessed that this had been a warning. Kelli and I had already decided to make no effort to recover the weapon for the time being, and now there was no point. I had little doubt that the area was being quietly monitored in hope of capturing whoever was responsible. It surprised me that they'd found Kelli's hiding place so quickly, but we would learn later that Lysandran weapons had a small transmitter embedded in them so that they could be traced and recovered.

"Vallencourt will take down the particulars, Ennis. I hope it's nothing serious."

The repercussions became more obvious over the course of the next several days. The contingent at Harwell house doubled in size and two small buildings were seized in Safehaven and used as security checkpoints. Random searches of homes, businesses, and travelers became much more common. Resentment against the invaders had faded somewhat because of their relatively benign rule but now there were open murmurs of discontent and anger. Colson was effectively relieved of his authority and a Lysandran named Orchistralus accompanied him at all times, giving instructions in barely intelligible fashion. The military officer and interpreter left that first day, returning to the larger base they occupied in Managansett.

Kelli never talked directly about the incident again, but there was a change in her demeanor that possibly only I noticed. She'd grown somehow harder, almost as though she resented the Lysandrans for having put her in a position where she'd had to kill. I tried to help her deal with it, but it was hard because she refused to discuss what she was feeling. I let the others know what had happened, and suggested that we put our other plans on hold for a while, since the Lysandrans were unusually alert at the moment. No one argued, but unfortunately we weren't the only ones planning things.

Brodie Bors was killed one morning when he and three others ambushed, or rather tried to ambush, a Lysandran security team. Brodie died on the spot, cut down by several rounds as he sat in a tree holding a totally inadequate hand weapon. Kimberly Carter was wounded, managed to elude capture for a while, but was arrested at home a few hours later. Two others escaped, apparently uninjured, and I was reasonably sure they were Evan Carter and Teddy Wilber, because both boys disappeared that same day. None of the Lysandrans were injured.

There was pandemonium in Safehaven. People argued in the streets, in their homes, in the shops. Some were angry that the recent incidents had focused so much Lysandran attention on our community; others wanted to storm the magistracy and liberate the Carter girl. This last would have been a wasted effort since she was already en route to Aladdin for interrogation. We never saw her again, and even years later no one knows exactly what became of her. The Lysandrans stepped up their patrols and Colson quietly moved from group to group, counseling patience and restraint. A few people even listened to him.

I spent a lot of time shuttling back and forth among Safehaven, the house at South Brook, and the farm. Sylandris was avoiding me again, and Mom told me he spent most of his time by himself, either shut up in his room or out in the fields somewhere. "If he was a human, I'd say he was suffering from depression. I think the two guards are uneasy about the situation as well. They talk together quietly all the time, and they watch him closely now."

I told her my suspicion that Sylandris was part of a faction that was losing influence. "Lysandrans seem to believe that defeats are almost always permanent. If another party establishes superiority, he'll accept the new status quo and make no effort to change it, even if he still feels that he was right. That's why they're so ineffective dealing with the rebels; it would be unthinkable for Lysandrans to rise against a conquering power."

"It's more than that," she insisted. "I think we've corrupted him. I made a comment the other day about wondering what it must be like to be one of his people, and he told me he was no longer certain of that himself."

I had no time for Sylandris' problems, however. There was farm business to be dealt with, followed by a short, private conversation with Zai and Jeb, and then the trip back home. First dusk was ending and a deeper darkness was spreading through the trees as I landed the flitter. Kelli was spending the night in Safehaven; her father's decline continued despite Suki's best efforts. I had eaten before leaving the farm and I was so tired that I'd had visions of my bed during the short trip.

The moment I entered the house, I knew that I wasn't alone. I don't know what subliminal clue told me, perhaps a hint of unfamiliar body odor, or a sound so low that I didn't consciously hear it. In any case, when I called up the lights I was crouched warily, wondering if Gaunt had sent another messenger, or if Evan Carter was hiding in my kitchen, or perhaps I had an apolitical burglar. We locked the doors when we went out, most of the time, but the house wasn't a fortress; it wouldn't take much effort to get past the safeguards.

I was considering a rush for the kitchen to get some sort of weapon when a figure stepped out of the shadowy hall. It was a good sized human, wrapped in a dark cloak that looked almost Lysandran. Then the cloak was drawn back and a familiar voice filled the room.

"Hello, Ennis. It's been a long time." The voice sounded pleasant, friendly.

It took me a couple of tries to find my voice, and when I did, it was neither friendly nor welcoming. "Hello, Melody. What are you doing here?"

CHAPTER THIRTEEN

Melody looked very much the same as she had when she left Safehaven. She was older certainly, and there was a short scar on her temple that I didn't remember. But she remained fit and moved with a lithe grace that I both remembered and envied. She came out into the light and smiled, but it was guarded, and her eyes watched me alertly. Physically she wasn't very different, but I realized I was talking to a stranger who just happened to have been someone I knew a long time ago.

"I'd like to say I'm just looking up old friends, but that wouldn't be true. I was sent to you by someone who thought you might be able to help me."

"Help you do what?" We were both still standing, and I felt no inclination to offer her a seat. After all, I hadn't even invited her in.

"Stay out of sight. I've become a bit of a celebrity with our visitors." I must have looked blank, because she elaborated. "You know, the Cranes? They're taking Aladdin apart piece by piece looking for me."

"You always were popular." She cracked a smile and I relented and gestured for her to sit down. "Can I get you something, or have you already raided the kitchen?"

"A cold drink would be nice." I took my time getting it, so that I could organize my thoughts.

"So why are the Lysandrans looking for you?"

She took a long, slow sip and when she raised her head, her eyes were staring at something not in the room with us. "I killed a few of them. They get very upset when inferior beings don't act the part."

In that instant I knew what she'd done, but I had to ask anyway, just to be certain. "You're the assassin who got into their headquarters, aren't you?"

"Yes." She didn't seem particularly proud or happy, which made me feel a little better. "I'm surprised you've heard about it. They keep most of the bad news bottled up."

"I'm not completely cut off here. I've had word from the underground from time to time."

She looked surprised, then nodded to herself. "Gaunt's people. We've been trying to make contact with them, but they're very careful."

"You're not part of his organization?"

Melody shook her head. "Gaunt works out of Tyrada and sometimes Casper. We think he has agents in Aladdin but we've never been able to identify any of them. No, Gaunt didn't send me."

"Then who did?"

She wet her lips and lowered her voice. "Your sister Cille sent me. She said things were quiet down here and that you had the resources to keep me out of sight for a while. They have security surveillance tapes of me and it would jeopardize our entire group if I stayed where there was a good chance I might be captured."

I was stunned, but my eventual response was to laugh at myself. I'd known all along that Cille wasn't likely to hide in a dark basement and wait for things to get better. It shouldn't have surprised me to find that she'd become an underground leader, but somehow it did, and it upset me as well. But I'd have to think about that later. "Not as quiet as you might think." I told her about the botched ambush, the Lysandran Kelli had killed – although I didn't identify her, and mentioned that there had been several other recent incidents, but I didn't identify any of the participants and I didn't tell her that Kelli and I had recruited our own little resistance group. "Gaunt has people stirring things up here to take some of the pressure off the cities and thin out the occupation forces."

She bit her lip. "Then maybe I should go elsewhere."

I shook my head. "No, you're as safe here as anywhere. We have places you should be able to stay out of sight." There were the caves where Cille had stayed briefly, and Jeb had quietly built up caches of supplies in two or three remote locations in case we were forced to go into hiding. "I warn you, though. It probably won't be as comfortable as what you and Cille may be used to, wherever she's been hiding."

If Melody detected my not particularly subtle effort to find out where Cille was located, or at least under what conditions she was living, she ignored me, but she did seem actually grateful. "Thanks. Cille said I could count on you, and I remember you as a friend, but so much has changed since the Cranes came, I'm never certain of anything anymore. You seem like a different person, much more mature and wary."

"I guess we've all changed a lot since the invasion." I was about to say something about how different she was, but then I remembered Martin Harwell's death. No matter how justified it might have been, she'd committed the crime cold bloodedly and had covered it up afterward. I couldn't say that I was truly surprised to hear that she'd killed again.

"So will you help me?" Suddenly she seemed much younger, more vulnerable, and I softened and assured her that she'd come to the right place. It wasn't until later that I decided her change of demeanor had been calculated to evoke just that kind of response in me. It was then that I realized that I still admired and respected Melody, but I didn't particularly like her any more.

She spent the night in our store room. I thought about calling Kelli to give her a guarded version of what was going on, but there was always the possibility that the Lysandrans were monitoring com traffic despite their assurances to the contrary. Early the following morning, I told Melody to stay inside and out of sight, probably unnecessarily, then went into Safehaven. Kelli was already up and ready to go when I arrived, but her face looked drawn.

"He's not doing well, Ennis. It's like the life is draining right out of him. He seems older and smaller every time I see him, and his mind wanders. Last night he was talking about Lemayel as though he were still here."

I sympathized as best I could, then told her about our unexpected visitor. Her expression didn't change but I could tell by the set of her shoulders that she wasn't happy about the situation. "What are we going to do with her?"

I'd given that some thought. It was possible that we could have passed her off as a new hire for field work, but there had already been one random search of the barracks by a Lysandran patrol, and it seemed to risky. On the other hand, one of the caves in the Serrated Hills had been pretty well stocked, and Jeb had even moved in bedding and spare clothing. It wasn't luxurious, but it was habitable, and it had the advantage of being well concealed. We could take her there during the night, although even that was somewhat risky; if a Lysandran patrol flew over using infrared, they might not spot us while we were moving along a ravine, but for at least part of the trip we'd be out in the open. The alternative was to brazen it out and go by day. Jeb had fashioned a crossbow for himself and made a point of spending some of his free time in the forest there, hunting skimbats and other native pests for sport, while secretly carrying in more supplies.

The house looked deserted when we got home and I wondered briefly if Melody had decided to seek help elsewhere. But she was waiting inside, not revealing herself until it was obvious that we were alone. Kelli greeted her hospitably if not warmly, and the brief, inconsequential conversation that followed was cool and proper, though both women seemed to relax toward the end.

"How long do you plan to stay in the area?" asked Kelli, finally bringing up the subject at hand.

Melody shrugged. "I have no idea. Until I hear otherwise, or more likely until you hear otherwise. The Cranes may all look the same to us, but they can tell humans apart, and they know what I look like." Actually, I had little difficulty telling most Lysandrans apart now, although they did vary considerably less than human stock. The hue of their skins was the most obvious distinction, and their faces were as differentiated as our own. But I'd had more leisure to study them from close proximity, particularly Sylandris and his guards, than had most humans.

I commed Jeb and asked him to drop off some tools when he had a chance, our pre-arranged code indicating that I wanted to see him. He showed up within the hour, showed no reaction when I told him about Melody and what I wanted him to do.

"Tonight would be best. It's going to be stormy and they don't do as much patrolling when the weather is bad. I can swing by at dusk, pick her up, and leave the flitter at Barbecue Hill. We'll have good cover from there and it's only a half hour or so each way."

For more than one reason, I was impatient to have Melody out of my home. Jeb's plan was sound. When we presented it to Melody, she nodded. "Whatever you think's best. Frankly, a nice cozy little cave sounds very appealing right now. Except for one day spent in the cargo hold of one of your barges, I've been traveling on foot ever since I left Aladdin."

I had business to deal with that day, mostly negotiations with the consortium that was trying to set shipping prices on the Jackknife all the way to Junction. I didn't get home until late in the afternoon, and by then there was a noticeable thaw between Melody and Kelli, who'd made her up a package of fancy foods to take with her. "Jeb's a dear, but he'd live on the same three meals forever if left to his own devices, and I suspect the supplies he's packed away will be pretty monotonous."

A few hours later, Melody had gone off with Jeb, and I found myself feeling considerably relieved by her absence. It wasn't her fault, of course, but Melody's arrival had underlined for me the increasingly dangerous game we were all playing. As conquerors go, they Lysandrans hadn't been too repressive so far. But I was beginning to think that what was bothering Sylandris was not so much frustration about their inability to understand us, but fear that they were learning too much, and that the knowledge was corrupting his superiors.

The level of unrest in Safehaven grew steadily, though I'd have to admit that much of it was independent of our efforts to stir things up. On several occasions, objects were thrown at Lysandran soldiers, resulting in three arrests. Sean Mercuriopolous was badly beaten by two Lysandrans when they caught him trying to set fire to one of their guard stations. He ended up recuperating while locked in one of the two cells in Colson's makeshift jail. We tried to do our part as well. Dan Kater actually managed to disable the steering system on one of their transports right under the noses of a security guard. The Lysandrans could eat human food if they took some sort of supplement, but they periodically received shipments off their own supplies as well, and Suki managed to contaminate part of one of these so badly that they destroyed the entire consignment. Jeb and I set another fire at the Harwell farm, but other than disturb their night's rest, it did no real damage.

There was more and greater violence elsewhere. Some of the reports that reached us were false, some greatly exaggerated, but the preponderance of the information convinced us that the rebels, both Gaunt's group and others, were stepping up their campaign. There were stories of ambushed patrols and snipers almost every day, mostly from the northwest, presumably carried out using the weapons smuggled in from offworld.

The most significant incident, if it wasn't a fortuitously coincidental accident, was the explosion of a Lysandran shuttle shortly after takeoff from Aladdin Port. The wreckage fortunately fell in an uninhabited area, but the military command in Aladdin was livid. A citywide curfew went into effect, and was later declared in Casper and Tyrada as well. Colson told me that he'd actually received contradictory instructions from the Lysandran military authorities, the first time that had ever happened.

"If they were human, I'd say they were panicking. But it's a funny kind of panic, if that's what it is. They seem more confused and surprised than frightened or angry. Say what you want about them, they've always appeared to be disciplined and well organized up till now."

"Sometimes you can wind a spring too tightly," I said quietly. It was reassuring to hear that the Lysandrans were capable of making serious mistakes, but it was also worrisome. Their responses to violence up to now had been restrained by human standards. I wondered how much longer that would last.

I wouldn't want you to think that the Lysandrans were the only things we thought about at the time. We continued to manage the farm, turning a much smaller profit than usual thanks to disruptions in our shipping patterns, some unusually cold weather, and a particularly bad bluebug infestation. We even had another wormswell out in the rollers, although it was small and did very little damage. The west pier construction project was completed, we completely refurbished the larger north pier, and Mom talked us into upgrading the field hands' barracks. Every few weeks we'd get a recording from Cille, but there was never anything of consequence in it. We still didn't know for certain where she was hiding, and she never mentioned the underground or even the Lysandrans except in passing. But it was good to know that she was still alive and apparently well.

Melody made her cave quite comfortable. I only visited her there once, ostensibly accompanying Jeb on one of his hunting trips, and only for a very brief time. She seemed to have adapted to the solitude reasonably well, although she was obviously starved for conversation. She wanted to know if I'd heard anything further from

Cille and I admitted that I had, but that her own situation had not been mentioned. "I doubt that she'd record anything like that. If it fell into the wrong hands, it could compromise your safety."

"I wouldn't expect her to record anything, but she could have sent a messenger." She sighed. "I guess I should have known this wouldn't be a short term situation." She glanced around the cave. It was well lit, but shielded so the light wouldn't spill outside after dark. "When I joined the underground, I didn't expect it to be so literal."

We talked for a while, and I felt something of her old charm. But I had changed and she had changed. There was something different in her voice, her posture, the way she always took a position where she could watch the cave entrance, even a certain wariness if I moved suddenly or approached too closely. It made me uncomfortable after a while and I fumbled for excuses to leave, finally found one that seemed plausible and escaped.

Two days later, Kelli's father died. A Lysandran patrol had chosen his house for a random search. When he hadn't responded to their arrival quickly enough, they'd smashed open his door. He came out of his bedroom shouting and waving his arms and they raised their weapons. Although rumors spread through Safehaven that he'd been killed by the soldiers, the truth was that he had a stroke and died at their feet. They did call for medical assistance, perhaps even promptly, but he was beyond help when Suki arrived.

Kelli had never been very emotionally demonstrative, and she received the news with apparent calm. I sensed the danger signs immediately, of course. Suki had come up to the house to deliver the news personally rather than use the com. Kelli insisted on brewing salsa tea even though no one really wanted any, and I could have told by the precision with which she arranged the cups on the tray and measured out the tea that she was under great stress even if I hadn't already known the circumstances. Suki must have sensed something as well, because she finished her tea quickly and took her leave.

I tried to talk to her about it, but all she would say was "Not now." If she cried during the night, I never heard her, and she was up before me in the morning. Over breakfast, she asked me if anyone had come up with some new way to harass the Lysandrans. I mentioned a few ideas that had come up recently, most of them rather petty, some impractical.

"Those are all children's games," she said with unusual heat. "We have to do something serious, something that will make them hurt the way we're hurting." I remembered that she was the only one of our group who had actually killed one of the invaders.

"We don't have the resources for anything more serious. The few small arms we've been able to hide won't penetrate that body armor they've taken to wearing. They've confiscated most of the explosives." Jeb had been experimenting with organic fertilizers and some of the chemicals in common use for soil treatment or insect control, but so far all he'd been able to manage was a noxious smelling smokebomb.

"Well we have to do something." Her voice crackled with tension.

"We will, Kelli. I promise." She subsided them, but I didn't think she was mollified. I had planned to spend the day at the farm but I commed Jeb and made alternate arrangements, not wanting to leave Kelli by herself. But even though I stayed with her throughout that day, I'm not sure that she was anything but alone.

Our impotence did not afflict the underground elsewhere. The Lysandrans were still not interfering with personal communications, although there were persistent rumors that they had begun monitoring the com lines more closely. Even after making allowances for exaggerations and mistakes, it was obvious that the rebels had become more organized, more ambitious, and more effective. The military commander at Linden was killed by a sniper, who died as well after a brief chase through the hills north of the settlement. One of the barracks compounds near Tyrada was overrun by a large and well armed force. There were reliable reports that between forty and fifty Lysandrans had been killed, some by their own people when it became obvious that their wounds were too serious. Half a dozen humans died there, and one was captured, a man named Devenwell, who was reported to have died of natural causes several weeks later, but since he was still a prisoner at the time, it was widely believed that he had been tortured to death. In fact, the Lysandrans never mistreated their prisoners that we know of, except to euthanize those with disabling wounds, a fact that is not unfortunately true of our own side.

There were several incidents of sabotage at Aladdin spaceport. At least one shuttle was misdirected and badly damaged when it landed on a drainage filtration bed instead of a reinforced pad. There were several power failures at critical times, and the orbital communications array was slightly damaged by a bomb. Lysandrans could no longer travel the streets in small parties, even armed, and humans had been banned from the Lysandran quarters, which had been consolidated into one large compound surrounded by a makeshift wall and armed guards. The existing buildings had been modified and supplemented, and all had walls reinforced to resist explosives. A few rockets and makeshift mortar rounds had been fired into the compound irregularly ever since the occupation began, but there were no reliable reports of any resulting damage.

Kelli relished every rumor and I think she fooled herself into believing even those stories that were obviously false. On the other hand, she seemed uninterested in the plans our little local group was making, and didn't participate in the small forays we made, breaking the windows at the Harwell farm one night, setting fire to one of the reinforced guard stations that had sprung up on strategic corners in Safehaven, We all shared her frustration to some extent; we knew that our activity was more prankish than rebellious. But we lacked two important elements. We didn't have the equipment required for a more serious assault, and frankly we were short of targets. The Harwell farm was heavily guarded now; we'd almost been caught during our rock throwing spree. Safehaven was monitored day and night, usually by groups of three soldiers based in the guard stations during the day, by hovering military flitters using infrared and other sensory equipment by night. They were frequently in the magistrate's office, and continued to conduct random searches of other buildings, but followed no pattern that we could predict and use to lay a trap. While off duty, the military contingent lived in a riverside warehouse they'd converted, and which was surrounded by very alert perimeter guards.

Jill Garner and Suki both spent considerable time recording their movements, trying to detect patterns, weak spots. They received fresh supplies every ninth day from an armored transport flier that would not have been economical for use commercially but which was faster and less vulnerable than the barges we employed for our own shipments. Although Lysandrans could get along quite well consuming human food and breathing our atmosphere, there were some trace elements that required supplements. They had also hermetically sealed one portion of the warehouse and used canisters of pure oxygen to recreate an atmosphere closer to their own. I imagine they received some form of electronic mail from home, and we knew for certain that they occasionally received personal packages, but we were surprised not to be able to discern any form of entertainment. No one had ever heard Lysandran music, if such existed. Their reading material all appeared to be instructional or historical. I had once invited Sylandris to watch a holofilm with me, but when I told him that it was not a true story, he had seemed puzzled. The next time I offered, he declined, and I never suggested it again.

I was beginning to get seriously worried about Kelli, although much of the time I fooled myself into believing she was going through a normal period of grief. She had become obsessed with the Lysandrans and was frequently irritable and impatient when we got our little cell together to discuss options. She was only slightly placated when Dan Kater managed to sabotage one of their fuel cells, causing a patrol skimmer to crash rather violently into the front of Sean Mercuriopolous' tavern. The pilot was hurt badly enough that he was evacuated by air for medical treatment, but we never did find out whether or not his injuries were so severe that he was euthanized. Grant Colson told me later that the incident had been dismissed as an accident. The Lysandrans continued to have blind spots about the conduct of a guerilla war.

Kelli and I didn't talk much about other things, although I made frequent efforts to break the silence. When we made love, it was quick, intense, and oddly impersonal. She disposed of her father's estate dispassionately and efficiently, and the only time she showed any hint of loss was when she visited his alcove in the small cemetery building in Safehaven. I realized that I was making excuses to visit the farm because it was so difficult to be around her when she was so obviously in pain and I was so obviously unable to help. Remorseful, I almost neglected my duties for a while, and probably made things worse by hovering so much. We didn't fight, but when we talked, it was never about what we should have been talking about.

I had expected, and hoped, that her fervent desire to strike back at the Lysandrans would cool as the days passed, but it didn't. At times I was actually glad that we didn't have the opportunity to engage in more direct action, because I feared that she would do something foolhardy. I was caught in whirling tidepools of ambivalence about the whole situation, and when our cell met, I frequently let Jeb or Suki lead the discussion even though I had been informally proclaimed cell leader. Kelli always attended, but she rarely contributed, and was almost always openly dissatisfied. I felt trapped by the situation, unable to move forward, unwilling to step back. I wished profoundly that something would happen to alter the status quo.

I got my wish, but not in the way I had intended.

Most of my day had been spent at the farm, plotting next year's crops and market strategy with Mom, Jeb, and Zai. Garner Elsevier had given notice and moved to Casper to take a position there, and none of us were particularly upset by his departure. Garner was something of a bully and he'd mildly mistreated a worker recently. It had taken considerable effort to smooth over the injured man's feelings. The four of us sat around a terminal evaluating various scenarios, then plotting likely yields against a trends analysis of demand. Jeb favored moving almost entirely to staples.

"Things are too unsettled right now. People aren't willing to take chances even in their diet, and they're certainly not willing to spend credit unnecessarily."

Zai, on the other hand, thought the mood was changing. "The occupation is more than two years old. People are wary, but they're getting tired of being frightened all the time, and they're overdue for some illogical discretionary spending. Since they can't buy the exotic items like holofilms, VR games, and other things that we used to be able to import, they're going to have to settle for what's available. And let's face it, even before the Lysandrans came, there wasn't much of a luxury business on Aragon. If we offer something even as trivial as an unusual grain or fruit, someone's going to buy it."

I leaned toward Zai's position because the small crop of delicacies we'd produced during the last two seasons had turned a good profit, but Mom had grown more conservative as time passed and she supported Jeb. We eventually worked out a compromise with which we were all equally dissatisfied, so it seemed likely to be a good one.

That day would be the last time I talked to Sylandris for a very long time. He was sitting outside on the porch, watching first dusk settle around us, and I almost walked past him without speaking. I hated to admit it to myself, but I rather liked Sylandris despite the conditions of our meeting, and given Kelli's current mood, it seemed particularly traitorous to offer him even a few polite words. We had talked about his vulnerability in our cell meetings, but not even Kelli wanted to cause trouble at the farm where Mom might possibly be in danger. Dan Kater had argued that we were drawing unwanted attention to her by not acting against him, so we'd decided to stage some minor incident as camouflage, but to date we hadn't come up with anything workable.

"How much longer will you be visiting us, Sylandris?"

His head slowly turned to look up at me. "Are you asking me to leave your home, Ennis Baxter? Am I no longer welcome? Have I done something so objectionable that you withdraw your hospitality?"

"You were never welcomed into our home or our world, Sylandris. Nor were you or your people invited." I paused to let that sink in, then relented and settled into a chair beside him. "Had you come openly and in friendship, that might have been different. We are not as much unlike one another as you believe."

He nodded, a gesture he'd picked up from us. It made him seem more human, more a person. "I no longer know myself what I believe about such things. In some ways, you are right; in others, we are more different than any of us might have guessed. Or at least, we were. You have changed me, Ennis Baxter, you and your mother and your world. You may have changed my race as well. Only time will reveal the result of this merging."

"You've been here since the invasion," I said slowly. "Don't you miss your family? Your friends?"

"I have duties and they have required that I remain here." There was a whispery undertone in his voice that I had never heard before. I was certain that it reflected an emotional state, but had no idea what it might be. Sadness? Regret? Grief? Anger? Frustration? They all seemed possible. "Duties, yes. I have more duties than I have friends or family, Ennis Baxter. Would it be a grave insult if I numbered you among my friends? I know that you must share the animosity of your people toward all Lysandrans, but I would like to think that beneath it all, we have touched one another on some level. You have always treated me with respect even though there is no clear dominance relationship between us."

"Can respect be mutual if one being is dominant to another?"

"Certainly. I respect my superiors for their achievements and judgment. They respect me for the able performance of my duties." He hesitated. "Although there are, I admit, some who feel I have not fulfilled my potential in that regard."

"Because you have not figured us out?"

"No. Because I believe that I have. My conclusions do not sit well with those who have reviewed them, and it has been suggested that I be more assiduous in discovering a more palatable truth."

"I thought Lysandrans believed that there was only one truth, one optimal answer to every question."

"You are correct, Ennis Baxter. Lysandrans believe that there is one preferred solution to every problem, that every question has its answer, and that the answer can be reached by logical thought. The problem is that I am no longer certain that I am still properly speaking a Lysandran."

I was still puzzling over that when I got back to the house. Kelli was waiting inside, sitting quietly in a chair facing the door. Although she remained still, I had a sense of frantic, invisible motion and I knew something was up even before she spoke.

"We've had visitors while we were out," she said quietly. "They're gone now but they've left us some presents." She nodded toward the oversized wicker storage bin we kept in the corner. It was normally filled with old clothing, blankets, and other materials we would eventually take to the Safehaven recycling center. I've never pretended to be psychic, but there was a sense of ominous danger almost tangible in the room, and I walked to the basket on shaky legs.

There was a bit of an anticlimax when I opened the lid, because staring up at me was the sweater I'd torn while inspecting the underside of the east pier a few weeks earlier. Hesitantly I reached out and pushed it aside. Beneath it lay four military issue assault lasers, rechargeable, each wrapped in transparent plasticene.

"Was there a note?" I asked, my voice suddenly hoarse.

"No, nothing. But I think the message is obvious." She stood up and crossed the room, caught my upper arm with both hands. "I think they want us to turn up the heat." The pleasure with which she said it made my skin crawl.

CHAPTER FOURTEEN

Kelli had found a note when she returned home, containing one of the code words we'd been given and directing her attention to the basket. She hadn't touched them, had just destroyed the note and waited for me to return. There was no possible way I was going to leave those weapons in the house overnight. We'd already been searched once by a Lysandran patrol and they'd been quite thorough. Kelli seemed reluctant to part with them, but she conceded the point. It was not a risk worth taking. There was a small cave not far from the house, hardly more than a crawlspace. Jesper and I had played in there occasionally as children, but it was a tight fit for me now and I scraped a shoulder getting them inside. I figured they'd be safe from the elements, wrapped as they were. It was located in a small gully about twenty minutes walk away; I wasn't about to risk carrying them in a vehicle, particularly at night. Kelli insisted on coming along, and I wondered if she didn't trust me to tell her where I was hiding them. Her enmity toward the Lysandrans had become the dominant force in our life, and though I shared her desire to restore Aragon's freedom and expel the invaders, I worried that it had become an obsession with her, that she was more interested in revenge than freedom.

Our wedding anniversary was only a few days away. We hadn't planned much in the way of public celebration, but it would provide a good excuse to assemble all the cell members. I tried to look enthusiastic as I mingled with the two dozen guests who overwhelmed our small home, but I kept looking past the party to what must follow and it made me nervous. It wasn't difficult to convince people to leave at a reasonable hour; no one had been feeling very festive lately, and they knew there was a good chance they'd be stopped and searched if they were traveling late at night. Eventually the seven of us were alone.

I watched them carefully, gauging reactions, as I told them about the weapons. Zai was her usual inscrutable self, Jeb nodded gently and looked serious. Jill Garner and Suki North were openly uncomfortable. Only Dan Kater betrayed any enthusiasm, and it was cautious. Kelli seemed to be watching them as well, and she spoke up irritably.

"This is what we've all been waiting for, isn't it? Now we have a way to do some real damage."

"It certainly gives us more options," admitted Suki. "But there are still only seven of us and four weapons. We're hardly in a position to storm their compound."

"They usually fly patrols at night. We could ambush them, shoot them down." Dan looked around the room for support.

"Their flitters are too well armored for that," said Jeb. "A laser would cut through it eventually, but we don't want to be waiting around that long."

Kelli made an impatient gesture. "They're still sending out parties on foot. They're vulnerable."

I glanced toward Jill. She'd been collating our information on Lysandran troop movements. "They're out at early most mornings and they continue well into the evening. There are a few random search patterns, but they've pretty well settled into a handful of predictable ones. We can't pinpoint the exact time they'll reach a particular spot, but it's very unusual for them to follow an alternative route. In Safehaven proper the patrols are pretty small, but out in the countryside, there's always at least six, sometimes eight."

"But we'll have the element of surprise on our side." Kelli's eyes danced around the room, watching people's reaction. "And we won't be fighting a pitched battle with them. We kill as many as we can in the first few seconds, then escape while they're looking for cover."

I'd been silent up to now, because like it or not, everyone except Kelli and Jill deferred to my opinion, and I wanted to know how the others felt before I said anything. "We're not going to devise a plan tonight, but we need to start thinking about what our next step should be. Dan, why don't you and Jill go through her data and decide which of the patrols gives us the safest, simplest opportunity. We'll have to go over the ground where we plan to hit them and make sure we can get to cover quickly. Unless we manage to kill them all in the first few seconds, which seems unlikely, they'll call for help."

Suki had been staring down into her lap, but now her head came up. "They only have three military flitters here now; they sent the other two to Managansett." But they can still respond to an attack anywhere in the area within half an hour, faster if they're already in the air."

"Is there any way to predict where they'll be?"

She shook her head. "I've been watching them take off and land from the aid station, and if there's any kind of pattern, it's too sophisticated for me. They tend to be less active at night though."

"They're not much use in wooded areas," interposed Jeb. "But they can illuminate a lot of ground with their lights when they're out in the open. And they're faster than the flitters we're used to."

"All right, are there any other targets we should consider?" I looked around the room. Surprisingly, it was Zai who spoke up. "There are only three of them out at the farm. And the Harwell place is vulnerable."

My first reaction was to veto any action at the farm. I told myself that I didn't want Mom to be involved, but I knew I was also reluctant to move against Sylandris, even if I wasn't ready to reciprocate and call him my friend. It might be possible to pick off one of the guards. "Let's leave the farm out for the time being. It's one of the few places we can get together without attracting attention and if they post more soldiers out there, we're just going to make things more difficult for ourselves. How many do they have guarding Fossicker's group?"

"I counted six the last time I was there." Zai personally delivered food and a few other supplies to the research group, for which we were paid at slightly higher than the market rate. "Plus four civilians. The civilians have weapons, though, but I'm not sure how much threat they pose. They've reinforced the walls, and there are lights and motion detectors all around the place. We wouldn't stand a chance attacking openly with four weapons, but we might be able to snipe at them. The guards are alert but they're frequently exposed."

"Can you and Jeb come up with some specific plans?"

The exchanged glances and both nodded.

"All right. Why don't we take a couple of days to think things through and then meet again. And if anyone thinks of something else, bring that up as well."

We adjourned a few minutes later. Kelli didn't say anything, but she seemed disappointed, as though she'd been expecting us to charge out to begin slaughtering Lysandrans that very evening. I tried to talk about it, but she insisted she was exhausted and went to bed. I followed, but it was a long time before I got to sleep.

Ten days later I killed a sentient being for the first time.

We had decided to raid the Harwell farm first because it seemed to be a marginally easier target. The surrounding fields hadn't been worked in years and were heavily overgrown, discipline among Lysandran civilians appeared slightly more lax, and because we had a lot more freedom to choose the timing of our attack. The buildings and immediate grounds were better defended than a patrol would be, but it was also a good distance from the areas where the flitters usually patrolled. Kelli seemed satisfied once we'd decided, but she was openly impatient during our preparations.

I spent the day before our attack alternating between wild excitement and intense dread. Kelli, Dan Kater, Jill, and I carried the lasers. Jeb and Zai had packs filled with smoke bombs, while Suki acted as control center. We had worked out a simple code so that we could use the coms, and Suki had a receiver tuned to the Lysandran military band. She was the only one of us who spoke more than a few words of Lysandran, although she was far from fluent, and she would be the only one who could transmit, since we didn't want the enemy locating us by tracing our transmissions. Zai and Jeb went in first, planting the explosives in strategic spots just outside their passive defense perimeter. The fuses were commercial ones and could not be traced; every farmer on Aragon had a box or two of them around in case of bluebug infestations. The airborne agents we used to kill them were strong enough to make a human very ill and the countermeasures were always taken from a distance. The smoke was designed to cover our escape, so our raid was going to be short and violent.

We approached from the rear of the house, Kelli and I from the east corner, Dan and Jill from the west. They had the advantage of a deep, jagged gully to cover their approach; we were taking advantage of what had once been Harwell's biggest orchard and which was now heavily overgrown with konga vines and bristlethorns. We were slightly behind schedule because the underbrush was heavier than we had anticipated, but we reached our positions before the first shots were fired. Barely.

The distinctive flashes of laser fire started almost immediately. I heard a window break – explode actually. We were just beyond the perimeter alarms, thanks to Zai's observations, but it almost seemed as though the Lysandrans had been waiting for us. There was immediate answering fire from the house and from some point outside. Another pair of shots splashed harmlessly against the rear wall and I heard at least one of the aliens shout something. A door slammed and two figures rushed out into the night. They used their own weapons immediately, and Dan and Jill began their planned retreat, returning fire sporadically so that it was obvious that they were withdrawing. The Lysandrans immediately pursued them.

That's what we'd been counting on. The floodlights revealed four crouched shapes moving toward the far corner of the building. I turned to signal Kelli but she was already on her feet and her laser hissed softly. I joined her, trying to target the figure closest to us, but he moved more quickly than I expected and when I tried to track him, I lost him behind a tree. We were out of time; those inside were almost certainly calling for help. I looked for another target, saw one stagger and go down, but a split second later the Lysandran moved again and scuttled into cover before I could target him.

"We have to go," I whispered to Kelli, who was still firing almost indiscriminately.

"Not yet!"

"Yes, now!" I moved toward her, crouched over. When I touched her thigh, she jumped away, not having seen me approach, and that saved her life, because an explosive round whooshed past us and impacted against a tree, showering us with splinters and knocking us both from our feet. I sat up, stunned, and saw something rising from the brush, illuminated by a stray laser flash. It was a Lysandran, and there was no possible way he had reached us from the house this quickly. He must have been stationed outside and wisely held his post in anticipation of just what we had planned. The flash faded instantly and I couldn't see him, but I remembered where he'd been and I raised my weapon and fired frantically, three quick blasts. One of them struck home because there was a scream that sounded as though it could have been human. It lasted only for a second.

Kelli was on her feet, and she helped me up. She was still looking toward the buildings and held her weapon up, but this time I grabbed her arm firmly. "We're leaving, Kelli. Now!" Mercifully, this time she obeyed.

As it was we were caught in the smoke, although the night breeze had changed direction in our favor so that we were quickly beyond it, following our prearranged escape route. We crossed into Baxter property before checking in with Suki. None of us could return home until it was clear that no one had been taken, alive anyway, and Kelli and I sat concealed behind a windbreak until everyone else was far enough from the attack site that they could use the com without drawing attention. Then we returned the weapons to the cave and went home.

We heard the official story the next morning. If Kelli was disappointed that only one Lysandran had been killed, she didn't make an issue of it. I felt nauseated but also a bit proud of myself. I had experienced doubts about whether I would actually be able to cause the death of another intelligent being, and now those doubts were over. It would be easier the next time, and the time after that, and with that realization came a sense of accomplishment. Years later I would feel very differently. What I did, what we all did, was necessary, and I feel no guilt about any of those who died at our hands. But I do feel badly that it was easier each time. Killing, no matter how justified, should never be easy.

Kelli wanted us to start planning our next raid immediately, but I insisted that we let things cool down first. Suki informed us that patrol activity had been dramatically increased. "They've brought back one of the flitters from Managansett, and it looks like they're planning to expand the barracks." She was right; a new wing was added to the heavily guarded compound, but not for additional troops. The occupation force was already overcommitted. Instead they brought Fossicker and his crew into Safehaven and abandoned the Harwell place.

It was several days before we found an excuse to get together as a group again. Everyone except Kelli was happy with the results, however limited. When she brought up the question of an attack on one of the patrols, Dan and Jill sided with her immediately. The others shared my opinion that we needed to let things sit for a few more days first. I countered with the suggestion that we target one of Sylandris' guards. "But not Sylandris himself," I cautioned. "He's one of the few sources of information we have about them, and he's in some kind of disfavor with his superiors. Sometimes he says things that I suspect he's not supposed to be talking about and I don't want to lose the chance that he might let something helpful slip."

Jill and Dan seemed amenable to that, and only Zai objected. "If you kill one of his guards, won't they just withdraw him like they did Fossicker?"

It was a good point, but irrelevant. Two days later a flitter picked up Sylandris and the two guards and took them up north. Mom later confessed to me that she'd been very surprised to discover that she started missing him almost immediately. "He was never quite able to figure out whether I was dominant to him or subservient, and there is no such thing as an equal standing between two Lysandrans, so he always acted with exaggerated politeness but with a kind of haughty undertone. I might have found that offensive except that he recognized the contradiction and it rather amused him, I think."

Kelli was delighted with the news, because that left us with only one active plan, ambushing one of the Lysandran patrols.

For a long time afterward, I felt that the disaster that followed was my fault, that I should have convinced the others to be more patient, to plan more carefully, to wait for an optimal opportunity, as Sylandris would no doubt have insisted. But I didn't. Kelli and I had one of our very infrequent arguments the night before we met and made our fatal decision, and I was sulking a little and more than slightly discouraged by my inability to convince her. So it was the normally quiet Zai who led the argument for restraint, with Jeb and I providing lukewarm support. Suki had just finished treating two teenaged girls who were beaten by Lysandran soldiers after they threw paint on the windows of one of the guard posts and she was on the warpath, pushing her into the activist camp. And so it was that we decided to lay a trap for the patrol responsible for the west end of Safehaven and the Carter and Pakarang farms.

This particular patrol covered most of the streets in the western half of Safehaven before setting out into the countryside. Sometimes they crossed the Pakarang farm first, then swept back across Sobriety Carter's property before returning to town. Occasionally they reversed themselves, but they covered almost exactly the same ground, just in a different order. In either case they had to cross the Middling Creek, either on the main bridge or the small footbridge slightly to the north. The former was safer because it was well lit and there was little cover nearby to conceal attackers, but the latter was more direct and faster.

We would set up to hit them on the small bridge, and if they didn't show the first time, we'd try again until they did. There was plenty of cover, including a small hidden cave in one of the steep walls that faced the creek, some very heavy brush, and even an extensive run of ragged, exposed rock with lots of nooks and crannies ideal for concealing assassins. Our plan was to kill as many of them as we could while they were crossing, by dividing ourselves into two teams again, one at each end of the bridge. We still had a few smoke bombs left to cover our escape, but Jeb had warned us he couldn't build any more with his existing stock of supplies. It wouldn't do to arouse suspicion by purchasing more fusing material or any of the other chemicals right now.

Zai and I managed to talk the others into waiting for a dark night, one with heavy cloud cover and preferably some rain. Kelli must have prayed to the weather gods because the sky darkened the following morning and the clouds showed no sign of breaking up throughout the day, although the only rain we had was a short, stinging downpour late in the morning. We met at a deserted spot in a remote corner of Carter's property and redistributed the weapons.

Kelli and I were to take the west side of the bridge, Dan Kater and Zai would cover the east. Suki was serving as coordinator again while Jill and Jeb would cover our retreat. Jeb had fashioned some makeshift rocket launchers to fire off the smokers this time, and we hoped that we could confuse any survivors and make good our escape before help arrived. In retrospect it still seems a good plan to me, and the disaster that followed was a combination of bad luck and our own ineptitude rather than a flaw in our thinking.

We arrived shortly after full dusk and carefully scouted the area to make sure that we were alone. It had started to drizzle and turned cool enough that it was actively unpleasant. I would like to say that I had second thoughts, but the fact was that excitement had overcome, or at least masked, my fears. Kelli and I found good cover only a few meters apart, affording us an excellent view of the bridge and most of the area beneath it. Dan and Zai disappeared into the darkness and took up their positions, while Jeb and Jill were just over the lip of a nearby hill, ready to lob smokers into the area. Suki was further off this time, sitting on the roof of a building in the west end of town. From there we hoped she'd have a better chance of spotting a flitter if any of them started toward us.

We knew the approximate window of time through which the patrol would pass us, if they came this way, and we'd arrived well beforehand. The wait was excruciating, physically as well as mentally. I was squatting in a cleft between two large basalt plates, but there was an overhang that made it impossible for me to straighten completely without stepping out into the open. It wasn't long before my ankles and thighs began to ache, and what small stretching I was able to manage didn't help much. Even worse, the rain had intensified, and there was a steady stream pouring down through the rocks. The runoff would hit little irregularities and spit out in all directions, so that the overhang didn't keep me as dry as I had hoped. Then it began to pool where I was standing, and although my boots kept my feet dry, they didn't keep them very warm. What passed for winters were mild on this part of the planet and I didn't really own any good, cold weather clothing. I preferred to stay in out of the rain rather than be outfitted to deal with it.

Time crawled past and my excitement died down to embers. I'd been staring out into the darkness for so long that my eyes had started to imagine movement where there was none, so when there actually was a change, it took a few seconds for me to believe what I was seeing. Four Lysandran soldiers were crossing the bridge; another pair followed a few paces behind them. The bridge wasn't flat because of a large, humpbacked boulder that lay half in, half out of the water. We had agreed to fire when the first soldier reached the point where the mild incline evened out and started down. I raised the laser to my shoulder and moved the sights to the center of the bridge, and suddenly all of my discomfort was forgotten.

They were silent as they crossed. Among themselves, Lysandrans form friendships just as do humans, but they have an antipathy toward casual conversation. Sylandris rarely spoke to his guards, for example, even though they'd lived pretty much isolated from their fellows for well over a year. Their weapons were in their hands, and their heads slowly moved back and forth as they walked.

Kelli fired first, perhaps a bit too early, and I joined her. Pale beams shot down from the east a split second later. I'd aimed at one of the two leaders, and he fell sprawling on the wooden planking, although I don't know if it was my shot that hit him. One of the second pair spun around, dropped his weapon, and fell back over the side. His partner jumped over after him and scrambled for cover beneath the bridge while the other leader raced away from me. He never made it; either Dan or Zai brought him down. I looked for the third pair and saw them running for cover in the underbrush at our end of the bridge. Although I fired twice, I don't think I hit anything. Kelli was concentrating on the soldier partially hidden below us, but he'd managed to find enough cover to thwart her..

Something exploded above me somewhere and sand and small stones came crashing down past my protective overhang. Someone had fired an explosive round, and a second one splintered a large, gnarled native tree a second later. Three Lysandrans were dead or wounded, one was under the bridge, and two were scrambling through the brush and were not in position to have fired at us. I aimed at the brush where the two soldiers had concealed themselves, starting a small fire with my shot, and a split second later the rock I was leaning against shook as another explosive round impacted against it. There were obviously more than six Lysandrans in this patrol, and some of them had remained behind to cover the others as they crossed the bridge.

It was time to leave.

As if answering my thought, there was a series of six pops in rapid succession as the smokers were fired. One hit the water and did no good, but the others all began emitting billowing clouds of dark smoke that made the night even murkier than it had been before. I climbed up the ledge toward Kelli, who was already moving above me. The smoke didn't reach this high, but it had already put a thick wall between us and the soldiers. All we had to do was stick to our plan and escape into the countryside before a flitter could reach us.

I'll never know what possessed Kelli to turn, shoulder her weapon, and fire down into the murk. Possibly there was an eddy in the smoke that revealed one of the Lysandrans and it was just too tempting to pass up. Maybe she was just overcome by the heat of the moment and couldn't resist a last gesture of defiance. For whatever reason, she took the shot and the flash of discharge must have pinpointed her location for our unseen opponents. The thunderclap of the explosive round knocked me off my feet and I sat down hard, stunned, almost deafened. I held onto my weapon by reflex rather than intention. My mind kept telling me to get up, grab Kelli, and get out of there, but my body didn't want to move. The smoke was rolling up the hillside toward me but the cloud cover overhead suddenly opened up, letting in a slice of starlight that laid a lightly glowing hand on the ground in front of me.

It was just bright enough to show me Kelli's body and even in that dim light I could tell that she was dead. Most of the upper half of her body was gone.

I'm not sure exactly what happened during the next few minutes. Some survival instinct must have taken over because although my conscious mind remained there, stunned, staring at what had been my wife only moments before, my body took itself elsewhere. I don't remember anything else from that moment until I stumbled in the darkness and hit my knee against a rock hard enough to send flaring pain up my leg. That brought back a limited amount of sanity and I stopped, looked around, and realized that I had no idea where I was. Off in the distance, I could see floodlights spearing down from overhead, at least two sets, moving in an obvious search pattern.

There was a stand of trees nearby and I hobbled in that direction for cover, unnecessarily as it turned out. The Lysandran flitters were moving steadily away from me. The pain dulled but my leg stiffened and I found myself limping. I was still carrying the laser so I used it as a makeshift crutch. The woods thinned quickly and I found myself on the edge of a cultivated field. Regular rows of young spongemelon plants stretched as far as I could see in the dark, and I realized I was on Tonobi land. Theirs was the only farm besides ours that grew spongemelon commercially any more, and our fields were over toward the Jackknife.

I turned north, taking advantage of the cover offered by a windbreak even though it appeared that I was in no immediate danger. Staying roughly parallel to Baxter Road, I walked for over an hour, bypassing the house. My knee began to hurt again, grew steadily worse, and I tried to concentrate on the pain and forget what had just happened. I would have to face it sooner or later, and the consequences, but for the time being, it was too great a disaster. I concentrated on the need to return the laser to concealment in the small cave. Once that was accomplished, I would consider the next step.

Obviously I was in shock and not thinking clearly. I walked right past the small slope that led down to the cave and had to retrace my steps. The ground was slick and wet but somehow I managed to keep my feet under me. An unmarked path, almost invisible even by daylight, led up to the entrance, a horizontal slit through which I was forced to crawl. No light penetrated inside so I worked by touch alone, wrapping the laser in one of the plasticene covers and hiding it carefully behind a small, serrated ridge of stone.

My first thought after that was to go home and reassure Kelli that I was all right, but Kelli wouldn't be there. The fact of her death hit me more forcefully then, and I lay back with my arms covering my eyes and surrendered to my grief. I'm not sure how long that lasted, but eventually I fell asleep, and when I next opened my eyes, my knee wasn't hurting as badly any longer and a small puddle of light was creeping slowly up through the cave entrance.

It was morning.

CHAPTER FIFTEEN

It was a warm, bright morning, and for a few seconds I was disoriented, wondering if everything I remembered from the previous night had been just a dream. But my clothing was still damp and my knee was sore, and I couldn't delude myself for long. The reality of Kelli's death rushed over me again, but this time I was able to hold onto something of myself and deal with it. At least for the time being. There were other issues of more immediate concern.

I'd missed our planned rendezvous, and I didn't know if anyone else from our group had been killed or captured. Once they identified Kelli's body, they'd be looking for me even if the others had all escaped. Jeb was the only one who knew the location of the cave where I'd been caching the weapons so I decided to leave the laser where I'd hidden it, but I couldn't remain there myself. I thought about using the com but decided against it. Our prearranged codes didn't cover this situation, and I didn't dare speak openly, even obliquely.

I set off for home and some clean, dry clothing, but not so precipitately that I took any risks. There was pretty good cover for most of the route, although I had to cross open fields on two occasions. Cautious as I was, I almost walked into a trap, because everything looked quiet and deserted as I neared the house. Some sixth sense must have warned me, because I crouched in the brush at the rear for a long time, watching and listening, and when something moved, just briefly, behind one of the small windows, I realized I was not alone. It might have been Jeb or one of the other cell members, but I didn't think so. We all knew how important it was to do nothing out of the usual, to be where we were supposed to be. At least one and probably several Lysandran soldiers were waiting for me to come home.

So I didn't.

The farm was out of the question as well. There were a few people in town I thought I could trust, but I was reluctant to put any of them in jeopardy. The Lysandrans would almost certainly be looking for me, and for the others if they had identified anyone else, and they'd be stepping up the random searches. But I had to go somewhere. I retreated from my home, wondering if I'd ever return, and tried to think.

Fortunately, food was no problem. Rubbage and cornfruit were both in season, and although they didn't taste particularly good raw and unseasoned, they filled my stomach and helped stop my hands from shaking. I thought about returning to the cave and retrieving the laser, but it was awkward to carry and if the Lysandrans found me, there was little chance that I would escape a second time. At the moment, I was more interested in getting away than in fighting to the death. Up until this day, I had resented the Lysandrans, but I hadn't actually hated them. That had all changed with Kelli's death, and I was determined to live long enough to see them pay for what they'd done. If Sylandris had popped out of the bushes with a cheery greeting, I would have strangled him on the spot.

I spent most of that morning huddled in the lower branches of a windbreak on what had once been Abe Chandler's farm. Tonobi owned the land now, but after Abe moved up north, he had hired one of the Valentine twins to manage it for him and she'd done an indifferent job. The cornfruit rows were too far apart; she could have increased her yield by a good ten percent if she'd spaced them correctly, and I'd noticed that when she'd harvested the cornfruit she'd let the droppings rot on the ground. They wouldn't have sold for top price, of course, but she could have ground them into meal and made a slight profit.

The morning seemed to stretch on forever, and the image of Kelli's mutilated body kept popping into my mind despite my best efforts to concentrate on the present. Shortly after midday, I couldn't stand the inactivity. I had seen one flitter in the distance a short time earlier, but it might have been a civilian vehicle and in any case, it had not come in my direction. I followed along behind the windbreak until it ended, then sprinted for a small woodlot. I had some vague plan to hide out at the Harwell farm, which was presumably deserted now, but while I was making my way through the trees in that direction when I realized that a much better alternative was available.

I did end up spending the afternoon on what had once been Harwell property, although I never ventured close to the actual buildings. It had occurred to me that the Lysandrans might well have left some sort of passive surveillance equipment here, and while I was probably exaggerating their resources, at the time I was unwilling to take the chance. The land hadn't been cultivated in years, but some of the former crops had gone wild and I was able to forage for enough to keep me going. Many of the fields were so overgrown that they provided excellent hiding places. I waited impatiently for darkness to fall.

At first dusk, I moved south on a circuitous route that would take me well clear of the scene of the previous night's attack. I reached the heavy forest to the south without incident, and never saw another living soul, human or Lysandran. Once there I began to make better time because I'd traveled this area in the darkness on several previous occasions but it was still quite late before I knew I was close to my goal. I was only a few dozen meters away when a voice behind me made me freeze.

"I wondered how long it would take you to get here." It was too dark to see her face in the shadows, but I recognized Melody Miller's voice immediately.

"How did you know I'd be coming?" It was the first time I'd spoken in more than a day and my voice was rough and unsteady.

"Jeb came by a while back and asked me to be on the lookout for you. He figured this is where you'd end up if they didn't catch you."

"Jeb's all right then? How about the others?" I realized then that we'd never told Melody about our group, unless Jeb had spilled the beans today.

Melody stepped out into the open and I could see her face, indistinctly, in the starlight. Her voice changed. "You know about Kelli?"

I nodded. "She's dead." That's all I could say.

"Jeb said to tell you everyone else got away. Malvolio has a broken wrist but there were no other serious injuries."

Malvolio was our code name for Dan Kater. "They're looking for me."

"Quite avidly, according to Jeb. He told me to keep you here. There are enough supplies for both of us for a while and he said he'd arrange more when things calmed down a little. So I guess we're going to be roommates."

"Not for long." I looked around. "Let's go to the cave. I don't feel safe here."

We didn't speak again until we were inside and past the dogleg that prevented anyone outside from seeing the dim light from the alcove where Melody had been living. I noticed that she'd already set up a second makeshift bed. "You were pretty confident I'd be heading this way, weren't you?"

"Where else would you go?"

"North," I answered promptly. "As soon as things settle down a little, I'm going up toward Aladdin to find Cille."

"She's not in Aladdin." Melody raised her hand to her lips, as though she had said something she wanted to take back. "I can't tell you where she is, Ennis. I'm sorry."

"That's all right. I know she's at Lake Lilith."

Melody gasped. "Who told you that?" Her tone confirmed what I had actually only suspected.

"She's my sister, Melody. I know how she thinks." I sat down on a smooth outcropping and crossed my arms over my chest. "There's nothing else I can do here to help. This is a small town; I'm too well known. The only way I can hope to avoid being caught is if I hide in a cave and let things happen without me. Maybe there was a time when I could have done that, let other people decide the fate of Aragon while I stood by. But that day passed when Kelli died. I want to fight back, Melody, and I can't do that here. Now you can tell me what I need to know to get in touch with her, or I can figure out something on my own. But in either case, I'm going to Lake Lilith just as soon as I think it's safe to travel."

I thought she was going to argue the point, but she just shook her head. "It's late and I'm tired. You look exhausted. Let's talk about it in the morning."

"All right, but you're not going to change my mind."

But the following morning, she made no effort to argue. Instead she announced that she was coming with me. "You were right last night. Hiding in a cave isn't going to help get the Cranes off Aragon. And we'll have a better chance of arriving safely if we travel together."

It sounded good in theory, but the practice was considerably different. Jeb returned to the cave two days later, supplementing the meager amount of information we'd been able to glean from the public com lines. We could listen, but not transmit. He confirmed what I already knew. "They've been out to the farm every day at least once and they've offered a reward for your capture. Every barge and flitter that tries to head out of the area is searched and they've increased the daylight patrols." A ghost of a smile passed briefly over his face. "But they've cut back at night. After dark, only flitters go outside of Safehaven proper."

Zeb wasn't very happy when I told him what we were planning. "I can't do any good here, Zeb. We'll send word as soon as we're safe. I need for you and Zai to watch after my mother while I'm gone."

"She's a strong lady. She doesn't need or tolerate much looking after, but we'll do what we can. What else do you want me to get for you?" He'd brought two changes of clothing with him, concealed in his fishing tackle box.

"A couple of backpacks for one thing." I gave him a short list of items I'd written down the previous day. "But don't bring them here. They'll be watching you more closely than before and I don't want you getting into trouble. Do you remember the large split rock south of the west dock?"

"Sure do."

"Leave the supplies in the tanglebrush some time in the next two days, or better yet have one of the hands bring the stuff out. We won't move before then. Is that old canoe still in the shed?"

"Yeah, but she leaks pretty bad. You wouldn't get far in her even if they weren't watching the rivers. They've commandeered some fast boats up on Lake Pudallah, and they run regular flitter patrols down both waterways. I don't think you'll be able to sneak through."

"Not planning to, and the canoe only has to stay afloat long enough to get us to the west bank of the Swift. We'll sink her ourselves once we're across just to be safe."

"Don't tell me the rest. I can't let slip what I don't know. The supplies will be there tomorrow. Anything else I can do?"

"Yes." I took a folded piece of paper from my pocket and handed it to him. "Give this to my mother." It was a totally inadequate effort to reassure her, but I couldn't leave without making at least some effort. "Don't get caught with it, and have her destroy it as soon as she reads it."

Jeb put it in his pocket. "All right then." He held out his hand and shook mine and he wished us both good luck. Then he was gone. I wondered if I would ever see him again.

We abandoned the cave as soon as full dark had fallen, and those last few hours left me irritable and jumpy. I was impatient to be gone, and Melody interpreted this as rashness and lectured me about the need to remain cool and thoughtful. My moodiness lessened considerably once we were on the move, and in actual practice I was more cautious than my companion. We crossed the Harwell farm, taking advantage of the heavy brush there, then turned toward Barbecue Hill and the Swift. The land due west of us was no longer under cultivation; it was the plot Zai had claimed for us in order to block the construction of an overland route from Safehaven. The soil was too acidic for most of the crops we raised, but every second year we planted something just to hold our claim.

It took us a good portion of the night to make our way up the Swift to the west dock, picking up the two backpacks on the way. A military flitter passed by at one point and we hunkered down in a tangle of vines and waited until they were out of sight. Jeb had offered to bring us one of the lasers, but they were too big to conceal easily and we didn't dare take one. Melody had a small handweapon, a vermin killer, but only a dozen rounds of ammunition, and it wouldn't be much help against an armored Lysandran. I had forgotten to ask for a key to the boat shed, but Jeb must have left it unlocked for us. We wrestled the canoe outside, and I was glad for the darkness because if it was in as bad shape as I remembered, Melody might have balked at using it to cross the fast moving river.

We were only a few meters from shore when she whispered angrily at me. "This thing leaks like a sieve."

"So paddle faster," I answered. "We can probably make it to the other side before it sinks."

"Probably!" But she didn't say anything else and paddled more energetically.

We did make it across, just barely, and mostly because we got caught in a fast, crosswise current that did a lot of the work for us. But our feet were thoroughly soaked by the time we jumped ashore. I pushed the canoe away from the river bank, and it turned and angled out into the darkness. It would either sink quickly or it would be carried downstream and possibly confuse the pursuit, if the Lysandrans ever found it at all. If they thought I'd headed into the wilderness, that was all to the good.

I won't bore you with a detailed description of our journey northward. It was tedious, uncomfortable, and only occasionally dangerous. We ran out of food north of Managansett, which we avoided because of the heavy Lysandran presence, scavenged a little, stayed hungry a lot. Occasionally we saw people, humans only, but we always avoided them. There hadn't been a lot of collaboration with the invaders, who apparently had never thought of paying for information until quite recently, but there were a few people who had embraced their vision of a united, homogeneous human society. As Cille would have said, everyone performs their own personal dance toward perfection, and some of the steps look pretty strange to the rest of us.

It took us twenty four days to reach Junction. I had suggested bypassing the town but Melody insisted that she knew someone there whom we could trust. My reluctance faded with the depletion of our supplies, and when we finally reached the Madisons' home, I was so tired and hungry that I deferred to her judgment. Fortunately the Madisons were as good as she claimed. They let us spend two nights in a cramped, smelly, but well concealed room in their root cellar, and they gave us as much food as we could carry when we left.

From Junction we traveled due north toward Aladdin, paralleling the paved road for the first several days, and we started traveling during the daylight instead of only after dark. I suggested turning northeast, directly toward Lake Lilith, but Melody talked me out of it. "The terrain is too rough. What you gain in distance you'll lose twice over in speed. We're better off going straight to the capitol first."

I was concerned about entering Aladdin, given the heavy Lysandran presence there, but Melody assured me that we'd be safe. "Or relatively so anyway. We won't go into the city proper and we'll have to watch out for patrols. They were already heavy when I left, and they're probably worse now."

We would have made better time if we could have walked on the road, but the surrounding country wasn't as bad as it might have been. Aragon's native flora consisted predominantly of umbrella shaped trees which constantly shed their lower branches as they grow taller, and featherlike grasses that shoot up to about shoulder height but which are so filmy that it is easy to walk through them even at their most dense. We could hear the commercial traffic on the roadway a couple of hundred meters away, primarily big cargo autolorries carrying produce from Safehaven and Managansett, and occasional manufactured goods from the small production facilities in Junction. Sometimes we'd hear the distinctive sound of a flitter but we rarely knew whether they were human or Lysandran. Their vehicles sounded much like ours for one thing, and they'd also confiscated a large number of private vehicles. We avoided exposing ourselves to any of them.

Eventually we crossed the incomplete roadway to Linden. Construction had ended with the invasion. The following day we began to see signs of human settlements, and once we even backtracked to avoid two women who were swimming in a small, clear pond. Melody suggested we revert to night travel and once again I deferred to her judgment. She knew this area much better than I.

Although we continued to monitor the public news on our coms, we were more intrigued by what was not said than by what was. There were occasional references to the trouble in Tyrada, but the nature of that situation was never described and it would be several days before we learned that the Lysandrans had withdrawn from the city completely in the wake of a violent uprising and were threatening to level it if the rebels didn't surrender their arms and submit. In Aladdin, there was a first dusk to dawn curfew in the vicinity of government center and the main Lysandran base, and restrictions on movement in several other parts of the city. Much of the spaceport was off limits to humans at all times. The remnants of the new Assembly had adjourned and refused to reconvene, leaving the Lysandrans with no organized body with whom to communicate.

Melody described the layout of Aladdin and its suburbs in great detail, but I had trouble keeping it all straight in my head. My first hand knowledge of the city predated the invasion, and I'd never ventured outside the commercial district during my visits. She led me through a maze of satellite communities, clusters of residences and small businesses that had grown up on the outskirts of the city proper. It was no longer possible to avoid other humans, so we acted as though we had nothing to hide. Our cover story was that we had spent the last two weeks hiking through the wilderness studying native Aragonian plantlife.

Hard currency was rarely used on Aragon and I was only carrying enough to buy us one meal, and not a fancy one. Fortunately, Melody had access to a credit line created by the underground for just such occasions, and we spent the night in small but comfortable rooms at an inexpensive hostelry. The following morning she went off on her own, because she doubted her contacts would reveal themselves if they saw her with an unfamiliar companion. She was gone for four hours, and I was more than slightly anxious when she finally returned.

"Everything's set," she assured me. "Someone will meet us this evening. I hope you're not claustrophobic."

I raised an eyebrow. "Not that I know of. Should I ask why that's an issue?"

She smirked. "You'll find out."

That evening, I spent four very cramped hours squeezed into an unlighted compartment concealed inside a trash hauler and municipal maintenance vehicle. It was empty when Melody and I climbed down through the gaping jaws, slid open the concealed inner panel, and crept inside, but that didn't last for long. The hauler followed its usual route through the city, robotic arms sweeping up containers of refuse and dumping them down on top of us. It was loud, uncomfortable, and the odor was overwhelming, a blend of lubricants, organics, and decomposition. There was barely room for the two of us, which was probably just as well. The ride was so rough that a single passenger would have emerged bruised and battered.

After the first two hours, we took on no additional trash, and there were no stops for a very long time. Sleep was impossible, but I had sunk into a sort of stunned somnolence when we finally came to a halt. The body of the hauler began to rotate and we slid around the inside of the hidden compartment, almost deafened by the sound of the trash being voided from all around us. When the noise finally stopped, I asked Melody if this was the end of the line.

"Not quite. We're at the recycling station east of the city. If there aren't any Crane patrols in the area, they'll let us out on the way back."

"And if there are patrols around?"

"Then we find as comfortable a position as possible for the ride back into the city and try again tomorrow night."

Fortunately, things went our way.

Three figures whose faces were concealed by scarves helped us out of the compartment because our limbs were so stiff that we couldn't manage it unassisted. They led us inside what appeared to be a utility building of some sort, but I couldn't identify it because there were no lights except those on the hauler, which moved away immediately. We were hustled through a small, dark room and down a staircase into a damp, cluttered storage area. Melody exchanged a few words with a tall woman who lifted a small, non-standard com unit to her mouth. A second later, there was the a faint whir of machinery and a section of the wall slid up out of the way, revealing a surprisingly large, well lit interior. There were four people sitting at a table inside. Three of them were strangers but even in the dim light I recognized the fourth.

"Come in Ennis, Melody." Cille stood up and came around the table and before I realized that I was moving I had my arms around her and we were embracing each other.

The next couple of weeks were a blur and seem even less distinct when I look back on them now. I spent most of that time in a complex of tunnels beneath the partially completed resort complex at Lake Lilith. Everything above ground was carefully maintained to look as though it was not being maintained. Part of the tunnel system, meant to house the servomechanisms and human staff to support the facilities above, was left in disrepair, but there were concealed entrances to other sections which now housed the planning and administrative headquarters for a fairly extensive resistance movement. Cille shared leadership of the group with two others, Vedric Graham, a retired Navy officer whose face seemed to be set in a permanent scowl, and Tristan Tcho, a local businessman whom the Lysandrans incorrectly believed to be sympathetic to their cause

I saw very little of the two men during my stay at Lake Lilith, and not a whole lot more of Cille, although we did spend much of that first night together, catching up on all the little things we'd been saving up since she'd gone into hiding, most of which were probably quite trivial. It was the act of sharing rather than the subject of that sharing that was important. Melody vanished sometime the following day, sent out on some mission whose nature I never learned.

Most of my time was spent with Carlos Torres and Laura Mizushima, who were assigned as my tutors. Carlos was relaxed and friendly but Laura was all business all the time. They made me memorize the street plan of Aladdin and its outskirts, and weren't satisfied until I could describe in reasonable detail most of the more significant buildings and landmarks. I also learned to maintain and use a variety of weapons including, surprisingly, captured Lysandran assault lasers.

One of the problems hindering efforts against the Lysandrans had been the tracer components lodged in each of their weapons. The tracers were incorporated into the triggering mechanisms in such a way that it could not be easily removed without rendering the weapon unusable. It could be done, but Lysandran response times were much shorter. The entire trigger assembly could be discarded more quickly, but that left the weapon inoperable. At just about the same time as Melody and I were hiding in the cave near Safehaven, a team at Lake Lilith had managed to build a replacement module that worked, most of the time. The underground had already accumulated a score of workable but untraceable Lysandran lasers, and was actively looking for ways to acquire more.

Eventually my instructors decided that I was no longer completely ignorant and I was given a job in the data section, collating information on troop movements within the city, comparing reports from dozens of observers, trying to determine patrol patterns, troop strength, and anything else that might be helpful. The season had changed before I left the hidden compound, disguised, carrying false identification, and accompanied by two experienced companions who gave me a guided tour of central Aladdin under the pretense that we were looking for a site to open a small arts and crafts shop. The Lysandrans were everywhere in the city during the day, but once darkness fell, they retreated to those areas where humans were subject to the curfew.

I guess I passed that informal test, because I started spending more and more time in the city, eventually becoming an "employee" at a real estate development firm using my fictitious identity. For a while I acted as an observer, feeding information back to headquarters, then as coordinator of a series of harassing missions against the Lysandrans, disrupting their communications network, sabotaging equipment, but never confronting them directly.

The situation in Tyrada had become static after a major Lysandran counterattack destroyed much of the city but failed to oust the rebels. The relatively ineffective response to Gaunt's rebellion puzzled me until I noticed that our surveillance indicated that the invaders were still slowly reducing their numbers on Aragon. It was well disguised as normal troop rotation, but it wasn't long before we were certain that there were fewer troops arriving than departing.

The company that acted as my cover also oversaw construction projects and I was delighted to discover that the Lysandran military had approached the owners about managing the reinforcement of a portion of the perimeter around the main barracks area. Emily Donergan, my theoretical boss, suggested that I take a temporary assignment as assistant to the project manager. Two Lysandran officers would also supervise, and from the outset it was obvious that they were watching for any sign of sabotage, but we finished the job exactly as it had been contracted. Their defenses were marginally improved, but in return I managed to gain detailed intelligence about the layout of the compound, security arrangements, and most interesting of all, manpower levels. As we had already suspected, Lysandran troop strength had been significantly reduced, and most of their civilian contingent had either withdrawn to the capitol or left the planet entirely. I reported everything to Lake Lilith, but it was obvious that even with their depleted resources, the Lysandrans would be able to brush aside anything we could presently throw at them.

Although I was closer physically to Cille now than I had been, I saw her infrequently and most of our communications were verbal messages repeated by couriers. She assured me that she had gotten word back to Mom that I was alive and well, and that in turn she'd learned that the Lysandrans had not retaliated against her because of me. Jeb and Zai were apparently all right, but the farm was under closer surveillance than before, and Dan Kater had gone into hiding for reasons unknown.

Short summer gave way to false autumn, then warmed back up for long summer. I began to feel more like a clerk than a revolutionary. Lysandran troops periodically made forays against Tyrada, but the city somehow managed to remain free of their control. A similar uprising in Casper failed with great loss of life, and I began to feel frustrated and impatient. And then one night I thought of something, and I got up and wrote it down, and in the morning when I woke up and read it, it still made sense. I thought about it off and on over the course of the next three days and finally decided that I shouldn't keep it to myself. On my next report back, I requested a meeting and a few days after that arrangements were made for me to visit an "old friend" on the eastern edge of Aladdin. At first dusk on a particularly muggy night, I met with Vedric Graham and two others and told them what I had in mind. They asked a few questions, looked at one another, and then Graham asked me what I needed to get the job done.

That was the first step in my transition from assassin to mass murderer.

CHAPTER SIXTEEN

Nothing in their experience could have prepared the Lysandrans for the human race. Once defeated, all of their previous opponents had been content to stay that way. They'd never had to deal with a guerilla war before, and consequently they had never developed tactics to deal with the situation in which they were currently entangled. Most of the adjustments they did make were taken from their investigations into human history, but they never learned enough fast enough to make a difference. They made repeated efforts to prop up the fragments of the Assembly, but most of the representatives had long since returned to their homes, and those who stayed in Aladdin refused to convene. The pretense of a local government was dropped completely as control of the countryside began to slip.

One of their biggest failings was inadequate protection for their physical infrastructure. They knew enough to keep their troops well protected, to make it difficult for their enemies to use captured weapons, and they had learned some rudimentary counter insurgency tactics. But they were not rigorous in defending supply lines and supporting facilities. Power to their base was cut off six times before they finally moved a generator inside the perimeter. They purchased or requisitioned large quantities of local foodstuffs, but they were lax about inspections and often had to throw away large quantities of deliberately adulterated grain and fruit.

It was one such oversight that I'd noticed while I was visiting the main compound in Aladdin.

Physiologically, Lysandrans and humans were amazingly similar. Both races could eat the same foods, although they needed to take trace mineral supplements and as it turned out humans reacted badly to certain items in their cuisine. We also breathed the same atmosphere, although Lysandrans were used to a slightly richer mix of oxygen and a different blend of trace gases. Although they could survive indefinitely and without serious harm breathing Aragon's air, it apparently caused them some mild discomfort, or perhaps it was just that they found a mix closer to their own pleasurable. For whatever reason, they had sealed off a good sized building within their complex, formerly a small flitter hangar and repair shop, and adjusted the atmosphere inside by piping in supplementary oxygen and other gases. Off duty soldiers congregated inside in the Lysandran equivalent of a nightclub, although they never used anything equivalent to human intoxicants to alter their mood, nor did they dance, play games, or even listen to music. The whole concept of the arts was foreign to their species.

The club building was as well shielded and fortified as the barracks proper. The oxygen tanks were inside the perimeter as well, but they sat in a series of latticelike metal cradles that were exposed and vulnerable. Their laxness was understandable. In their eyes, destruction of oxygen tanks would be an inconvenience but hardly a disaster. They weren't nearly as devious in their thinking as are humans.

Graham sent a team of four to work with me. I only saw one of them again afterward, and she had a different name that time, so I don't think I ever knew who they really were. The team consisted of an explosives expert who talked too much and whose left kneecap was still tender from surgery, a pair of laser equipped sharpshooters who talked too little, and a thin, intense teenaged girl who carried a crossbow in a rugged plasticene case.

The weather was against us. In order for my plan to succeed, the wind would have to come from the southeast, and although that was not unusual at this time of year, it perversely blew from the north for five consecutive nights, then teased us by reversing itself during the daylight. The team had a legitimate reason for being in the city but we still had a bad few minutes when a Lysandran patrol showed up at the hostelry to examine their papers, although they seemed satisfied.

On the sixth night, the wind cooperated.

The sharpshooters, whom I privately thought of as Thud and Blunder, assembled their weapons, wrapped them in cloth, and took positions flanking the archer and I as we approached the perimeter wall. Our explosives expert had done his job and he wasn't mobile enough to go with us on the actual operation, but he wished us luck. We stayed well clear of the motion detectors and infrared sensors, and skirted the areas where live patrols were active. The area immediately adjoining the oxygen tanks was well covered but we didn't need to get very close. Our archer unlimbered her crossbow as we took our positions on top of a rusting storage container. From that vantage point we could see the Lysandran compound fairly clearly. The security lights bathed the entire area.

"Are you sure you can reach it from here?" I asked for at least the fifth time..

She looked across at the target, then back to me. "Easy. I can put a shot behind it if you want."

"You have to get a direct hit. This won't work if we don't get a single, massive release."

"I'll hit the target. If the package does what it's supposed to do, you'll get what you want." She had accepted a second specially made quarrel disdainfully, insisting that it wouldn't be needed.

Blunder stayed with us while Thud scouted around to make sure we wouldn't be surprised by an unscheduled Lysandran patrol. I insisted that we wait until there was a fairly brisk wind, and my throat was dry when I finally told her to make her shot.

She was as good as her word. The quarrel struck exactly where it was supposed to and the explosive package when off with a sharp crack and a dull thump. The largest of the containment tanks split open like an overripe cornfruit. The detonation sounded frightfully loud to me, but only because I was expecting it. Two Lysandran soldiers popped into view, weapons ready, staring in the direction of the explosion.

I had been counting in my head, and now I turned to Blunder and nodded. He raised his weapon, took aim, and fired. The thin red beam found the refuse bin directly in front of the one time hangar and started a small fire. It wasn't serious and would have burned itself out quickly under ordinary circumstances.

My companions were already preparing to descend to the ground and make their escape, but I was frozen in place. The cloud of pure oxygen released from the tank was invisible, but it had to be moving in the right direction. As long as it didn't become too dispersed too quickly, it should do what I had planned.

The walls of the hangar building were plasteel, one of the most durable substances known to humankind, and normally inflammable. But large concentrations of pure oxygen change the rules. Given an ignition source, even metal will burn in the presence of a rich enough atmosphere. One of the guards turned toward the burning trash bin while the other started to speak into his wrist com, and then the invisible cloud of oxygen reached the flame and enveloped the front of the hangar and a split second later the concussion knocked me from my feet.

The results of my plan far exceeded my expectations. The fire and explosion blew a large hole in the hangar wall and the flames poured through. I was a bit dazed when I regained my feet, and I blinked uncomprehendingly at the chaos below. Figures came running out of the ruined building, trailing streamers of flame, racing back and forth in a panic. It looked vaguely familiar to me and it was only later that I realized that it had reminded me of the wormdance I'd seen the night we'd doused it with flammables and set it alight. It was horribly beautiful but I felt a pang of guilt. What had happened to Cille had been an accident, and I had finally made peace with myself about my part in that terrible day. But this night was intentional, and it had been my idea. Those frantic burning figures below were unwelcome invaders, the enemy, and one part of me was wild with excitement about striking this blow, but another part knew that regardless of the right or wrong of it, the Lysandrans thought that they were doing what was right, just as we believed that fighting for our freedom was right, and I wondered why it was that intelligent races, human and otherwise, had to spend so much time killing and maiming each other in the pursuit of good.

I might have stood there, transfixed, for much longer, dangerously longer, but Thud or Blunder – I don't know which – climbed up and dragged me away.

Lysandran reaction to the attack was, by human standards, quite muted. There were no reprisals against the people of Aragon, although the curfew was extended to include most of the urban area, and it was more strictly enforced if you were caught. There were more patrols the first few days, but things rapidly returned to normal. It was an open secret that the Lysandrans could not long sustain such a high level of activity. Nearly a hundred of them died as a result of my plan, half of them in the fire and explosion, the other half euthanized by their own people when it was obvious that they would be permanently disfigured or disabled.

We also heard rumors of duels among some of the top officers of the occupation army. Apparently longstanding dominance patterns were now being questioned, subordinates deciding that their superiors were losing control and making their bids for self promotion. The siege of Tyrada continued to be a standoff, and there was renewed trouble in Casper, Linden, and other locations. The Lysandrans stopped drawing troops away from Aragon, but they made no effort to bolster their remaining forces.

I continued to accumulate information on their activities, most of which seemed to me to be of no value. I hadn't seen Cille for several days, although I'd had messages from her. She did let me know when Zai Kreller came to the city on business and even helped arrange for me to meet with her very briefly in a public diner, just long enough to exchange greetings and a bit of news. "Your mother is doing well and wanted me to tell you not to worry. We haven't been bothered much lately. Our friends seem to be very busy. Someone set off a bomb under one of their flitters the other day. Blew the stabilizer right off."

"Anyone I know?" I figured it was Jeb, and she gave me a look that confirmed it. "Colson says they're going to withdraw from Safehaven completely and watch us from Managansett." We only spoke for a few minutes, not daring to prolong the conversation, and I returned to my room feeling homesick and depressed. I hadn't allowed myself to think much about Kelli's death, or most of my former life, concentrating entirely on maintaining my cover and doing my new job, and seeing Zai again had brought it all rushing back.

The winter was colder than usual that year. We had snow a few times, though never a heavy accumulation. Casper and Tyrada were blanketed with it for several weeks, however, and operations against the Lysandrans came to a virtual halt there. Even in Aladdin, there seemed to be no real progress. I was beginning to chafe a bit at the inaction when I received the summons to Lake Lilith. This time I could travel openly on assignment for my boss rather than in the belly of a trash hauler.

There were about two dozen of us who were briefed that day by Tristan Tcho and another man whose name I don't recall. Contact had finally been made with Gaunt's organization, which would allow coordination of our separate efforts to oust the Lysandrans. His people had captured and disabled a large number of military weapons in Tyrada and were storing them, but they had been unable to replace the discarded components. We would be sending them enough replacement triggers to convert what they had as soon as we could manufacture them.

"We're not ready to fight the Cranes openly yet, but we're getting close." Tcho was in constant motion when he talked, walking back and forth, rubbing his hands together, gesturing dramatically. "Basically they've withdrawn into three armed camps, here, Casper, and their forward operations base near Tyrada, and there are still a few smaller groups scattered elsewhere."

"What about Linden?" someone asked.

"They abandoned Linden and Managansett two days ago, and it looks like they're preparing to pull out of Farrell and Junction fairly soon. We know they've asked for reinforcements, but based on what they're doing, we don't think they got the answer they wanted. This consolidation will make them harder to hit, but it also gives us more freedom to maneuver." What he didn't tell us was that the Lysandrans had not taken their human collaborators with them, because within their own culture the withdrawal would simply have resulted in a change of dominance patterns. I heard later that the magistrate of Junction was hanged in his own office and there was a widespread and violent witch hunt in Linden.

Our work now was to quietly move forces into place around the remaining enclaves without attracting the attention of our adversaries, and equip them adequately. Once they'd converted the captured weapons, the rebels in Tyrada would significantly outnumber the opposition there. Other than the flitters, the Lysandrans had never landed any of their armored equipment on Aragon, having assumed that a show of force would be sufficient to establish dominance without actually engaging in protracted ground warfare. Tcho was confident that Gaunt's people could overrun the forward base once they were armed. "The Cranes have earthwork ramparts and sentries, but nothing to stop a determined push. But Gaunt's people will hold off until we're ready. If we hit them everywhere at once, we think they'll collapse. They can't move their reserves around fast enough without splitting them up."

As a realtor, I was well situated to find safe locations in which to stockpile weapons and provide assembly areas. A bogus investment company had been created retroactively in the city records, and they had more than adequate, though entirely fictitious, financial resources to pay for the rental of the dozen or so buildings that would be required. I was no longer working under Graham's intelligence group but reported to Tcho in implementation and supply. The change suited me; I'd grown tired of the endless reporting of trivial data since our successful attack on the hangar club. I tried to see Cille before returning, but was told that she was not presently at Lake Lilith, so instead I left a cheery, innocuous, and unsatisfying message.

I had no great difficulty obtaining leases on the properties I wanted. The economy and the population of Aladdin had both declined dramatically during the past two years and there were vacant buildings almost everywhere. The weapons came in small batches, smuggled in both assembled and in parts. There was a respectable number of converted Lysandran weapons and a handful of Concourse assault lasers left over from the Navy contingent. Chemical grenades began to show up as well, and a few sets of body armor, though not enough to outfit the numbers we'd need for the battle that was coming. As the days passed and the year crawled toward spring, I felt a mounting impatience. It was no longer anger at the Lysandrans for invading our planet, taking away our freedom, or even killing our loved ones. By then it had evolved into an exhausted frustration and a desire to get this over with, one way or another, so that I could look around and decide how much of my life remained to me.

The uprising took place on the tenth day of spring. The first attack was in Casper, preceding the rest of us so that some troops would be drawn off to reinforce the garrison there. Then Gaunt's forces attacked the forward base near Tyrada, using Lysandran assault weapons for the first time. They took heavy losses but breached the perimeter and eventually overran the entire installation. A very large number of Lysandrans surrendered and were disarmed and imprisoned in their own barracks.

Things didn't go quite as well in Aladdin, where our attack started with first dusk. Three tunnels had been dug under the outer defensive walls surrounding their base, but someone had miscalculated or missed one of the surveillance posts because the assault team was spotted as they emerged and we lost the element of surprise. Several large explosions followed as holes were blown in the perimeter wall. We lost a lot of people in the next few minutes;

the man in front of me as I ran through dropped without a sound and never moved. The Lysandrans harried us with laser fire from small and heavy arms, and a dozen flitters lifted off.

Then things began to shift in our favor. Graham's munitions experts had constructed crude missiles which eventually brought down about half of the enemy's air cover, and armed and armored civilian flitters engaged the others. Although we continued to take losses on the ground, we outnumbered the enemy. The Lysandrans retreated slowly but steadily to their inner perimeter. That left the power generators exposed and we knocked them out quickly, which cost the Lysandrans not only the lights but most of their remote surveillance and automated defensive systems.

We settled into siege mode, building small redoubts all around the inner camp. The few surviving Lysandran flitters landed inside their considerably shrunken perimeter, but they stopped firing at us unless we presented an obvious target. I spent most of the night crouched behind a stack of packing crates, trying to make sense of the coded messages racing across the com lines. Shortly after first light, a heavily accented Lysandran voice broadcast in clear, offering to negotiate a surrender.

It looked like we'd become dominant on Aragon again.

No one had told me that Cille was involved in the fighting, but I should have realized that she wouldn't have been willing to remain in the Lake Lilith base. I only found out later that she personally met with the Lysandran commander and accepted his formal gesture of submission. He was openly puzzled when she insisted that the Lysandrans relinquish all their weapons. Having acknowledged human dominance, it would never have occurred to him or his troops to resume hostilities unless some extraneous incident altered the dominance pattern. But she was adamant and he agreed to her terms. Teams were sent in to collect the weapons, but they were carefully selected. There were some who would have happily slaughtered the disarmed Lysandrans where they stood.

The days that followed passed for me almost like a dream. With the surrender of their high command, all of the remaining pockets of Lysandrans had stopped fighting. For the most part, they were not mistreated by our forces, who took their weapons and arranged for their transportation back to Aladdin. Their former headquarters had been transformed into a military prison. Several dozen soldiers were killed by an angry crowd in Casper despite efforts by Gaunt's people, probably half hearted, to protect them. Within five days, there were no living Lysandrans anywhere on Aragon except those imprisoned in Aladdin.

Unfortunately, the same was not true of the space surrounding Aragon.

There were no longer any of the largest of the Lysandran ships in our system, but there were four medium sized warships and at least eight smaller ones orbiting above us. One of the former and three of the latter were visibly damaged but remained crewed and presumably maneuverable. Human military wisdom said that planetary bombardment was impractical, but we didn't know if anyone had told that to the Lysandrans. When the orbiting ships did nothing in the next few days but transmit feeble and badly phrased demands for the release of the prisoners and the restoration of Lysandran control, our anxiety level dropped considerably. We remained blockaded, but we were no longer part of the Lysandran Comity.

The surviving members of the original Assembly were all brought to Aladdin, although there was considerable disagreement about the legitimacy and practicality of that decision. One third of the elected representatives had died, and a handful of others either refused to serve or were unable to for other reasons. Gaunt was invited to take a seat but he sent one of his people in his place, insisting that he was too busy helping rebuild Tyrada to invest time in politics. Tcho and Graham were also included in the new Assembly as non-voting advisors.

After some occasionally rancorous haggling, an interim government was established with three presiding officers who would rotate the position among themselves on a regular basis. New elections would be held before year's end, with a structure only slightly different from that we'd used originally. The triumvirate consisted of Marco Fong, who had been one of Gaunt's chief confidants, Lee Amitsu, Aladdin's city administrator, and Cille Baxter, my sister. Cille and I had actually been able to sit and talk together a few days earlier. She'd been free of her other responsibilities for almost an hour. But on the day she was appointed, I was back at home.

I confess here that I was a bit disappointed to find the farm in such good shape. It's always a bit of a blow to the ego to discover that people can get along quite well without you. Mom, Zai, and Jeb had managed things well, and although they hadn't turned a profit, they'd covered most of the losses we might otherwise have suffered. The same could not be said for most of the other farms in the area. A few of the smallest still had their heads above water, but Carter, Tonobi, Pakarang, and Aguilar were all virtually bankrupt. Needham's bank had gone under because its guarantors were offworld. There were empty storefronts in Safehaven for the first time and Suki North was running what amounted to a soup kitchen, aided by Dan Kater, who had returned from his self imposed exile. No one was homeless, but no one was thriving either. I suppose the situation was technically worse in the big cities, but there they had an active infrastructure working to correct things. Safehaven seemed to have lost its heart.

I stayed at the farm. The very thought of returning to the house Kelli and I had shared made me sick to my stomach. Mom seemed to understand. She'd had all of the furniture replaced in the room that had until recently housed Sylandris and I moved in there. Jeb and Zai kept my mind occupied with farm business and Mom asked me about Cille over and over again, even though there was little I could tell her. They talked on the com frequently now, but Cille was far too busy to come home. I suggested that Mom visit her in Aladdin, but she just shook her head and said she'd wait until the time was right.

Although I thought I'd been keeping up a pretty good front, my depression and sense of loss must have been pretty obvious, obvious enough to prod Zai out of her habitual reticence. She found me sitting on the porch one evening, watching the last of the light as it was leached from the sky, and she plopped down in a chair beside me without speaking. We waited together in silence until full darkness had fallen before she spoke, and I think this somehow made it easier for her. She'd never been an emotionally demonstrative person. I'd seen her irritated but never mad, solemn but never sad. Or at least so it seemed to me.

"This must be very difficult for you," she said finally.

I glanced at her, surprised that she'd spoken. "It's a bit of an adjustment. I'll manage. Once I've caught up on the planting cycles and reviewed the contracts for next year, it'll all come back to me."

"I wasn't talking about the farm."

After a momentary hesitation, I sighed and shifted uncomfortably in my seat. "I miss her, Zai. It didn't bother me so much before because I kept busy, working against the people who killed her. Now that it's done, I wonder if I should even have come back here. Everything I do, every place I go, will remind me of things we did or places we went together."

"This is your home, Ennis." My name sounded strange from her lips. She almost never called anyone by their familiar names. It was a mark of disrespect back within her home culture. "Kelli's ghost isn't going to come back to haunt you, and if it did, she wouldn't want to see you throw away everything you have because of her."

I opened my mouth to say something, but my mind couldn't find the right words to say, and I was suddenly blinking back tears. Zai reached over and took my hand in hers, squeezing reassuringly, and she didn't say anything either. We stayed that way for a long time before she rose and disappeared into the darkness, and after a while I stood up and went to bed. It didn't stop hurting that evening, but the pain wasn't as sharp the next day, and after a while I realized that an invisible wound had finally begun to heal.

The Lysandrans in orbit hadn't forgotten us nor we them. They broadcast calls for us to realize our error and set free their captive troops, who numbered approximately one thousand. The provisional government responded by threatening to executive all the prisoners if any attempt was made to land fresh troops or take any other reprisals. I'm not sure if we would actually have followed through on the threat, and neither apparently were the Lysandrans, who fulminated and rattled their sabers but did little else. We were actually pretty certain that the orbiting ships didn't carry enough personnel to mount a serious assault anyway.

Weeks passed, and the season turned and things approached something approximately normality. In the bigger communities, several score collaborators were tried and sentenced, in most cases to a mixture of house arrest and community service, along with forfeiture of all land titles and voting rights. It was only in Tyrada that resentment was high enough that a few individuals were actually imprisoned. The mines were reopened but the city itself was half destroyed and would require years to recover its former vigor. Safehaven was lucky in this regard. Once the guard posts were torn down and the barracks building restored to its original purpose as a warehouse, there were few signs of the occupation, other than a plaque in front of the magistrate's office commemorating those who had died. Kelli and her brother were both listed there, and it would be a long time before I could pass through that intersection with feeling a fresh wave of grief.

Our local economy improved slightly, although still not enough to make the farm profitable. We continued to eat into our reserves, although not so badly as did our neighbors. The government offered tax relief and talked about temporary subsidies, but the legislature itself was in debt. There had never been any significant export of food from Aragon, so it might seem as though we would be immune to the economic doldrums, but the truth was that without the influx of credit from offworld investors and the sale of our small but growing pre-war manufacturing base, our customers lacked the ability to purchase anything more than the basics to survive, and that drove down the prices of everything. One of our three major distributors had already become insolvent and the others weren't much better off.

Since the farm had run just fine without me for over a year, I decided that I could be spared and set out to survey the situation first hand. I'd been to Linden once very briefly, but never to Casper, Tyrada, or most of the smaller settlements. Traveling by flitter, barge, and sometimes on foot, I went on a lengthy grand tour, partly to give myself time to adjust to the new shape of my life, partly to evaluate our markets and determine whether it was practical to form our own wholesale distribution service. I was shocked by the devastation in Tyrada, where Gaunt had just declined to become city administrator by acclamation, retreating into his usual seclusion.

I met with Cille twice in Aladdin during my travels. Although she was obviously busy, she made time for me and if she was secretly impatient for me to be gone, she never let it show. I think, I hope anyway, that I gave her the opportunity to sneak away from her responsibilities for a while and pretend she was just a young girl again. On both occasions she had initially seemed serious and somehow even older than I was, but ended up laughing enthusiastically as she told me about the foibles of her fellow legislators. During our second visit, I asked her about the Lysandran prisoners.

"They're actually puzzled as to why were keeping them confined. They say that since they've acknowledged that we're dominant, we can trust their parole."

"Sure. Unless fresh troops land on the planet and the dominance pattern is called into question again."

"It's a real drain on our resources to guard them and feed them, but we can't release them to their fleet because they'd be back a few days later with new weapons. And we have a limited supply of their dietary supplement. We've communicated that to their friends in orbit, but the response was roughly that it's our problem, not theirs. We're dominant down here so we're responsible."

"Do you know what happened to Sylandris?"

She nodded. "He's not on Aragon. Apparently he was sent home in disgrace."

"Oh? What did he do?"

Cille chuckled. "He recommended that Aragon and the other colony worlds be abandoned and that his people withdraw from all contact with the human race, because our culture was corrupting traditional Lysandran values."

CHAPTER SEVENTEEN

It was on the day following my second visit with Cille that things changed again. I was at a hostelry in Aladdin on my way back home from Casper when the orbital battle started. We'd been able to monitor Lysandran activity above us fairly closely although we had little knowledge of what they might be up to elsewhere in the system. One of the smaller ships had departed shortly after the uprising, but the others were still in place, and repairs were being made on those with obvious external damage. They were monitored at all times so that they couldn't stage a surprise landing, although that would have been difficult in any case. Graham had recommended that large vehicles be parked on the spaceport landing pads to make them unusable, and the government had taken his suggestion. Although it was possible to set individual troop transports down elsewhere, there were few other locations suitable for a mass landing.

After dining alone in a small café, I'd returned to my room, planning to make an early night of it so that I could leave for home at the crack of dawn, hitching a ride or paying passage down to Junction. Traffic was steadily increasing again, and although there was no commercial service yet, most of the transports along the route were more than happy to supplement their income by taking on passengers. I had in fact started to undress when a bright starburst lit up the entire sky directly facing my window. Blinking, somewhat alarmed, I stuck my head outside and looked up.

That initial glow was probably the explosive death of a Lysandran warship. The Navy caught them completely by surprise, striking with a force far larger and more numerous than that which they opposed. Most of what followed was invisible to the naked eye, although there were numerous smaller flashes and streaks of light resembling shooting stars. Most of the Lysandran vessels that were actually destroyed had been on the opposite side of the planet at the time of the attack, so no one on the ground witnessed their death throes even at a distance. The activity was quite intense for almost an hour, after which it died off very quickly.

I listened to my com, trying to find out what was happening, but the official announcement simply indicated that there had been a military engagement of some kind in orbit above Aragon. Although I could have commed Cille directly, I figured she'd be busy enough without having to deal with her older brother's curiosity. Like almost everyone else in Aladdin, I watched the sky until quite late that night, long after there had ceased to be anything to see, wondering if our liberation was now complete. The answer to that question turned out to be more complex than I would have guessed.

The following morning I was up early, but my plans to return to the farm were on indefinite hold. There was an official news release now, confirming that the Concourse Navy had in fact attacked the orbiting Lysandran vessels. "As of this moment, it appears that the system is clear of the enemy. Those ships which weren't destroyed in the engagement have fled. There are presently at least twenty Concourse warships orbiting Aragon and an unknown number elsewhere in the system. Communications have been established between the commander of the strike force and leaders of the Assembly."

It was holiday time in Aragon. Everyone was walking around exhibiting a cheery smile, and since most businesses had not bothered to open, the streets were filled with milling crowds. Sidewalk vendors were doing a thriving business selling brazed cornfruit and barbecued crab wings. I passed more than one group of musicians performing impromptu concerts on street corners. Aimlessly, I drifted toward government center, soaking up the infectious happiness around me.

The roar of the landing rockets caught me completely by surprise and for a few seconds I, like most of those around me, had a sudden sense of dread. The only shuttles that had set down on Aragon during the years of Lysandran rule had been military vessels carrying fresh troops and supplies. Shading my eyes, I looked up at the dark, gray shape settling down toward the spaceport, relaxing only when I recognized it as a standard human style landing craft. Even at that distance, the sound of its landing was loud enough that I missed the chirping of my com until after it had settled in place and cut its thrusters.

Cille was calling. "Ennis? Are you still in the city or have you left?"

"Still here. Decided to stay around for the festivities."

"Don't celebrate yet. There have been some complications. We've just called a special meeting of the Assembly to deal with the situation, and I'd like to have you there in the audience. We need to be able to demonstrate a unified response."

"Response to what? What's going on, Cille?"

"I can't talk over an unsecured communications line, Ennis. Just be there, please." She gave me a password to get past security, then broke the connection. My good mood began to dissipate. We believed that the Lysandrans had been monitoring private com lines, although as far as I knew it had never been proven. Who was Cille worried about now, and why?

Even with the password, I almost didn't make it into government center. The newly reconstituted city police had cordoned off the area, although not particularly efficiently. When I tried to get past the first check point, I was turned away, but I was able to bypass their perimeter altogether without much effort, and the entire line collapsed by late morning. The streets immediately surrounding Constitution Hall were so packed that even if you were to pass out, you would have been held upright by the press around you. Somehow I managed to make my way through to the more disciplined Assembly security guards, whose numbers had been visibly augmented by several dozen serious looking men and women who all wore the distinctive pickaxe insignia of Gaunt's rebel forces.

To my immense relief, they accepted Cille's password immediately and allowed me through. The corridors of the building proper were passable, though crowded, but the gallery in the Assembly chamber was packed, standing room only. I found a relatively good vantage point by climbing up onto the staging used by the cleaning crew, although it was buffeted constantly and was in constant danger of being overturned.

Most of the seats on the stage were filled, but I didn't see Cille anywhere. The representatives were all talking quietly among themselves, their amplifiers turned down. Although those in the gallery still seemed upbeat, there were clusters of faces below that wore masks of concern. I felt a prescient sense that everything was not as it should be.

There was a short but interminable wait before the proceedings started. A cluster of figures entered from behind the podium, one of whom was Cille, another Graham. There were two other civilians I didn't know, and three uniformed Navy officers. They were greeted by a standing ovation, to which I contributed cautiously. I couldn't see the expression on Cille's face from this distance, but I could see her posture, and I knew that she was tense. Something was wrong.

Graham let the applause continue for a few seconds, then raised his arms. The uproar slowly subsided, giving way to the constant susurration of a restless audience. Graham was silent for almost a full minute before introducing Cille as "acting Planetary Administrator"..

Cille stood and waited for a fresh but muted wave of sound to subside. "Thank you all for coming, particularly those of you who responded on such short notice. Let me introduce our guests." She turned to the three military officers, who stood in perfect synchronization. "Admiral Rafael Bhutto commands the task force which engaged and defeated the Lysandran fleet orbiting Aragon just a few hours ago." She had to stop then because the assembly and the galleries gave Bhutto a standing ovation. He nodded to the crowd a few times, his hands clasped behind his back, but did not speak. Cille waited an appropriate length of time, then raised one hand to signal for quiet. It came, though not quickly.

"With the Admiral are Captain Ivana Leskya from the corvette *Nostradamus*," she paused for another brief spatter of applause, "and Captain Paolo DiMarco, staff assistant to the admiral." A third but thankfully briefer ovation followed. "Admiral Bhutto has informed us that the Lysandrans are in general retreat, but still hold approximately half of the human worlds conquered in their initial round of attacks. Although they are clearly regrouping and are far from defeated, the Admiral believes that there are now sufficient forces in place here to forestall any attempt to recapture the system." She turned and gestured to the Admiral, who stepped forward.

"Let me first apologize for our tardiness in coming to your aid. Quite frankly, the Concourse was unprepared for a major war. Many of our ships were antiquated, the senior ranks were filled with inexperienced and largely unimaginative officers, and the rank and file had not received adequate training. Those problems have all been addressed and during the past year we have pushed the enemy steadily back. In order to achieve victory, we were careful to avoid incurring the same logistical problems that hampered the Cranes, adopting instead a methodical but unfortunately gradual accumulation of resources prior to each assault. But I can now safely say that we have them on the run, and it seems unlikely that they will present any further threat to your planet." There was another wild outburst of applause following the Admiral's words, and this time he even allowed himself to smile.

"Aragon will be integrated back into the Concourse as quickly as possible," he continued. "To that end, I have chosen Captain DiMarco to serve as military governor of Aragon." DiMarco stepped forward on cue, apparently expecting to be greeted with another swell of appreciation, but this time there was only scattered, uncertain applause. Admiral Bhutto's smile faded. He started to speak but Cille pre-empted him.

"Admiral Bhutto only announced his intentions to the senior Assembly members a short time ago," she said. "He gave us no opportunity for a diplomatic response. Although we cannot speak for the entire Assembly, we ourselves are unanimous in our rejection of the imposition of military rule on Aragon. We defeated the Lysandran invasion force without the assistance of the Concourse or its Navy, and while we welcome their presence in our system and will cooperate in any reasonable fashion requested," and she emphasized that last word, "we do not recognize that the Concourse has the authority to supercede our freely elected government with one imposed from the outside."

There was a rising murmur from the gallery and from the Assembly at large, and I was gratified to hear anger and indignation predominate. The Admiral seemed to realize that he was losing his support and raised both hands above his head.

"I understand your concerns. Believe me, the Navy has neither the desire nor the ability to administer your planet in the long term. But you must realize that the Concourse is in the middle of a war and that in times of war it is sometimes necessary to take extraordinary measures in the short term in order to secure our freedom. The installation of a military governor is meant only to bypass the time consuming procedural delays that might hinder a united effort by both of us to strike at the enemy. For the majority of the population, there will be no impact whatsoever. Your assembly will continue to meet and make laws to govern your planet. The governor will only veto them when they would interfere with the war effort, and his veto will expire immediately upon the cessation of hostilities."

There was more murmuring, and considerable arguing, on every side. Bhutto stepped back and glanced at Cille and those immediately around her. It was several minutes before any of them could speak over the crowd noise, and it was one of the officials I didn't know by name, but whom I later learned was Marcus Fong, who asked the question.

"What precisely would the Navy want us to do, Admiral?"

Bhutto seemed to take the question as acquiescence, because some of his good humor returned. "Nothing particularly onerous. We'd like to bring liberty parties down obviously; our people have been cooped up aboard ship for several months now. And we'll resupply here periodically, food primarily. I want to emphasize that we won't be confiscating what we take. Fair market value will be paid in standard Concourse credits. Profiteering will not be allowed, obviously. That's one of the things the governor will be monitoring. Conscripts will receive the same compensation per rank as will any other soldier or sailor."

He might have said more, but Cille interrupted him. "Military conscription is forbidden under the charter of the Concourse, Admiral."

"Yes, well under ordinary circumstances, that would be the case. But due to the war emergency, the Concourse has temporarily suspended that provision on all worlds deemed to be within the contested area. But once again, our conscriptees will be immediately discharged and returned to their places of origin upon the cessation of hostilities."

There was a great deal more, but most of it covered the same ground. Admiral Bhutto's patience visibly grew thinner, Cille and those around her became cooler and in some cases openly hostile, and the enthusiasm in the audience had been leached away almost entirely. It was Bhutto who finally brought a halt to that day's discussion.

He had just listened to one of the representatives present a tediously legalistic objection in a high pitched, whining voice that put everyone's nerves on edge. When the speaker paused for breath, Bhutto stood up abruptly and raised his voice loud enough to be heard even without the amplifier. "What none of you seem to grasp here is that this is not a request. The installation of a military governor will take place as I have outlined and you will conform to the military code as conveyed by his office and any other duly appointed representatives of the Concourse Navy. This debate is futile."

He glanced directly at Cille as though challenging her to contest the point. She remained seated for a few seconds, then stood up and spoke in a level voice. "I believe that Admiral Bhutto has expressed his position clearly and completely. I am sure that he will understand that the Assembly needs to ponder this information at length and in private before acting officially. I suggest that we suspend the public session at this point. I imagine most of you will wish to talk to your constituents and reflect on the implications before committing yourselves to a course of action. If the Admiral would consider returning at the same time tomorrow, I believe we will be able to call for a vote."

Bhutto actually smirked. He must have interpreted Cille's remarks as a concession, assuming that the Assembly would balk at defying the Navy. Even from my remote spot, I could tell that it was just the opposite. Cille had just squared off for a fight and I wondered if the Admiral would ever know what hit him.

I returned to my room and arranged to hold it for another two days, then commed back to the farm and let people there know what was going on. Late that evening, my unit beeped for attention, and Cille's face appeared on the tiny screen. It was well past my usual bedtime – farmers are early risers and it's a habit I hadn't managed to break even while traveling – and I felt sleepy and depressed.

"I'm sorry to be calling so late, Ennis, but I've been rather busy. I assume you heard what went on today?"

"Yes I did. Have you decided how to respond yet?"

"That's not up to me, or at least not entirely." She sighed and for a split second looked like her younger self. "The Assembly is pretty evenly split between those who are indignant and those who want things to just quiet down and return to something like normal. I can't say that I entirely blame them."

"But Bhutto's demands were outrageous," I said with some heat. "He wants to return us to colonial status. Worse than that, in fact; involuntary servitude of any kind is a strict violation of the Colonial Charter Agreement."

"I know." She nodded her head. "And I'm glad to hear you say that. Even at the best of times, those of us in the Assembly tend to fall out of touch with the people we're supposed to be representing, and I've spent most of the last few years living in the basement of an unfinished resort complex. What do you think the reaction will be back in Safehaven?"

I thought about it. "Split, but with a majority opposed. There's always been some distrust of central authority there. And Managansett will be even more staunchly against a military government."

"Will you come again tomorrow?"

"If you want me to."

"I do. It's going to be very close, Ennis. I won't even try to predict the outcome." And she gave me a password to use and then she was gone.

I arrived early enough the following day to secure a seat for myself and stared down at the nearly empty legislative floor for a very long time before the representatives began entering and drifting toward their seats. Some looked thoughtful, some angry, some worried. I didn't see anyone who looked happy. Tcho and Graham showed up without Cille and I had a few minutes of worry before she emerged, walking beside Admiral Bhutto and his two officers. The latter kept their faces expressionless, but the smirk had returned to Bhutto's face. Once again I suspected that the Admiral was underestimating my sister; she might not prevail today but she was going to give him a good fight.

The last few seats filled below us, and when Cille called the Assembly to order, it became quiet immediately. There wasn't even the usual murmuring from the galleries. She summarized the events of the previous day calmly and objectively, and then asked Bhutto if there was anything he wanted to add.

"Not at all," he answered magnanimously. "I believe you've described the situation accurately."

Cille nodded. "Then what we are called upon to do today is decide whether, as the legal government of the planet Aragon, we are willing to accede to the demands of the Navy or whether we will exercise our sovereign right to reject them."

Bhutto's smile slipped a bit and he half raised a hand to attract Cille's attention. She nodded toward him. "Do you wish to add something after all, Admiral?"

He stood up slowly and let his eyes move around the chamber before speaking. "I only wanted to correct one small misinterpretation. Members of the Concourse are guaranteed sovereignty over their internal affairs. There are certain standards which must be maintained to avoid expulsion, of course, but only one planet has been cast out in our entire history. But members also accept an abridgement of their sovereignty in external affairs, and the war with the Cranes is about as external as you can get." He paused to let that sink in. "Compliance with Concourse resolutions in matters involving trade, exploration, colonization, and military campaigns is mandated by the Concourse Charter. This is not negotiable."

He subsided into his seat and Cille nodded to herself as though she'd expected, no, counted on just that response. She then called for speakers from the floor. A few representatives spoke briefly, about evenly split between compliance and defiance. None of them were particularly eloquent, nor did they bring anything new to the debate, which was essentially very straightforward.

At last Cille saw no more raised hands. "If there is no one else who wishes to speak on this subject, it is time to take a vote."

A heartbeat passed and a deep, rough voice called out across the chamber, not boosted by an amplifier but still audible everywhere. "I would like to say a few words."

Every eye in the chamber turned to a heavy set, bearded man standing in the front row of the gallery directly facing me. Cille was caught as much by surprise as the rest of us, but she recovered quickly.

"I'm sure that your opinion is valuable, sir, but for practical reasons, we have ruled out participation by anyone not a member of the Assembly unless," and she nodded toward the Admiral, "their input is of critical importance."

"Well, I'm not sure whether you'd consider my words important, but as it happens I AM a member of this assembly, although circumstances have caused me to send a representative to serve in my place. My name is Gaunt and I represent Tyrada."

It took quite some time to quiet things down, during which Gaunt was ushered down to the floor of the legislature where he briefly clasped hands with the woman who'd been holding his seat before she left for the gallery. Then he turned and looked up at the podium and Cille raised her hand for quiet. "The senior representative from Tyrada has the floor."

"I was born on Aragon," he began, his voice pitched just low enough that we all had to strain to hear him. "I grew up here. I watched our people make a place for themselves, working within the colonial framework, planning for the future, creating a code of laws, and then achieving independence and the right to apply for admission to the Concourse of Worlds. It wasn't always easy, and sometimes we had trouble deciding which rights were more important than others, but we worked things through. Then the invaders came."

There was a wave of murmuring and Gaunt remained silent until it subsided. "The aliens came and took our rights away. Oh, not all of them, and they claimed to have only the best intentions. In their eyes, they probably did have our collective welfare in mind. They thought they were doing the right thing. They were wrong. So we rose up and fought them, and a lot of us died, and a lot of them died, and most of us lost something or someone in the process. But eventually we prevailed, and we have reclaimed the right to shape our own society, our own future." This was followed by applause. Gaunt waited motionlessly until it was quiet again.

"Now the Navy has found the time to come to our system and drive out what's left of the invaders, and we thank them for that assistance. The fact that we were left virtually alone to face our conquerors for four years was probably not their fault. But the fact is that when they arrived, Aragon itself was no longer in the hands of the enemy. Aragon had reclaimed its own freedom, as it should have. We can't rely on someone else to protect us. We have to be strong enough, and resolute enough, to fight our own battles."

I glanced down at Bhutto, trying to gauge his reaction. He looked puzzled, and wary. Gaunt had caught him by surprise and he obviously didn't like surprises.

"I lost a lot of friends in the process. I lost two fingers from my left hand." He raised his arm to illustrate his point. "I regret each and every sacrifice that had to be made, but given the same situation, I would do it again." He turned and looked directly at Bhutto now. "The Admiral has told us that in order to preserve our freedom, we must give it up. He assures us that this is an emergency measure that will end when the crisis ends, and I have no doubt that he believes that to be true. But know this. A freedom voluntarily surrendered is forever at risk. We never surrendered to the invaders and eventually we defeated them. If the Navy, if the Councourse, tries to impose its rule on Aragon, I will not surrender this time either, and I will never stop until I have defeated them as well. We did not sacrifice our friends and our family members to overthrow the Lysandran dictatorship just to make room for a human one. If they force this upon us, we'll fight them just as we fought the other invaders. And make no mistake, if instead you choose to agree to the Admiral's demands, you will be surrendering our liberty and that of our children."

He sat down abruptly while the galleries and some of the Assembly either applauded wildly or spoke in hushed tones among themselves. Bhutto was livid. Without even waiting to be recognized, he stood up and spoke. "The speaker's impassioned rhetoric makes good theater but not good sense. And his efforts to incite an insurrection are criminal and should be regarded as such!"

Cille nodded to Tcho, who apparently cut the power to Bhutto's amplifier, for his voice faded on the last word. "You've had your opportunity to speak, Admiral. I think it's time to vote. Press red if you feel that we should accept the installation of a military governor on Aragon and green if you wish to reject the motion." Cille wasn't about to miss the chance; Gaunt's words had undoubtedly swayed some of the fence sitters, and she wanted them to commit before they had time to reconsider. The voting lights came up very quickly on the display panel, and we didn't have to look at the numerical key to know the outcome. Better than two thirds of the display was a bright emerald green.

Bhutto had remained standing throughout the vote, and his expression had darkened. Without benefit of an amplifier, he bellowed loud enough to be heard. "Enough of this charade! You have no authority to accept or reject our supervision of your planet. You're overlooking the fact that the Concourse Charter overrides member governments in the event of a military emergency, which is clearly the case here.!"

Cille replied instantly, and her amplifier had been turned up loud enough to be heard clearly over the angry murmuring that swept through the chamber. "It is you who have overlooked the legality of the situation, Admiral. Aragon is not now and never has been a member world of the Concourse. We had applied for admission prior to the invasion, but our request was never acted upon. Aragon therefore is legally an independent world, not subject to the Concourse in any way. You have no legal authority here, and if you attempt to impose yourselves where you're not wanted, then it is you who will be ignoring the Concourse Charter. And the free people of Aragon will consider such action an act of war."

I believe that what followed might best be described as pandemonium. Everyone was up out of their seat, spectators and Assembly alike. At some point Bhutto and his satellites stormed out, but I never saw them go. There was never any formal adjournment, but eventually everyone was streaming out of the chamber. I wandered around the city aimlessly for awhile, trying to absorb everything that had happened, and I was quite close to the spaceport when the Admiral's shuttle rose on a tail of flame and shot upward into the sky. End of crisis, I thought to myself.

Rarely have I so misjudged a situation.

Eventually I started back to my room, but my com beeped while I was en route. It was Cille. "Ennis, can you come back to government center? Right away?"

I frowned. "I suppose. What's wrong? Everything seemed to go well today."

"Maybe, maybe not. But that's not why I need to see you. Please, come now. It's very important." I agreed and she gave me the address. It was too far to walk quickly, so I paid an exorbitant price for a ride in a commercial flitter, and even then I was forced to walk the last several blocks.

Cille had temporary quarters in a heavily damaged building that had once catered to our thin but wealthy tourist trade. She had a fairly large suite, although the luxurious furnishings had been largely replaced by more practical desks, terminals, communications equipment, and other less identifiable paraphernalia. Two guards reluctantly allowed me to pass inside, and I found myself in a milling crowd of technicians and dignitaries. I couldn't see Cille but I spotted Tcho and explained that I had been summoned.

"She's in there." He gesture toward the door to a smaller room, guarded by a heavyset woman who watched everyone suspiciously. She wouldn't let me pass until she had commed Cille for clearance. Then the door opened and I went inside.

There were only two people in the room, sitting opposite each other at a narrow table. One of them was Cille, sitting leaning forward on her elbows. Her companion was Gaunt, rebel leader and most recently politician. He had one hand tangled in his long, thick beard and was twisting it nervously back and forth. Cille glanced in my direction. "Come in, Ennis. Sit down. We have a lot to talk about."

I took the third chair and sat and in that instant I realized why Cille had asked me to come. For a second it was hard to breathe, but then I managed to inhale slowly and calm myself. I turned to Gaunt and extended my hand. "Nice to see you again, Jesper. We've missed you."

CHAPTER EIGHTEEN

Some months later I would have a brief, personal crisis, persistent feelings of inadequacy, as though I'd wasted my life or failed to meet my responsibilities. My younger sister Cille was as close to being head of the planetary government as our constitution allowed, and my younger brother Jesper was the leader of the Tyradan insurgents and arguably the man most responsible for the defeat of the Lysandrans. And me? I was a moderately successful farmer whose name was virtually unknown outside of Safehaven and perhaps Managansett. It bothered me off and on for almost a year, and it wasn't until later that I realized that it wasn't as important to attempt great things as to do a great job at the things you attempt.

The three of us tried to catch up on many years in just a few minutes, and failed horribly. Shortly after leaving the farm, Jesper had found the body of a solitary prospector who'd died in a landslide. He'd appropriated the man's identity and his profession for a while, with enough success to buy himself a share in the Tyradan mining operation. To my utter amazement, he told me that he'd visited the farm once, secretively, in order to see Dad before he died, and I realized that what I'd dismissed as a soothing deathbed illusion had been real. "I thought about staying around for a while, but it wasn't time. I still didn't know who I was then. So I talked to Mom briefly and then headed out."

"You talked to her?" My mouth must have dropped open. I know Cille's did.

"Sure. We've commed each other once in a while ever since. I made her promise not to tell either of you, said I'd disappear again if she even hinted that she knew where I was."

Personally I was torn between being annoyed with him and just being happy to have him back, but none of us had leisure to enjoy our reunion for long. There was a knock on the door and Graham entered. He acknowledged me with a nod and then looked at Cille, and his expression was not a happy one.

"It's all right. You can talk freely."

Graham looked my way again, but took her word for it. "Our observatory is reporting some interesting activity in orbit."

The atmosphere in the room visibly altered. "What kind of activity?" Cille's family voice was gone; she was a stranger to me in that moment.

"Two ships have changed orbit which, perhaps coincidentally, puts them in optimum position to land a shuttle in this vicinity. There's been some EVA activity consistent with safety checks prior to the launching of assault craft. Most of their intership communications have been in clear since they arrived, but now everything is going out coded."

"They're planning to attack us, aren't they?"

He nodded. "I'd say that was a safe guess. Bhutto's at least keeping his options open. He might try to bluff us first."

"That won't work," said Gaunt...Jesper.

"Will Bhutto actually risk it? Legally we aren't part of the Concourse. What he's doing must exceed his authority."

Graham shook his head. "We don't know exactly what else may have changed since we've been isolated from the Concourse. It's possible that there's precedent, that some other non-member world has already been forcibly recruited. But even if that's not the case, Bhutto may well believe that he can make a valid claim that there was no legally constituted government on Aragon. I know that most of the Assembly was elected, but there are some appointees as well." He glanced at Jesper. "It might be claimed that we had reverted to colonial status. In his place, I might use force, knowing that it would be years before the legal issues ever got resolved. By then the point will be moot, the war will hopefully be over, and Bhutto may even be retired."

Cille clenched her jaw and her eyes hardened. "I want the spaceport pads blockaded immediately."

Graham smiled slightly. "I took the liberty of obstructing all of the pads immediately following the Admiral's departure." The smile vanished. "That will make things more difficult for them, but it won't stop them. They can't put down as large a force, and their troops will be scattered, but there are enough suitable locations on the outskirts of the city for them to land a thousand troops or so."

"How soon will they come?"

He shrugged. "I suppose they could land tonight if they wanted to, although that might be rushing things a bit. If Bhutto puts top value on surprise, I'd say tomorrow, during second dusk or full darkness. On the other hand, if he thinks it's more important to intimidate us, he might land in broad daylight so that we can see what he's throwing against us and, presumably, surrender to a superior force."

"A thousand troops?" I sounded skeptical. "Formidable I grant, but can't we match that?" I looked at Jesper. "How many fighters can you raise?"

"Close to a thousand." But he shook his head. "In Tyrada, not here. It would take five or six days to move that many to Aladdin."

"We might be able to find almost as many here, but in the short term I'd guess only half that number would be available," said Graham. "And they're not as well trained or disciplined as the Navy, and I don't know that we could form any comprehensive defense in such a short period of time. There are too many different spots where they're likely to land, and they'll be heavily armed, armored, and well organized. We're a guerilla force, not a stand up army."

"I don't want a shooting war in any case," objected Cille. "There's been enough death on Aragon lately. If we can't make them see that they're wrong, then we have to convince them that they can't win this battle. How much warning will we have when they make their move?"

"They can disguise their transmissions, but they can't blind us. We'll see the assault shuttles detach. If they take a risky high speed descent, they could be on the ground in less than an hour. But I don't think that's going to happen because we don't have anything capable of destroying them en route. Bhutto's two officers spent a lot of time in the city. They'll have a pretty good idea what we can throw up in the way of defense, and I think they'll be pretty contemptuous of our chances. So we can probably count on at least four hours' notice."

"Best guess. Will they come by day or by night?"

Graham thought about that one before answering. "By day, sometime tomorrow. Bhutto doesn't want a battle either. He's planning to bully us into giving in to his demands so he'll want us to see what we're facing. And that way his people won't have to secure unfamiliar terrain in the darkness. In his place, I'd attack at first light."

"Which doesn't give us much time to raise an army." Cille's voice was uncertain for the first time.

"No it doesn't."

"How much resistance would it take to change Bhutto's mind?" It was another second or two before I realized that I was the one who had asked the question. They all turned toward me and Graham in particular acted as though he was seeing me for the first time. "We can get five hundred irregular troops into place before dawn, maybe a few more if we're lucky. If we had double that number, a Navy landing force could still overrun us, and we'll be spread out defending more target areas than they'll actually hit. We'd need two thousand irregulars to pose a credible defense."

"How many seasoned troops would you need to accomplish the same thing? On top of the five hundred we can already count on."

"Another five hundred might do it. We'd have the advantage of cover and they'd necessarily be attacking from open areas, which leaves them vulnerable. They'd still win in a pitched battle, but it would cost them dearly. But if we're going to wish for the impossible, conjure up a thousand veterans and their position becomes untenable."

"All right." I took a deep breath and then I had my brief moment of greatness, I suppose. That sort of thing is supposed to be exciting and uplifting, but all I felt was terror and uncertainty and a hollow sickness in my stomach. But Cille and Jesper and Graham listened and Cille nodded first, and then Graham, and after a great deal of argument and some modification to the original plan, Jesper came around as well.

Graham's assessment proved very accurate. He later confided in me that he'd looked up Bhutto's service record. "A competent, loyal, but very unimaginative officer. It wasn't hard to predict what he'd do." His only inaccuracy was his prediction that there would be six landing sites. In fact, Bhutto sent down only four shuttles, preferring to keep his troops close together so that they could act as a unit rather than attempting to launch multiple coordinated attacks. They came down on the north side of Aladdin, two vehicles side by side in one of the few open meadows in the area, two others on sites which had been cleared for construction that had never gotten underway.

The troops poured out and joined up quickly as our outlying pickets retreated in front of them. A few shots were fired by nervous irregulars, but the landing force didn't answer. They turned toward the city and began a methodical march forward through the suburbs, following a route which would allow them to occupy government center and the spaceport by late morning if there was no resistance. As our forces continued to retreat in apparent disarray, they grew more confident and were less careful about securing the areas adjacent to their line of march. We had reports that some of the invaders were singing as they advanced.

We made our stand at Dudley Square, a large open park in the northern sector of Aladdin. The advancing troops halted at the edge of the greensward when they saw the barricades we'd erected at the opposite end. The singularity of their attack had allowed us to move defenders around and there were probably four hundred irregulars facing a force of six hundred professionals.

A group of three officers came forward under a flag of truce. Graham went out to parlay while Cille, Jesper, and I watched from the roof of a four story bank building. They huddled together for a surprisingly brief amount of time before Graham straightened and Cille's com beeped.

"They wish to negotiate our surrender," Graham said calmly. "Colonel Yoon says that he has no desire to spill any blood today."

"Tell the colonel that we share his reluctance but that we believe his withdrawal would better fulfill our mutual desire."

There was a brief pause. "The colonel indicates that he admires our determination but points out that he has a superior force in play and that there can be no question of withdrawal."

Cille turned to me and winked before answering. "Advise the colonel that he has misjudged the situation. He is outnumbered and his forces are concentrated and surrounded. We do not require that he surrender, but we do insist that he agree to immediately desist from his illegal aggression against the free planet of Aragon and withdraw his forces to orbit."

There was a longer pause this time. "The colonel expresses his regret at the necessity to contradict you, but sees no reason to re-evaluate the situation."

Cille and Jesper exchanged glances and Jesper lifted his com to his mouth and spoke the code word. Almost immediately, figures began to step out from behind barricades, lean forward from windows, rise up out of camouflaged trenches. A large force erupted from the underground service areas behind the Navy position, taking cover among the smaller buildings they had passed moments before. There were approximately nine hundred newcomers, each wearing full body armor and carrying a military laser.

Our Lysandran prisoners surrounded Dudley Square methodically and completely, arms ready but not pointed at the human troops.

An almost physical silence spread across the area, and I swear no one, human or Lysandran, breathed for a full half minute. Colonel Yoon slowly pivoted and swept his eyes in a complete circle. Graham later told us that he never changed expression, that his breathing remained cool and even. I can't say the same for myself, or any of the rest of us on the rooftop. As the silence stretched, the tension was so great that I wanted to retch.

Finally, Graham's voice came from the com, and he sounded uncharacteristically emotional. "Colonel Yoon sends his compliments and admits that he may have misjudged the situation. He requests that we advise him as to our intentions."

I knew in that second that we had won.

We insisted that they leave their weapons behind, although it was more of a symbol than anything else. Aragon didn't have the troops to use them, and the Navy had more than enough equipment to reoutfit them. But we hoped it would send a message to Admiral Bhutto and his staff. And apparently it did, because there were no further attacks, and in fact no communication for several days. Then Captain DiMarco was sent down in a small personnel shuttle for consultations, during which he requested that Aragon accept a military advisor who would have no authority but who would be available for consultation with the lawful government of Aragon.

Cille asked him if Admiral Bhutto thought this was a viable arrangement. Captain DiMarco replied that he had no knowledge of Bhutto's opinion, as the Admiral had been relieved of his command and reassigned elsewhere.

It wasn't as much of a risk as it seemed, releasing the Lysandrans. At Jesper's insistence, their weapons had all been disabled. I hope Colonel Yoon never learned the truth, that we were prepared to surrender the city to him if he had called our bluff. I had argued in favor of letting the Lysandrans carry working arms, but Jesper had demurred and in retrospect he was probably right. Having accepted that humans were dominant, it's unclear where their new loyalties might have ultimately rested if it had come to an actual fight, and for that matter, they might well have proven overzealous or just plain ornery and have fired at the Navy personnel anyway. Lysandrans and humans aren't that much different, after all, and we've grown more alike in the years since the war.

There's not much more to tell. That wasn't the last exciting thing to happen in my life, but it was the last one that might be of interest to anyone else. I returned to the farm and have managed it ever since. Mom lived to see her two grandchildren, Kelli and Jon, grow up into handsome, willowy adolescents, and she died peacefully in her sleep. Yes, I married again, two years after the confrontation in Aladdin. Zai and I added love and passion to the respect and friendship we'd already felt for each other. I still miss Kelli and Zai is comfortable with that, and I think Kelli would be happy for me as well. Jesper comes to visit from time to time, but he never again occupied his seat in the Assembly and once Tyrada was back on its feet, he spent most of his time exploring or prospecting or both.

Cille served two terms as Planetary Administrator. The Lysandran Comity collapsed and sued for peace early in her second term. Aragon eventually did join the Concourse and she became our representative to the Standing Congress. She hasn't been elected chair of that group yet, but she's got her own committee and I don't think it'll be long before she's running the whole organization. She's married now as well, a Lithurian diplomat who seemed all right to me although he obviously wasn't good enough to marry my sister. Cille never did get an artificial skin; a new technique was developed during the war that teased the body into regenerating its own covering. She's quite beautiful now. She's also quite rich. Most of her personal investments had been off Aragon, so she didn't suffer the massive losses of those whose investments were confined to one small planet. About half of her wealth was subsequently donated to recovery operations, both as loans and as grants. Among the farmers who owe their livelihood to her intervention is Sobriety Carter, who rather shamefacedly acknowledges the irony of that fact.

Sylandris returned to Aragon with a small group of companions last year. They're living just outside Junction. Apparently he absorbed too many human habits and ideas to fit in comfortably back home, although when I visit him he constantly complains about the lack of a consistent, logical rationale for human civilization. But I notice that he stays here. Dan Kater and Suki North married and moved to Tyrada. Jill Garner took over Cille's seat in the Assembly. Jeb is married as well, although he still works for us. His wife is Aki Song's younger sister. About six months after the confrontation with the Navy, Melody Miller turned herself in for the murder of Martin Harwell and was sentenced to ten years of community service and forfeiture of her citizenship right. I testified as a character witness in her defense.

As I look back now, I'm reasonably content with the way I've conducted my life. I've made some mistakes, caused occasional harm, but always through ignorance or thoughtlessness and not through malice. I've helped build one of the strongest business empires on Aragon, but I think I've always been fair and honorable in my dealings with others, and I know that I've ignored opportunities because I didn't care for the consequences to others. I keep remembering something Cille told me once when we were talking about that long ago day when we burned the wormdance and almost killed her.

She told me that she didn't blame us because we were trying to do our best, even if the results were tragic. I think we're all like that most of the time, even Admiral Bhutto, even the Lysandrans. We all believe that what we're doing is the right thing, that our judgment of the situation is correct. Bhutto's mission was to defend the Concourse and defeat the Lysandrans, and our refusal to dance to his music must have seemed to him a distracting, childish tantrum, something to be swept aside for the greater good. Likewise the Lysandrans had benevolent intentions. After the war we discovered that all of their subject races had prospered under Lysandran rule. Their culture had adopted a mission, an imperative, and they really thought we'd be happier and better off once we accepted their dominance. Now we're dominant, of course, and I wonder if the Lysandrans are happier or better off than they were before.

But it's getting late now. I can no longer see anything outside my window and the lights are going off in the field hands' quarters. It's time for me to go to bed. Farmers have to get up real early if they want to get the day's chores done.

www.ingramcontent.com/pod-product-compliance
Lightning Source LLC
Chambersburg PA
CBHW072226170626
46813CB00003B/1102